ARE YOU SIGN **BLOG?**

You'll get the latest giveaways,
exclusive excerpts, c over reveals
and more.

Check out our complete list of authors, too!

No spam, no junk. That's a promise!

Sign Up Here

www.dragonbladepublishing.com

Dearest Reader;

Thank you for your support of a small press. At Dragonblade Publishing, we strive to bring you the highest quality Historical Romance from some of the best authors in the business. Without your support, there is no 'us', so we sincerely hope you adore these stories and find some new favorite authors along the way.

Happy Reading!

CEO, Dragonblade Publishing

Half a Chance

The Chances
Book 4

Emily E K Murdoch

© Copyright 2025 by Emily E K Murdoch
Text by Emily E K Murdoch
Cover by Dar Albert

Dragonblade Publishing, Inc. is an imprint of Kathryn Le Veque Novels, Inc.
P.O. Box 23
Moreno Valley, CA 92556
ceo@dragonbladepublishing.com

Produced in the United States of America

First Edition January 2025
Print Edition

Reproduction of any kind except where it pertains to short quotes in relation to advertising or promotion is strictly prohibited.

All Rights Reserved.

The characters and events portrayed in this book are fictitious. Any similarity to real persons, living or dead, is purely coincidental and not intended by the author.

Additional Dragonblade books by
Author Emily E K Murdoch

The Chances Series
A Fighting Chance (Book 1)
A Second Chance (Book 2)
An Outside Chance (Book 3)
Half a Chance (Book 4)

Dukes in Danger Series
Don't Judge a Duke by His Cover (Book 1)
Strike While the Duke is Hot (Book 2)
The Duke is Mightier than the Sword (Book 3)
A Duke in Time Saves Nine (Book 4)
Every Duke Has His Price (Book 5)
Put Your Best Duke Forward (Book 6)
Where There's a Duke, There's a Way (Book 7)
Curiosity Killed the Duke (Book 8)
Play With Dukes, Get Burned (Book 9)
The Best Things in Life are Dukes (Book 10)
A Duke a Day Keeps the Doctor Away (Book 11)
All Good Dukes Come to an End (Book 12)

Twelve Days of Christmas
Twelve Drummers Drumming
Eleven Pipers Piping
Ten Lords a Leaping
Nine Ladies Dancing
Eight Maids a Milking
Seven Swans a Swimming
Six Geese a Laying
Five Gold Rings

Four Calling Birds
Three French Hens
Two Turtle Doves
A Partridge in a Pear Tree

The De Petras Saga
The Misplaced Husband (Book 1)
The Impoverished Dowry (Book 2)
The Contrary Debutante (Book 3)
The Determined Mistress (Book 4)
The Convenient Engagement (Book 5)

The Governess Bureau Series
A Governess of Great Talents (Book 1)
A Governess of Discretion (Book 2)
A Governess of Many Languages (Book 3)
A Governess of Prodigious Skill (Book 4)
A Governess of Unusual Experience (Book 5)
A Governess of Wise Years (Book 6)
A Governess of No Fear (Novella)

Never The Bride Series
Always the Bridesmaid (Book 1)
Always the Chaperone (Book 2)
Always the Courtesan (Book 3)
Always the Best Friend (Book 4)
Always the Wallflower (Book 5)
Always the Bluestocking (Book 6)
Always the Rival (Book 7)
Always the Matchmaker (Book 8)
Always the Widow (Book 9)
Always the Rebel (Book 10)
Always the Mistress (Book 11)
Always the Second Choice (Book 12)
Always the Mistletoe (Novella)
Always the Reverend (Novella)

The Lyon's Den Series
Always the Lyon Tamer

Pirates of Britannia Series
Always the High Seas

De Wolfe Pack: The Series
Whirlwind with a Wolfe

Noble titles throughout English history have, at times, been more fluid than one might think. Women have inherited, men have been gifted titles by family or gained them through marriage, and royals frequently lavished titles or withdrew them as reward and punishment.

The Chance brothers in this series agreed to split the four titles in their family line, rather than the eldest holding all four. It is a decision that defines their brotherhood, and their very different personalities.

Get ready to meet a family that is more than happy to scandalize Society...

Chapter One

November 1, 1812

AND JUST AS she knew they would, everyone was looking.

"Miss Edith Stewart, the flourishing rose—"

"Yes, yes, we don't need all that," muttered Edie, pushing past the footman announcing every arrival in a loud, clear voice.

Her arm was tugged as though by a solid weight. Turning, she saw her father's impassive, pale face.

"We'll stay," he said quietly. "For all of it. Start again, man."

Edie swallowed all her protests, standing as they were on the top of the steps that led down into Lady Romeril's ball, and glared at the footman. He had the goodness to look ashamed of himself, but when your father was a baron, a glare was typically insufficient to make servants do what you wanted.

"Ahem," said the footman, evidently a little lost. "Erm. The Right Honorable Baron Stewart. Miss Edith Stewart, the flourishing rose, as chosen by our queen, Queen Charlotte…"

Edie suffered through it as eyes turned throughout the elegantly appointed ballroom. Apparently, the beautifully playing musicians, the chatter and gossip already flowing through the place, and the punch table were insufficient to hold the room's attention.

No, they had to stare at her. And over a ridiculous title, one that meant nothing, that suggested naught but—

"—and Ireland," finished the footman, his cheeks pink. "My lord."

"Thank you," Edie's father said stiffly, his narrow shoulders held back.

Then, and only then, did he step forward to enter the ballroom.

Holding on to his arm and wishing to goodness she had refused to attend this one, Edie kept her head high as her father would have wished but ensured never to permit her attention to settle on a single person.

Meeting someone's eye, after an introduction like that, was liable to suggest scandal. Either that she thought herself above her station, as merely the daughter of a baron, or that she—heaven forbid—was attempting to attract attention.

"Now, what did we agree?" murmured her father almost without moving his thin lips.

Edie sighed but made sure not to let her shoulders show it as they came to a gentle stop just to the side of the wall. Really, this was ridiculous. She was four and twenty, and—

"Edie."

Plastering a genteel expression on her face that would convince anyone looking at them that nothing was amiss, Edie said in a singsong voice, "Dance with as many gentlemen as possible. Never dance with the same gentleman twice. Only one glass of punch. Smile with the ladies. Only discuss—"

"Excellent," said her father at the same time as Lady Romeril approached them.

"Ah, Lord Stewart, Miss Stewart, I thought I heard you announced," declared their hostess, moving toward them in a rush of green silk. "Twice, I believe. How remarkable. Wanted to make an entrance?"

Edie's cheeks burned as her father merely gave their hostess a charming smile.

"Oh, you know how it is. The echoes in a place as wonderful as your ballroom," Lord Stewart said easily. "A hostess such as yourself, who is so careful and dedicated to her guests, you were clearly concentrating to make sure we were sufficiently welcomed. As, I thank you, we have been."

He reached out, took the eagerly proffered hand, and brushed his lips across the shapely woman's gloved knuckles.

Lady Romeril, against all expectations of the room, giggled, her golden ringlets bouncing across her cheek.

Edie tried her best not to roll her eyes.

David Stewart, the fourth Baron Stewart, who greatly enjoyed being a lord, had been a charmer all his life. That was what her mother had said. Lady Stewart had been grateful, according to the family tales, to even be noticed by the handsome, amiable gentleman when she had first been presented to court.

And become a flourishing rose, or some such nonsense.

Edie didn't see it herself. Oh, Father was charming in that old-fashioned way. All obsequiousness and bows. But he wasn't—

"—too kind, I assure you," said Lady Romeril, fluttering her eyelashes.

Everyone around them was staring—*staring*. And well they might. Edie had never seen Lady Romeril flutter her eyelashes in her entire life.

Her father was still speaking smoothly. "—and there was no better place for my young Edie to appear tonight, not after last week's pronouncement."

Both he and Lady Romeril peered at Edie, who attempted to keep her face impassive.

"Yes, yes, very impressive," said Lady Romeril, her eyes sharpening now that she was no longer being admired by the handsome, silver-streaked widower Lord Stewart. "And you are delighted, aren't you, Miss Stewart? To be declared so?"

Edie hesitated.

Only for a moment. The instant she caught her father's eye, she uttered the trite, little statement they'd rehearsed.

"It's an honor, to be sure," she said, flicking out her fan and fluttering it before her.

Lord Stewart's eyes narrowed.

Admittedly, the fan had not been part of the agreement—but really, did he expect her to be gawped at all night without a fan to retreat behind?

"I do hope there are equally as impressive gentlemen with whom my daughter might become acquainted," her father said to Lady Romeril. "I am sure you will understand the delicacy of such a matter, my lady."

Edie tried not to groan. *Does he have to be so obvious?*

"Yes, yes, I quite understand," Lady Romeril responded. "In fact, there are a few gentlemen I would suggest. First of all…"

Without engaging any muscles that weren't required for the subtle movement, Edie took a small step backward.

There was no response from her father.

Attempting to hold her breathing, Edie took another. And a third.

By the fifth step backward, she was sufficiently out of earshot and could give a heavy sigh as she reached the ballroom wall.

Dear God, but she hated this.

She hadn't wanted to come in the first place. The argument had been brief, for Lord Stewart always got his own way, particularly when it came to appearing in public. But Edie had been most stringent in her argument.

"I have no wish to be stared at," she had said only minutes before in the carriage as it had pulled up outside Lady Romeril's London home.

"And neither do I," her father had replied, against all evidence to the contrary. "But it has to be done, my dear. If we are to find you an apt husband—"

The heat of the ballroom was pushing the memory aside. He was a good man, her father. Overbearing, certainly. Overly worried about the world's opinion, and too obsessed with his own reputation. But he would never make her marry a man she did not wish to.

That he wished her to marry, and soon, and to a great title...

That had been clear from the instant she had entered Society.

"—heard? A Danish prince, they say. Yes, I thought that outrageous too, but the scandal sheets said—"

Edie's head turned.

A pair of ladies, probably only a few years older than herself, was standing just to her left. Their fashionable gowns were trimmed with gold thread, and while one had tiny freshwater pearls entwined in her light-brown hair, the other had a most alarming trio of feathers woven through her black tresses.

But what they were wearing was immaterial. It was what they were speaking of that had drawn Edie's attention.

"—read it myself this morning," the befeathered lady was saying in a hushed tone that nevertheless carried the few feet between them. "The entire scandal sheet was—"

A passing trio of gentlemen arguing profusely about a card game walked between Edie and the gossiping ladies, entirely obscuring their speech. When the men had disappeared into what must have been the card room, Edie took a slight step to the left.

"—but I haven't seen him about the place," the woman with pearls in her hair said loftily. "And I am sure I would know a prince when I saw one."

Edie had read that precise scandal sheet that morning. *Whispers of the Ton.* It was her favorite, and despite her father's constant mutterings that he would forbid the thing within the house, he hadn't ever followed through on that threat.

She wasn't sure why. Perhaps he believed it evidence of husband-hunting activities.

The very idea!

"There you are," said a smug voice she knew all too well.

Ensuring a delightful smile was on her lips as she turned, Edie saw with a sinking feeling that her father had appeared. Beside him was a man with grizzled, gray hair and a moustache that had clearly been recently dipped in port.

Her hopes sank even lower. *Oh, Father, what are you thinking?*

"This," Lord Stewart said, his chest puffed out in evident delight, "is His Highness, Henrik Olafson, the Crown Prince of Denmark."

Edie remembered herself just in time. After sinking into a low curtsey—so low, her knees almost touched the floor—she rose and beamed as prettily as she could manage.

"Actually, I'm not the crown prince," said the man awkwardly. "I'm just a minor noble. The title of 'prince' is a courtesy for—"

"Prince Henrik," Lord Stewart said firmly, "wanted to be introduced to you, my dear, for a dance. Isn't that wonderful?"

Edie looked helplessly into her father's eager eyes. "Yes. Very wonderful."

For there was no point in arguing with him, was there? At least not here in public, where anyone could overhear them. The whispered mutterings that would follow them after such a disgraceful display could never be outrun.

Not even if she somehow became the wife of this clearly embarrassed nobleman.

"Off you go, then!" trilled her father, pushing the gulping Prince Henrik toward her. "Listen, I think they're about to start a Scotch reel. How fortuitous!"

Fortuitous, indeed, Edie thought dryly as she accepted Prince Henrik's arm and allowed herself to be led to the center of the room. *Except for the fact that we're at a ball.*

Of course, she could not deny that as the flourishing rose of the Season, she was receiving far better treatment than other ladies seeking husbands. Even if it *was* almost a new Season and she had not yet secured a match. She knew her time at the center of Society was growing short. Part of her hoped to fade into the crowd with a new crop of debutantes come January, but her father would be disappointed. He wanted her married while she still held the title, however superfluous. But what was her father thinking—a prince?

Prince Henrik bowed low as she took her place in the line, and Edie allowed herself a small amount of pleasure in the opening bars of the music. Dancing was, after all, a most splendid pastime. The way the music thrummed through her, the beat matching the pulse of her—

"I am sorry, but I will not marry you," said Prince Henrik as he stepped forward to take her hand.

Edie was so utterly surprised by the bland pronouncement that she almost tripped on her skirts.

Almost. One was not a flourishing rose for nothing.

"Goodness," she said lightly, as though men frequently informed her of such things. "I was not aware that a proposal had been offered, my prince."

She had guessed at "my prince," after his comment about not being the crown prince. How did one address a prince who was not a prince?

Trying to recall the brief conversation she'd had with the man while weaving through the set, Edie maintained a light and easy smile on her face.

You never know who could be watching.

"I apologize—my English is not strong, and I do not understand your customs," Prince Henrik said stiffly, taking her hand once more and turning her about in a circle before returning to the line of gentlemen. "No offense is meant."

"No offense is taken," said Edie, curiosity curling around her heart. "And—And I do not know your customs, my prince, so forgive me if I also speak out of turn... But I have no wish to marry you. So you see, there is no problem."

The grizzled man's face softened. "Ah. That is good."

"Yes, I rather think it is," Edie said quietly, adding to herself, "though my father will not be pleased."

She could see him. It was difficult not to, standing as he was right at the front of the watching crowd, nodding eagerly whenever she caught his eye.

Despite herself, Edie could not help but chuckle. He was a dear man, her father, even if he was ridiculous at times. He had plainly thought he'd done a spectacular job, finding royalty at the ball to introduce her to.

Such a shame that Prince Henrik Olafson had no interest whatsoever in marrying her.

"You do not come here to be married?"

Edie winced at the man's unrefined manner, but she could not deny the truth of what he said. "I suppose I did."

He nodded curtly as he took both her hands, promenading her slowly down the set. "I do not."

"I see," Edie said, not seeing at all.

And then Prince Henrik's cheeks crimsoned, just out of the corner of her eye. As she turned, she noticed his gaze had fixed on someone in the crowd. Someone else who was watching, who appeared to have the same level of great interest as her own father.

It was a gentleman of perhaps Prince Henrik's age. He wore a military uniform she did not recognize—Danish, probably—and had such a look of adoration in his eyes, Edie felt quite rude observing it.

The stranger saw her curious expression and turned away.

Edie looked at the prince. He was blushing furiously. "I see."

His forehead wrinkled immediately. "I would not wish you to presume—"

"It is of no matter to me whom anyone loves," Edie said softly so they could not be overheard. "Not when two people love and admire each other. It is none of my business, and I... I wish you happiness, my prince."

For a moment, she believed she had overstepped. Prince Henrik said nothing as he returned her to her place in the set and the musicians trilled their last notes. Applause rang out around the ballroom.

And then he smiled. "You are very charming, Miss Stewart."

"Just make sure to tell my father that," Edie said dryly. "Now, I'm going to hide—I mean, help myself to a glance of punch."

Her partner nodded, then bowed low before striding off in the other direction toward a worried-looking gentleman who had been watching them closely.

Edie sighed to herself as she meandered to the punch table. It had a very handy column behind which she could remain out of sight of the general crowd.

Well, you never know a gentleman's preferences by looking. Hopefully, Prince Henrik and his... *friend* were happy. They certainly appeared to have enough affection between them to ensure more happiness for themselves than most.

The glass of punch was unwelcomingly tepid in her hands. Were her hands warm, or was the punch a tad more potent than she had expected?

It mattered not. Edie took a large gulp of the liquid, affecting a coughing fit that was not completely false, and ducked behind the column.

There. At least she could stand here in peace for five minutes.

"—talk of the town," a low voice was muttering. "I never would have imagined it—the Earl of Lindow, married!"

"Worse, to a woman of no fortune and as far as I can tell, no family," replied another gentleman's voice with a hint of skepticism. "I heard from one quarter that she's the penniless daughter of a vicar!"

"Not anymore, she's not," replied the first voice. There was a trace of admiration in this one. "She's a countess now. I suppose we shall have to hope Lord Lindow doesn't lose his charm, even if he is married. He was a terrific gambler."

"Dice and cards, yes, and the man knew his way around a racecourse like no other," said his companion pensively. "I wonder if the Countess of Lindow will permit such pursuits?"

"In fact, I heard…"

Precisely what the man had heard, Edie was never to discover. They moved away, glasses perhaps filled with punch by now, leaving her to wonder at the gossip following this Earl of Lindow.

It sounded as though he had married for love. At least, she could fathom no other reason why a peer such as an earl would marry a penniless woman as described by their chattering.

Married for love.

Her lungs tightened, just for a moment, before Edie forced herself to inhale more naturally. It did happen to some. Her parents may have been a match for other reasons as well, but they'd certainly held a strong affection for one another. One heard about such things. One hoped for—

But there was no point in getting her hopes up. Not with the moniker most unwillingly bestowed upon her by the queen. Not with her father lurching about in search of a suitor.

And now that she came to think of it, her father had not sought her out after her dance with Prince Henrik. A flicker of excitement pulsed through her. Had she finally found a hiding place where even Lord Stewart could not find—

"You," said a stern voice, "are hiding."

Edie jumped so rapidly, she almost spilled her punch down her cream, silk gown.

She turned with a weak smile to her father. "Not hiding, precisely, merely standing in an out-of-the-way—"

"Don't give me that, Edie. I know you," said Lord Stewart with a twinkle in his eye. "And you were hiding."

Her shoulders slumped. "I'm being paraded."

"Nonsense," her father said briskly. "Nothing quite like attending a ball, particularly one hosted by such a woman as Lady Romeril, to force the young bucks to sit up and take notice. Particularly when one is—"

"A flourishing rose," Edie said wearily in unison with her father.

It was starting to become tiresome. Nothing had prepared her for the onslaught that coming into Society would bring. The instant she had arrived at court and had that terrible pronouncement declared over her, she'd been unable to move for invitations arriving at home.

Her father, of course, had been delighted.

"Just like your mother," he'd said just yesterday. "I knew you had it within you, Edie. You are beautiful for a purpose."

And that purpose, Edie thought dully as her father glanced about the place, seeking another insipid gentleman to whom to introduce her, *is to hook a rich, eligible, and by all accounts fashionable young man.* Then they could parade about together.

"I would prefer to go home," she said softly, placing a hand on her father's arm.

He did not appear to hear her. Oh, he heard that she had spoken—but her actual words appeared immaterial. "Everyone wants to meet you, Edie."

Edie sighed.

They wanted to meet the flourishing rose. They wanted to gawp at a woman who had officially been declared beautiful—and by a queen, no less. They had no desire to actually meet her. Speak with her. Know anything about her more than her name and her dowry, and to see how beautiful she was.

A sick sort of roiling tension curled in her stomach.

"Absolutely everyone in the *ton* wants to meet you," said her father insistently, patting her hand as it rested on his arm. "The whole world wants to meet Miss Edith Stewart, the flourishing—"

"Yes, that's exactly the problem," Edie said with heating cheeks.

She was not one to be rude, but wasn't this getting ridiculous? After all, none of these people who supposedly were so eager to meet her knew anything about her, save the inane title she had been given. They did not know her character, her preferences, her sense of humor. They did not even know if she had any of these.

And yet they were desperate for her company?

It's all so false, Edie could not help but think as she followed her father's gaze and looked out over the crowd filling Lady Romeril's ballroom. All of it—it was all an act.

Some people did not wish to be here at all and yet had plastered smiles on their faces. Some had merely plastered plaster, white powder and rouge everywhere—and not only on the ladies. Her keen eye could tell the "natural" looks were not so natural. The artifice of jewels and feathers and gold and silver thread overwhelmed the eye. It was all so... so false.

"—and I don't think that previous gentleman was quite suitable," her father was saying, his voice dull as he continued to look about the room. "You stay here, my dear, and I'll go and find someone more appropriate."

"Appropriate for what?" Edie asked testily, her pulse thrumming at her rudeness.

Lord Stewart blinked. "Why, for you to charm and wed, naturally. Now be a dear, and stay here."

"But—"

He was gone before Edie could make any sort of remonstrances to the contrary.

Not that it would matter, she thought dully. Kind and gentle as her father was, he was still Baron Stewart. Painfully aware of that, in fact. Nothing would do but his only daughter—his only child—being married off to someone eminent and impressive.

Edie flicked out her fan and attempted to hide behind it. It was raised too high to be graceful, but there it was. She had little desire to be mentioned in the scandal sheets tomorrow for her inexpert fan wafting. She had no desire to be mentioned in them at all.

No, it was reading them that gave the most happiness.

Her eyes followed her father's meandering journey through the ballroom just as she was knocked a step back by an overenthusiastic mama with what appeared to be seven daughters.

"Careful there, Josephine!"

"Yes, Mama…"

Edie had been forced closer to the wall, which in her opinion was no bad thing. Firstly, because it kept her out of the way of most of Lady Romeril's guests, but secondly, because it brought to view something she had not previously noticed.

An alcove hidden by a curtain.

Lady Romeril had decorated her ballroom most splendidly, and by all accounts, she altered the decorations with each celebration. This evening, floor-to-ceiling bolts of shimmering silk hung from the ceiling, making the walls appear like those of a tent. It was a very captivating idea.

It also, however, hid the fact that just to Edie's left was an alcove. The fabric had fluttered at the rush of movement from the mama and her many daughters, revealing a recess of several feet. There were candles in there, and two chaise lounges.

A place to hide.

Edie did not have to think. Her instincts, her need to be out of sight even for just a moment, overrode all other sensibilities.

Stepping slowly toward the fabric hiding the alcove, Edie was careful to keep her fan fluttering nonchalantly as though she were merely meandering around the ballroom.

And then, heart in her mouth, she ducked into the alcove.

Immediately, it brought blessed relief. There was no other place to hide in Lady Romeril's ball, but this afforded protection the like of which Edie had not expected to find in such a crowded, overwhelming space. There was a scent here of sandalwood, blackcurrant, and vanilla, most delightful, filling her lungs and causing flickers of delight.

Quiet, and solitude. The chaise lounges looked particularly comfortable, frilly though they were in red taffeta, and the window—

"I do apologize," said the man lounging by the window, an arm resting on the sill. "But this hiding spot is taken."

Chapter Two

IF THERE WAS one thing worse than a ball, it was being invited to the damned thing.

Frederick Chance, Viscount Pernrith, smiled tightly at the footman who examined his invitation closely. The angular man brushed a finger across the inked name, as though testing whether the ink were still wet.

"Is there something wrong with my invitation?" Frederick asked politely.

It took every ounce of strength within him to keep his voice level, but he managed it. He always managed it. No matter the situation in which he found himself, no matter how the rudeness around him, he was always the calmest one in any situation.

He had to be.

The footman cleared his throat. The noise echoed around the impressive hallway of Lady Romeril's residence. Frederick definitely did not glance around to see just how many people were staring.

He knew they would be. There was always someone willing to gawp at a gentleman in difficulty. The gossip would only increase when they discovered who it was…

"Nothing wrong, no, sir," said the footman vaguely. He was still staring at the piece of card.

Frederick's jaw tightened. "My lord."

The footman looked up. "What?"

"It's 'I beg your pardon', and I am 'my lord', actually," said Frederick, trying his best not to sound as testy as he felt. "And that is my invitation, and I am entering now."

Ignoring the spluttered protests of the liveried servant, he snatched the invitation back, stuffed it in his waistcoat pocket, and marched into the ball.

God knew why. It wasn't as though he actually wanted to be here. Any Society occasion was just another excuse for people to pity him, as Frederick well knew. It would be all about the *ton* tomorrow, how Viscount Pernrith had had a spat with a footman—a mere servant!

But then, they would say, his lungs tightening, *"You know where he comes from..."*

The place was packed. Lady Romeril had outdone herself, as usual, in both decoration and volume of invitations. Frederick could hardly move off the top step, where another liveried footman appeared to be having significant difficulties.

"The Duke and Duchess of... His lordship, the Right Reverend... Ah, my lord," the man said, mopping his wide brow with what appeared to be a sopping-wet handkerchief. "They come so quickly, you know, it becomes impossible to announce everyone properly. Here, let me do you. The Right Honorable—"

"That's enough," said Frederick softly.

There was no unkindness in his voice. No true censure, beyond the fact that he wanted the man to cease yelling his name.

But it was too late.

"—The Viscount Pernrith!" screeched the footman, apparently delighted he'd managed to get an entire name spoken before the individual had descended the stairs.

Frederick prepared himself. It was always the same. Why he had deigned to accept the invitation from Lady Romeril when he'd known there was going to be so much of a fuss, he did not know. Something dark within him, perhaps, had known he had to put on a brave face for the world. Had to appear in public.

His brother Cothrom demanded nothing less.

In truth, it wasn't so bad. A few gentlemen raised eyebrows at the sound of his name, but their conversations barely halted. A lady or three glanced around more out of habit, he thought, than any actual interest. They looked him up and down, swiftly noted the stylish yet relatively inexpensive jacket and breeches, along with the Hessian boots, which had seen finer days, and turned away.

And that, it appeared, was it.

Frederick let out a long, slow breath he hadn't noticed he'd been holding. *It's going to be a quiet ball, then.*

"My word, look at you," said a sneering voice. "Didn't think we'd see any of your kind hereabouts."

The tension that had so recently departed from his shoulders immediately returned—and trebled when Frederick turned and saw who had spoken.

Mr. Lister. The most irritating man in the *ton* at the moment. The devil rarely had a civil tongue in his head and saw no problem with making mischief.

Frederick did what he always did when in public and allowed a slow, unreadable smile to creep over his face. "Mr. Lister," he said politely, bowing.

The other man did not bow. Striding over to the viscount, the diminutive Mr. Lister said nastily, "I'm surprised Lady Romeril bothered to send you an invitation, I must say. I did not know your kind bothered with such things."

The musicians were starting to play now. Gentlemen led their partners to the lines and Frederick almost allowed himself to be distracted.

But only for a moment. He was not here to dance. Or to find a partner.

What woman, after all, would wish to be partnered with him?

"I must say I do not know what you mean, Mr. Lister," he said as politely and calmly as he could. "I can see Viscount Braedon over there, dancing with a lady, and I passed Viscount Donal and Viscount Wynn in the entrance way. There appear to be plenty of viscounts, *Mr. Lister.*"

Try as he might, Frederick could not keep his irritation from causing him to emphasize the second-to-last word perhaps a mite too long.

That had to explain the fiery fury in the man's pinched expression. "I didn't mean viscounts, you fool. I meant—"

"I know precisely what you meant," Frederick said, his voice continuing cold. "And yes, I know I am invited only on the request of my brother, William Chance, Duke of Cothrom. I do not need you to tell me that."

Despite the reminder of Frederick's superior connections, Mr. Lister's sunken eyes gleamed. "So you know you're not welcome, then?"

It was impossible to talk to such people. Especially when one's blood was boiling, and all one wanted to do was shout at the man that yes, Frederick didn't belong anywhere, wasn't welcome anywhere, and he was sick and tired of it.

Not that Frederick would permit such an outburst. Particularly not in public.

So he strode away. There was no point in arguing with the man.

Mr. Lister shouted something after him—of course he did—but there was no possibility of hearing the rudeness over the loud chatter, and the scrape of knives and forks on plates coming from the dining room, and the musicians, and the conversation of the dancers.

His three brothers had undoubtedly been invited. Lady Romeril would not have been so forgetful as to include the most scandalous Chance brother on her invitation list, and entirely forget William Chance, Duke of Cothrom; John Chance, Marquess of Aylesbury; and George Chance, Earl of Lindow.

The family with four sons—each with their own title. Yes, the

Chances were not a family the *ton* would soon forget.

Admittedly, only two of the brothers would own Frederick in public, but that did not halt him from glancing about the room seeking a friendly—or at the very least familiar—face.

They were nowhere to be found. The startlingly sky-blue eyes of the Chances were absent. There was no one here who would happily talk with him.

And so Frederick was able to do three things in very quick succession.

First, he was able—just about—to force himself to forget that every single person at this ball pitied him. No man wanted to be pitied. Particularly not for *that*.

Second, he swiftly picked up not one, but two glasses of punch that had just been poured by an exhausted-looking footman.

And third, he managed to slip behind a long, silk hanging over a recess he'd known was there.

Frederick inhaled deeply in the small room that had been hidden by the silk. The noise of the ball was muffled here—it was amazing the difference that silk made.

It was also impressive just how swiftly his nerves calmed, now that he knew he was alone. Out of sight. Unlikely to be judged, to be pitied, to be spoken to like that goddamn Lister had.

Here, in the little alcove that had never been obscured from view at any of Lady Romeril's previous balls, he could hide. Sit here for a few hours, drink his punch, then leave. He had been announced—it wasn't like Cothrom could complain he had not attended. But he wouldn't be subject to the *ton's* nonsense. He could just hide here.

Frederick sighed heavily, rolling his shoulders as he walked to the window. Fatigue was threatening to tempt him toward the taffeta chaise lounge, and if he fell asleep here and was found later...

Well. Then even Cothrom wouldn't be able to stop the gossip-mongers.

He placed the two glasses of punch on the windowsill and stared at the mottled glass. It shimmered with the light of the few candles left in here. The night outside made it impossible, thanks to the candles, to see through the glass. All he could see was his own reflection.

Blond hair—hair that was never tidy, no matter what he attempted to do with it. A sharp jawline with a smattering of light-gold beard that he probably should have shaved before he'd departed for Lady Romeril's ball. And eyes—hazel eyes. Eyes he hated.

Not the sky-blue Chance eyes all three of his brothers had inherited from... from their father.

In short, a gentleman of sorts and a man who had no business being a viscount.

Frederick's jaw tightened. *Well.* He had to live with that, he supposed. For the rest of his life. And that was all there was to it. As long as he could continue hiding here—

A flash of white in the window. Movement. The reflection danced, impossible to decipher. And there was a sound.

Frederick turned around.

The most beautiful woman he had ever seen had appeared, as though by magic, to stand behind him. She was holding her own glass of punch and her cheeks were flushed, as though she had managed to escape... well, a Mr. Lister of her own. Perhaps the very same man.

She had the sort of elegant figure that made artists salivate. Curves and swells precisely where one would have wanted them. But it wasn't her figure that was so captivating, though Frederick did find it rather difficult to drag his gaze upward.

No, it was her face.

The woman was exquisite. Delicate, golden-brown eyes surrounded by serious brows that nonetheless appeared to be potentially laughing at any moment. An aquiline nose that perfectly balanced the face, above a pair of lips that were eminently kissable. A soft pink, like the interior of a shell. The bottom lip was fuller than the top, and

Frederick found his throat drying as he imagined what it would be like to—

No, he couldn't think that way. He had to make her leave, didn't he? For her own sake. They were alone.

"I do apologize," Frederick said, leaning an arm on the sill in an attempt to look as languid as possible. "But this hiding spot is taken."

The delicate pink that had hitherto suffused the woman's cheeks became a brilliant, searing red.

On any other woman, it would have spoiled her looks. Become blotchy, reminded the onlooker that everyone had faults, and would have resolved the tension seeping into the small alcove.

As it was, Frederick was astonished to find it beautified her even more. There was a charming shyness to her now that only heightened her appearance. An appearance that, try as he might, he could not tear his eyes away from.

Dear God, but he wanted her.

Frederick immediately pushed the thought aside. A woman like that, even bother to give him the time of day? It was unheard of. No one wished to associate with Viscount Pernrith. Anyone who knew his history knew that he was not a suitable conversationalist for a young lady, let alone a dance partner.

Let alone a partner.

Swallowing the thought, Frederick tried to look away from the woman. Tried.

"I do apologize," the woman said in a light, soft voice that was sunshine and early-morning rain. "I did not believe this place to be occupied."

"No need to apologize," Frederick said through a hoarse throat. Thank God he'd managed to sound normal. "May I ask if there is a particular reason you are hiding?"

He had attempted nonchalance and wasn't sure if he had succeeded.

There was something about nonchalance that meant it had to come across as unstudied. The moment you worked hard for it, the thing fell apart.

It was something gentlemen just seemed to know how to do. *True gentlemen*, Frederick thought darkly. *Not someone like me.*

"'Hiding'?" The woman raised a perfect eyebrow. "I wouldn't say I was hiding, necessarily."

Frederick hesitated. *Right.*

This was unknown territory. Oh, he knew that in Society, it was perfectly permissible for an unmarried gentleman and an unwed lady to converse—and for that conversation to veer into flirting.

If chaperoned. And within sight of the public. And introduced. None of which they were.

Which was probably why there was a frisson of excitement tumbling down his spine at the thought of speaking to this ravishing beauty without the knowledge of her parents, Society... or even of her name.

The trouble was, he was hardly one to flirt. He'd had no practice at the damned thing. So how should he—

"My name is Edie," said the woman, her cheeks calming and a glimmer in her eye making Frederick's stomach lurch.

Well. And other parts of him.

Edie. It was a pretty name, and an unusual one. Even if the accompanying woman wasn't so tasteful and refined, he would never struggle to recall that name.

"Frederick," he said, mouth dry. If she wasn't going to use her formal title, he wouldn't, either. "I don't suppose there is a particular person of whom I should feel envious, is there, Edie?"

Edie. It was scandalous, speaking her first name like this. She could be a duchess—no, Frederick corrected himself, glancing at her bare left hand. The daughter of a duchess, then. Or the daughter of a marquess.

And yet he had spoken to her as "Edie," and she—

She did not recoil. She did not glare at him, as so many ladies in Society did. She did not mutter about presumption, or scandal, or the shameful expectation of speaking to her.

She just... laughed. "Why would you be envious? There is no gentleman out there who has any claim to me. No more so than you, anyway."

Frederick's pulse was thumping now in a rhythm not unlike that of a torrid river.

Well, he may not have known how to flirt... but she did.

Edie stepped around the alcove, not advancing on him, exactly, but meandering her way to the chaise lounge without taking her eyes from him.

She was... inspecting him. *And it appears*, Frederick thought with a rush of desire he knew he should dam, *that she likes what she sees*.

"So if you are not hiding from a gentleman eager for your hand," Frederick said, attempting to keep his voice as light as possible, "why are you not out there? In Society?"

"I have no wish to be," came the genteel answer.

Frederick's focus flickered over the delicate wrist, the soft, shimmering skin in the candlelight, the curve of her waist just beneath—

"And why are you, Mr. Frederick, not out there?" Edie put to him, jerking his eyes back to her face. "Not breaking any hearts this evening?"

Frederick shook his head, the truth spilling from his lips before he could stop it. "Why would I want to be out there when I can be here, looking at you?"

This time, her flush was one of delight. Already, he was learning her habits. This intrigued him. This color rose from her collarbone, drawing his attention to it for only a moment. Then it rose once more to those brilliant eyes, that curved mouth, which had risen into a smile.

"But does your wife not mind you being in here?"

She had spoken lightly, but Frederick was no fool. He could see the shape of the question she would not ask.

And... she did not know who he was. If she did, she certainly would not be in here, conversing with him. And that meant he could have a little fun.

"Oh, she doesn't mind," he said nonchalantly.

He managed the tone exactly this time, so perfectly that Edie's face fell.

Frederick laughed. He could not leave her under that misunderstanding. "Or at least, she probably wouldn't, if she existed."

Edie met his gaze and there was a fiery interest there no woman had ever bestowed upon him.

His lungs tightened. There was no other word for it: he was stirred. She stirred him. Drew him in in a way no other woman ever had—or perhaps no other woman had wanted to.

But their flirtation was all it could ever be. A flirtation.

Ladies did not have flings with men like him. If they had flings at all, they were after they were married. When evidence of said fling could be passed off as a husband's child, and no one ever had to be any the wiser. He'd never been so rash himself—he knew the pain of growing up with a father who would truly own you.

And even if Edie had been married, Frederick thought ruefully, *and wished to... explore, beyond the marital bed, she would not choose someone like me.* Not if she knew his surname—knew his title. Knew the history of that title, where it and he had come from.

Not if she knew he was the former Duke of Cothrom's bastard.

No, the only reason she was still standing here with light in her eyes and a teasing laugh in the air was precisely because she did not know who he was.

"So," Edie said softly, finally stepping directly toward him now, her curiosity clearly overwhelming her. "Why are you here, then? Hiding?"

Frederick took a deep breath to fortify himself to tell the truth. Which would have worked, if he had not also taken in a great deal of the woman's scent.

Lavender. And rose. And something akin to hazelnut. A heady, potent mixture that could easily unravel a man if he wasn't too careful.

And Frederick did not wish to be careful.

The temptation to kiss her, to merely act on the instincts pouring through his veins, rose in Frederick. For a moment, he considered it. By God, it would be a pleasant way to distract himself from the evening. She was beautiful. Delightful to look at. Would she be just as delightful to touch?

"You can tell me, you know," Edie said softly, perhaps under the impression he held a great secret. "I won't tell anyone."

Frederick nodded, half-dazed by her presence. He had the strange feeling that she wouldn't. And perhaps she would not judge, either. Perhaps she would see him for who he was, the man he attempted to be, not the scandal that followed him.

Though his instincts honed over decades always told him to remain quiet, to stay unobtrusive, guaranteeing he was never the center of attention... this woman made him feel differently.

"It's not a secret, as such," Frederick began, quietly. "It's... It's just that—"

"Edie? Edie, I know you're hiding about somewhere—there you are!"

Frederick took a hasty step back as a gentleman at least three decades older than him pushed aside the silk and interrupted what had been a most riveting conversation.

And Frederick saw immediately he had made a terrible mistake.

"Dear God—Edie! You... You are alone!" hissed the man who was definitely the lady's father. "Alone, and with a gentleman! Do you wish to bring scandal down around your ears?"

Frederick swallowed. He had been foolish in the extreme to permit the conversation to go on for as long as it had. The trouble was, he had been happy throughout.

A conversation with a lady, and one so beautiful as she was... And because she did not know who he was, she had appeared to enjoy it too. If only—

She only enjoyed it because she did not know who you were, Frederick told himself sternly. *And now you have some explaining to do.*

He could feel the stiff disguise that he operated in public returning. It flowed down his spine, making his legs rigid, tightening his jaw, closing his hands into fists. He placed his hands behind his back.

"Good evening," he said woodenly to the newcomer. "May I introduce myself?"

"I don't need an introduction. I know who you are," snapped the older man. "And you should never have been talking to my daughter—and alone? You call yourself a gentleman, I suppose?"

The barb was perhaps warranted, but it still stung. *Thank God you didn't tell her who you were, and why that mattered,* Frederick could not help but think. *Then the damage would have truly been done.* Though he was certain she would learn the truth soon enough.

"—can't believe you would speak to such a man," Edie's father was muttering. He had grabbed her arm and was trying to pull her away, out of the alcove—away from Frederick Chance. "Of all the people—"

"But this gentleman has been politeness itself," Edie said, her eyes wide as she glanced over at Frederick. "I liked his conversation. I do not understand—"

"The outrage!" her father muttered.

Frederick hardly heard him. It was Edie's words that were ringing in his ears.

"I liked his conversation. I do not understand—"

No. No, she wouldn't have. Because he had not been man enough, gentlemanly enough, to explain why scandal had followed him all his life. Why he could never escape it. And why she would do better, far better, to disassociate with him.

Frederick swallowed, hard, then held his head high. He knew what had to be done.

"I quite understand, sir—"

"'My lord,'" snapped the older gentleman, "if you do not mind!"

She was a titled man's daughter. Frederick tucked that away for later, then barreled forward with his decision.

"I quite understand, my lord, why you would not wish your daughter to associate with me," Frederick said quietly. "If you will permit, I will leave now. You and your daughter can wait say, ten minutes, then leave together. No one will suspect any wrongdoing."

Not that they had done anything people might have suspected. They'd just had a delightful conversation, the like of which he had never had before, and his heart had fluttered, though it should have known not to come to life.

Frederick inclined his head curtly, then strode away.

Away from temptation. Away from scandal.

And toward a ball where he knew he was most unwelcome.

Chapter Three

November 3, 1812

LIFE WAS JUST as busy as it had been at the very beginning of the Season this year, and Edie was once again disappointed.

Well, it wasn't as though she were the only one. Pushing through the crowds that teemed in St. James's Court proved that. The whole of London, it appeared, had hastened to court the moment it was announced that the queen may appear at today's gathering.

The Royal Family.

Edie had grown up reading about them. Ensconced—or rather, entombed—in the countryside her entire life, never permitted to travel to a town larger than Winchester, the idea of the Royal Family had kept her imagination alive.

Actually meeting them… that had been more than she could ever have hoped for.

Being named the flourishing rose at the beginning of her first ever Season in town… it had been a dream.

A dream that had turned swiftly, thanks to her father, into a nightmare.

"My word, what a crush!" said Mrs. Teagan. "I had no idea it was going to be so busy!"

Edie grinned affectionately at the woman her father had welcomed so recently into their lives. "A chaperone," Lord Stewart had called her. A nanny, Edie considered her.

But there was nothing unpleasant about the widowed Mrs. Teagan, considering what sort of lady her father could have invited to take on the role of de facto mother. The woman was only about ten years older than her, light of foot when it came to dancing at home, and inclined to indulge Edie in most of her fancies.

Except, that was, her desire to avoid crowds.

"And yet it will all be worth it, naturally," puffed Mrs. Teagan, pulling herself through a trio of gentlemen who were craning their necks to see where some of their friends had disappeared to. "When the royals appear!"

Edie had thought so too, when they had arrived at St. James's Court over an hour ago. The imposing brick building had been nothing like what she had imagined when they had first visited at the beginning of this year's Season, but the interior was far more splendid. Little expense had been spared with gold gilt everywhere, the royal insignia of generations adorning artwork, sculpture, furniture. The very carpet had the royal standard woven into the delicate design, and the mullioned windows held crests of the very best families.

But the splendor of the palace could not overcome her disappointment when it started to become clear that she had been mistaken about the attraction the appearance of the royals would provide.

Oh, she was certain the hundreds of people would look around if Prinny decided to show his face, but Edie had read in *Whispers of the Ton* that he was in Brighton at present.

And that would explain, perhaps, why every eye in the place appeared to be turning around and looking for a source of entertainment. And why so many of their stares were falling on... her.

Edie's cheeks burned, but she couldn't prevent them from looking. *Flourishing rose.*

It had felt like an honor at the beginning. A joy, a triumph.

Until she had realized it only meant stares, and pointing, and treating her like a fool because she'd been given a label that was apparently declaring her beauty to the world, one that said nothing about her character.

"There she is—no, not that one—that one!"

"With the pearls? My goodness, she is pretty."

"—never heard of the Stewarts before. Who's her father? Is that her mother there?"

Edie froze. She had come here to be entertained, not *become* the entertainment. Could she convince her chaperone it was best they left? That if the Royal Family was not likely to make an appearance soon, they should instead—

"Everyone does seem to be interested in you, my dear," the plump-faced Mrs. Teagan said, squeezing her hand.

She meant it, Edie knew, as a compliment. As a wonderful success. As an achievement, something her father would have been proud of.

And he was. Edie knew very well that Lord Stewart would have been delighted to hear the crowds at St. James's Court were transfixed by her, rather than anyone of bluer blood.

But he's not the one who has to stand here and take it, Edie could not help but think, her stomach lurching painfully. He was not the one everyone gawped at, and pointed at, and commented on. Comments on her figure, her clothes, her jewels.

Anything, in fact, but actually speaking to her.

"My word, it is hot," said Mrs. Teagan, fanning her face, drawing attention to its rosy complexion, with her gloved hand. "How, this time of year?"

And Edie jumped on the excuse. "It must be the crowd. It is markedly hot, is it not?" she said brightly. "I believe there is a table over there serving lemonade. Please, Mrs. Teagan, stay here—do not exert yourself, please. Allow me."

The older woman's cheeks were pink, and there was a bead of sweat threatening to trickle down her left temple. "Well… well, if you do not mind—I will remain here, by the wall, and you—"

"I won't be a moment," Edie called over her shoulder, already striding toward the lemonade table.

She had chosen it purposefully. There were two other tables serving refreshments as far as she could see. One was offering sweetmeats, only likely to increase one's thirst and overall discomfort. The other was serving rosewater, which Edie would have infinitely preferred—if it had not been for the fact that the table was right in the center of the room, where anyone and everyone could ogle her.

The table proffering lemonade, however, was tucked back away from the busyness of the place. It was almost ignored, the guests at court today obviously preferring to see and be seen.

And that was why when Edie reached the lemonade table, she was delighted to find the crowd thinned, the footman uninterested in her, and space behind the table to stand out of the way.

Edie forced air into her lungs, grateful for the moment to halt. It was most ungrateful of her, she knew. Her father had brought her to London to find a husband, and being named the flourishing rose of the Season had been a stroke of luck neither of them could have predicted.

Yet here she was, hiding from the world, hoping no one noticed her. As she had done for months—for far too long this year. God forbid anyone actually speak to—

"Do you hide here often?" came a teasing, low voice.

Edie turned around and saw... Frederick.

Frederick, whom she did not know. He could not have been "Mr. Frederick." She had been bold enough to give him only her first name upon their introduction, and he seemed to have responded in kind. She had sought only to avoid any recognition from him at the time, if only for a short while. But he had proven more skilled at seeking the same from Edie. Despite her gentle and hopefully not suspicious questions put to Mrs. Teagan, the woman had been unable to help Edie discern who the man could be.

Frederick was a common enough name. She had no hints, no details with which to feed Mrs. Teagan to help her narrow down the many choices of Frederick in Society.

It was definitely the same man. The same tall languor, the same teasing smile, the same hazel-brown eyes as warm as sunshine and sweet as honey.

Edie swallowed. Not that she should have been thinking such things about a gentleman to whom she had still not yet been introduced. That was ridiculous.

Which did not explain why her stomach had lurched so delightfully when she had heard his voice. Why her pulse had skipped a beat when she had turned to see him, leaning against the wall there, as equally out of sight of the court as she wished to be. How delighted her soul was to have another opportunity to speak with him.

An opportunity that, this time, would not be interrupted by a well-meaning Lord Stewart...

"I-I have never hidden here before, no," Edie said, her voice trembling. She sipped her tepid lemonade to strengthen herself. "Have you?"

"Frequently," said Frederick with a grin. "One has to be seen at such things, but I'm not always... welcome, I suppose you would say."

There it was again—that hint of mischief, of danger, of scandal. Edie stepped forward, only two or three feet from the gentleman who proved to be such a mystery.

He had dropped hints when she had first spoken to him at Lady Romeril's ball.

"It's not a secret, as such. It's... It's just that—"

Yet there did not appear to be anything uncouth about him. Frederick was dressed well, his silk-green cravat matching his waistcoat. His hair was wild, to be sure, but Edie was not certain about the fashions of gentlemen in London. They were all so... so different from those in Woodhurst.

"So," said Frederick, glancing about with a grin. "Are you allowed to talk to me today?"

Edie could not stop the heat from blossoming across her cheeks and she did not wish to. Her father had always told her that she was most becoming when pink.

Not that I want Frederick to admire me, she thought hastily. Not at all. It was only… Well. He may as well admire her, if he was going to see her. And he was a handsome man. There was a seriousness underneath the teasing that spoke of a trustworthy character.

"'Allowed to talk to you'?" Edie replied, as lightly as she could manage while simultaneously thanking her stars it was Mrs. Teagan, and not Lord Stewart, accompanying her today. "I suppose not."

Her father had made himself perfectly clear, as the two of them had waited in the alcove at Lady Romeril's ball.

"I never want to see you with that man again," Lord Stewart had muttered in a low hiss. "To think, you'd found yourself—but you didn't know who he is."

"I *still* don't know who he is," Edie had been unable to prevent herself from saying. "Who is he, Father?"

"Never you mind," her father had said grimly.

His response had only piqued her interest and made it *more* difficult to forget the charming gentleman who had so swiftly vanished from her sight. When Edie had returned to the ball, hopeful to catch a glimpse of the mysterious Frederick and be formally introduced, he had been nowhere to be found.

Gone. Just like that.

"You suppose not?" A low voice brought Edie back to the present. Frederick's eyes were glittering. "Well, all the more reason to speak to me, I would say."

Edie laughed, despite herself, despite knowing this was precisely the sort of man her father had warned her about.

Rakehells. Rogues. Blaggards. Seducers. Philanderers.

When Lord Stewart had given her the list in the carriage ride from

Woodhurst to London, Edie had memorized it. After all, what would she want to do with a man like that? An association with such a creature would be abhorrent!

Or at least, so she had thought.

Now she was taking another step closer to the painfully magnetic Frederick, starting to realize just how ladies lost their reputation in a place like London. Why, this man could suggest they slip out of St. James's Court and find somewhere quieter to talk, and she...

Edie swallowed. She would go with him.

His charm and good looks did not hurt, but there was something more. Something she could not explain, not even to herself.

Perhaps it was the fact that he was so evidently forbidden. The sweetest treats were those stolen from behind the backs of others and enjoyed completely alone.

Edie cleared her throat. Not that she was about to do such a thing.

"Do you read the scandal sheets, *Edie*?"

I am not delighted he had remembered my name, she told herself firmly as an unbidden smile crept across her lips. *Not delighted at all.*

Still, she could not prevent her eagerness from containing some of that delight. "I admit I do like them. In fact, I think it probably fair to say that I love them."

Frederick nodded. "I prefer newspapers myself, but having perused them both this morning, they concurred. The flourishing rose is here."

Edie's gasp caught in her lungs.

Did... Did he not... Was it possible he did not know?

"I thought I'd come here and take a look," Frederick was saying, completely unaware of the thoughts rapidly firing through her mind. "Though the place is packed and that makes it difficult to see anyone properly."

Edie glanced distractedly to her right. It was becoming a crush rather than a gathering, he was right. She could just about see Mrs. Teagan, almost pinned to the wall on the opposite side of the room.

She should be concerned, she knew. She should be conscious she was alone, unchaperoned for all intents and purposes, and with a gentleman whom her father...

But all she felt was exhilaration. Mrs. Teagan would not be able to interrupt them, not for a good few minutes.

"Though in truth," Frederick said in a low voice, almost a caress. Edie turned to him, unable to stop herself, flushing at the intensity of his look. "In truth, I cannot believe there could be a woman here more beautiful than you."

And she was flattered. Edie could not help but be flattered, of course. Who did not want a handsome gentleman declaring that you were the most beautiful woman to be found?

And yet...

Edie pushed aside the rebellious thought that she knew was most unbecoming of a lady. She had to be grateful. She had to be flattered. To be anything else was... was unruly. Ungracious.

Not becoming of a flourishing rose at all.

"You have a very discerning eye, Frederick," Edie said aloud. Was that a spark of delight in his eyes, that she had recalled his name? "Are you a florist?"

The man blinked. "Am I a—my lady, I am a gentleman."

Oh, bother. She had offended him with her quip.

Blushing furiously at the mistake her attempt at flirtation had caused, Edie said hurriedly, "No, I know that—it was a jest. A bad one. I only meant—well. *I* am the flourishing rose."

It felt so ridiculous saying it like that. Her father gained great enjoyment declaring such a thing, but it was not something to which Edie had grown accustomed yet.

She was not certain she ever would.

The noise in the place was growing swiftly, so Frederick could speak naturally. That did not prevent him, however, from leaning forward. Closer. He was now merely inches away.

"You are Miss Edith Stewart?" he asked.

She nodded. It did not feel fair he knew her full name and she still did not know his.

"And what does that mean, Ed—Miss Stewart? What does being the flourishing rose mean?"

Edie swallowed the answer she wished to give. It meant a loss of control and a need to always look perfect. It meant everyone saw her and painted what they wanted to see upon her, then acted surprised when she had her own ideas, her own tongue. It meant her father had this ridiculous idea of her marrying a duke. A duke!

She looked into the open expression, the curious gaze, and realized the man was actually waiting for a reply.

A man, waiting to hear what she had to say?

Edie had never known the like. But then, she had never encountered a gentleman quite like Frederick... Frederick who?

Why was she so hesitant to end the mystery and come right out and ask?

"I suppose it means I am the most eligible woman in the *ton*," Edie heard herself say.

Frederick jerked his head at the crowd of people on the other side of the lemonade table. "More than all of them?"

It was the perfect opportunity, and Edie knew her father would never forgive her if she did not take it. Even if it was talking to a man her father clearly did not like. What reason he could have for disliking a man she was sure neither of them had ever met, she did not know.

And so despite her instincts, despite her wishes, Edie performed as she knew the flourishing rose should have. "Oh, yes," she said, fluttering her eyelashes. "I am more eligible than any other woman you meet, Mr. Frederick."

It would have worked on any other gentleman. Edie had seen the way they had looked at her. Possessive, as if she truly had turned into the rare flower her title purported her to be.

But Frederick was different. He took a step back, a furrow creasing his forehead. "I see."

Edie did not understand. All gentlemen who saw her desired her. She had not been mistaken in the hungry look Frederick had given her at Lady Romeril's ball. If they had not been interrupted…

Her imagination had given her plenty of different options in the succeeding two days, most of them ending in Frederick giving her such a kiss that her toes curled just picturing it.

Yet for some reason, he was now examining her… almost coolly.

"Truth be told, it's a tad irritating," Edie said in a rush, unable to hide the truth any longer. "I wouldn't say I'm half as charming as Miss Eaton, or as intriguing as the widow Lady Dalmerlington. Yet here I am. With a title I did not earn, or even seek to receive."

Something flickered across Frederick's face. Not darkness, exactly. It wasn't a shadow. If anything, it was the opposite of a shadow. It was a skimming light that shone in the man's eyes, as though he had seen something that sparkled just behind her. His expression changed so utterly that Edie gasped.

It had been—well, something she had never seen before.

Frederick smiled. "I admire your honesty."

"It is a quality I typically attempt to hide," Edie admitted.

Why she had done so, she was not sure. It was not good manners to admit to one's faults in public, particularly not when at St. James's Court and attempting, in her father's words, to "hook a husband."

But this man drew the truth from her in a way Edie could not explain. It was not just his good looks. There were plenty of good-looking men in Society, though she couldn't think of any in this moment.

It was more than that. There was a softness, a gentleness she had never encountered in another. This was a man, she felt, with whom she could be completely herself.

Utterly open.

Vulnerable.

"I understand what you mean about titles unearned," he said quietly. "It is a strange sort of burden, being asked to live up to a title you would not have necessarily chosen for yourself."

Edie stared. "You... You understand me perfectly."

It was the wrong thing to say, but it was how she felt. Never before had she been able to articulate just why being declared this Season's flourishing rose had felt so... so utterly wrong.

But he understood. Living up to a title you would not have necessarily chosen for yourself—that was precisely what it was.

Edie tried not to lean closer to the man, but it was difficult. There was a warmth radiating from him and she wanted to be washed in its waves. To be close to him. To know what it was to—

"As you are the flourishing rose, however," Frederick continued, "I don't think you would wish to be talking to me, then."

There it was again—that hint of a scandal in his past her father had been unable, or unwilling, to explain.

Edie found herself within mere inches of the man's face. She stepped backward hurriedly. She could not permit herself to give into that particular desire. *The very idea!*

"You know, my father clearly knows who you are," she said quietly. "He has evidently formed his opinion of you."

Frederick's jaw inexplicably tightened. "He *thinks* he knows me."

Now what did that mean? "But I do not even know your surname," Edie persisted, knowing just by *thinking* of him by his first name, she was going far beyond the bounds of polite Society, but she ignored the tug in her stomach signaling she had gone too far. "Or anything about you. My father—he wouldn't explain why I shouldn't be speaking to you."

His smile was brittle, somehow. All the cordiality had gone from it. "A lady should not be speaking to a gentleman unchaperoned."

"Like I am now?" Edie shot back.

Some tenderness seeped into Frederick's expression. "Just so."

"So tell me, Mr. Frederick. Why should I not be speaking to you?"

It was the question she wished more than anything to be answered.

Here they were, amidst the very core of the *ton*. The rules, regulations, and restrictions of what a lady could and could not do were determined here, by the Royal Family. It trickled down with painful speed, fashions changing so rapidly that Edie had already been forced to visit the modiste twice since her entrance into Society.

And here she was, standing beside a man to whom she had still not been introduced, talking as though…

As though there was something between them.

Frederick was grinning softly, his head tilted to one side. "If I tell you, then you'll feel sorry for me."

The idea of feeling sorry for such a powerfully built, enigmatic, attractive man was entirely alien to Edie. *The very idea!*

"I'm willing to take that risk," Edie said.

Then she did something utterly outrageous. She reached out and took the man's hand in hers.

"I'm willing to take a few risks," she said, heart in her mouth, gaze locked on the honey-brown eyes of Frederick. "Just tell me. I want to know—I need to know. Who are you, and why—"

"There you are! My goodness, the crush!" said Mrs. Teagan just behind her.

Edie and Frederick sprang apart. She had released his hand the moment she had heard the first syllable behind her, her chaperone's voice almost as familiar to her now as that of her father.

Heat burned through her. To think, she had almost been caught by—

"I think we should leave, Miss Stewart," Mrs. Teagan said decidedly, somehow ignoring Frederick's presence. "It's altogether too much here. Your father would never forgive me if you were injured. Come on."

There was no point in arguing with her. Edie had never been able to out-argue Mrs. Teagan.

Letting herself be pulled away, Edie glanced over her shoulder for one last look at the man who was starting to distract her far too much.

Her stomach jolted most pleasantly. He was looking at her, watching her leave—and with a possessive need that shot right to her core.

Chapter Four

November 5, 1812

*A*ND NOW ALL *I have to do*, Frederick thought with a groan as he lowered himself into the pristine leather armchair, *is forget all about Miss Edie Stewart.*

As though that would be easy.

"May I get you anything else, my lord?" asked the footman in such a hushed whisper, it was almost impossible to hear him.

It didn't matter. Frederick had been a member of the Dulverton Club long enough to know the routine.

Arrive and present one's greatcoat to the footman at the desk at the front. Be shepherded to the room one requested, whether it be the Smoking Room or the Chinese Drawing Room, or one of the many other rooms within the establishment. Find yourself a seat, be offered whatever you wished by the footman who was accompanying you, and be left in relative silence.

Relative, of course, to who else was in the room with you.

"Nothing, I thank you," Frederick said softly.

The footman bowed and departed.

Their voices had been kept quiet for a reason. The Reading Room at the Dulverton Club was exclusively for, as was obvious, reading. Absolute quiet—or as much quiet as could be found in the center of London—was requested at all times.

It was the perfect place to lose his mind in something else, Frederick told himself, and stop thinking about... about her.

Miss Edie Stewart.

It hadn't been too difficult to find out more about her, not with all the articles in the papers about the flourishing rose of the Season earlier this year. Her father was Baron Stewart, which meant Frederick himself was technically of a higher rank, but Frederick wasn't fool enough to think the precedence would be upheld.

It was clear Edie's father knew precisely that Frederick had been born on the wrong side of the blanket. Everyone did. He couldn't walk down a street in London without heads turning, gossiping voices muttering, and before you knew it, the news that the once-illegitimate son of the late Duke of Cothrom had been seen in such a place would spread.

The scandal sheets would be full of it. Was his mere existence to always be a scandal?

And yet Miss Stewart did not appear to know. Just how sheltered had the woman—

You weren't going to think about her, Frederick told himself forcefully.

He needed a distraction, that was all. Something to take his mind away from beautiful women who were completely out of his league.

A woman like that, with her beauty, her elegance, her reputation... she would hardly wish to be seen conversing with him. Not, that was, if she had any idea who he was.

So. A distraction.

The benefit and at times irritation of the Reading Room at the Dulverton was that one was expected to bring one's own reading material. The library, the floor above, provided a great deal of variety, but Frederick had neglected to go there first.

Well, no matter. There were three other gentlemen seated around the Reading Room, one of them quite close to him. The man, whom Frederick recognized as the Baron Packham, was at this very moment folding a newspaper to lay it aside.

Frederick leaned forward, hoping his voice would carry yet not contravene the rule on volume. "May I read your newspaper, as you have finished with it?"

He knew the moment the hawkish man dropped the paper onto the table beside him and met his stare with a cool, almost steely air, that he had made a mistake.

"Pernrith," said Lord Packham coldly down his sharp nose.

Frederick's jaw tightened. "Yes. I said, may I—"

"I heard what you said." Lord Packham did not bother to keep his voice down. He had attracted the attention of the other two gentlemen in the room, much to Frederick's displeasure. "I didn't know you were a member."

His tone was almost accusatory—as though he had been hoodwinked in some way.

Frederick knew precisely why, though by God, he wasn't going to give the man a reason to be correct.

Membership of the Dulverton Club was not a right, but a privilege. It was something most gentlemen wished for, but few achieved. It was only through the support of two of his brothers, the Duke of Cothrom and the Marquess of Aylesbury, that Frederick had even been considered.

Even if he'd been legitimized in order to inherit a family title, the stain of illegitimacy, it appeared, could reach quite far.

It did not surprise him that there were those who wished Viscount Pernrith had not been permitted membership. Still. Frederick had hardly expected a gentleman to be so frank about it.

"I merely wondered," he said in a low, calm voice he always used when someone was being rude, "if I may—"

"I heard you the first time, man. I'm not deaf," snapped Lord Packham. "Fine. Take it. I don't suppose you can afford your own, though why in heaven you think you should be here if that is the case…" His voice trailed away, but his expression was gloomy.

Frederick swallowed. He didn't wish to read the damned man's paper now, not after that exchange—but after requesting permission, and being given it, it would have been churlish of him to retract his request merely because of a man's rudeness.

After all, it wasn't as though he did not encounter such rudeness frequently.

"Thank you," he said shortly, reaching over and picking up the newspaper.

The instant Frederick had unfolded the newspaper and started perusing the front of it, Lord Packham's voice sounded in the room. Loudly. Far more loudly than necessary.

"But don't give it back to me after you've finished with it," sneered Lord Packham. "I don't want it, not after you've touched it."

Frederick's fingers tightened on the edges of the newspaper as irritation and rage flowed through him. It was insupportable! It was infuriating, to always have to receive such indignities!

And as usual, he remained silent. Though the anger coursed through his veins, Frederick said nothing. He never did.

Quelling his outrage was something he had learned at a young age, and he was far too proficient at it to cease now. Besides, as his father had once said to him gruffly, a long time ago, it only served to annoy the buggers even more if one did not rise to it.

And so, despite his desire to leave, to throw the newspaper back in Lord Packham's face and snap that it was a low-quality sheet, anyway, despite all the cravings to leave the place and not have to put up with this nonsense—

Frederick slowly turned over a page and continued to read the newspaper.

Behind the printed sheet, Lord Packham snorted. Then there was the sound of a person rising from a leather armchair, loud footfalls across the room, and the slam of a door.

Frederick turned another page.

Only when, by his calculation, he had continued reading for a good five minutes after Lord Packham had stormed out of the Reading Room, did Frederick lower the newspaper.

The other two gentlemen in the place were looking determinedly at their books. One of the tomes was upside down.

Frederick continued to read for another fifteen minutes. Then, rising as languidly as though he had just arisen from a nap by the fireside, Frederick folded the newspaper as small as he could, then stepped over to the grate that was blazing. He threw the newspaper in the fire.

It isn't as though anyone else would want to touch it now, he thought darkly. Leaving it on the chair would only create more work for the poor footmen who spent their lives clearing up after them.

Frederick had stormed—no, stepped out of the Dulverton Club minutes later, hands hastily thrust into gloves, his top hat jammed upon his head. Staying there meant only tolerating the glares, the whispers, the muttering. The guessing, the pretense of civility.

Why he bothered to go back there, he didn't know.

Fine, I do. It's the sort of thing gentlemen do, Frederick thought furiously as he strode down the street, fingers stuffed in his greatcoat pockets. The sort of thing his brothers did. The brothers who... Well. Put up with him.

Two of them had managed to see past the circumstances of his birth, in the main. Cothrom and Aylesbury were good chaps, as brothers went. Frederick knew he was fortunate they welcomed him into their homes, though it was only for the monthly Chance lunch. The next one would not be too far away, now he came to think about it.

But Lindow—

All thoughts of his third brother disappeared as Frederick turned a corner and almost walked headfirst into—

"Mr. Frederick!"

"Miss Stewart?" he said, half-dazed.

She couldn't have been here. He had spent the last few days determinedly not thinking about her.

Well. Thinking about not thinking about her, just before he'd then spent a happy hour or so most definitely thinking about her.

She was even more beautiful in the flesh than she had been in his memory, which was impressive. The dazzling exquisiteness in his mind was hardly something to be sniffed at.

The reality, of course, was better. The wintery wind had raised pink in Miss Stewart's cheeks, giving her a delightfully friendly look that made Frederick's stomach turn over backward. Her pelisse was drawn tightly around her—so tightly, it was just as fitted as the delectable gown she had been wearing at St. James's Court. The same gown he had, in a dream he had indulged in only last night, ripped off with his—

"Miss Stewart?" said the older, petite woman beside her, her jaw dropped open. "What is the meaning of this?"

Frederick blinked. *Ah.*

Yes. He and Miss Stewart had turned a corner, almost walked into each other, exclaimed each other's names—she, his first name—then stood, dazedly staring into each other's eyes.

Not the sort of thing a respectable young lady was supposed to do.

Well, he could attempt to recover this as best he could. Who was this, her aunt? He had read about Lady Stewart's passing. Strange, they looked nothing alike.

"Miss Stewart," Frederick said, attempting to clear his voice of any longing. She could see that in his face, surely. He didn't need to make an addle-pate of himself by having it so damned obvious in his tone. "How pleasant to see you again. And this is…?"

"Mrs. Teagan, my chaperone," said Edie faintly, her eyes wide with evident concern.

As well they might be. Chaperone, that made sense. That left Edie in the tricky position, Frederick could see, of needing to introduce him to her chaperone.

The trouble was, it seemed Edie still had no idea who he was.

Frederick permitted himself a grin. Well, it had been pleasant while it had lasted. He had never had more than five minutes of conversation with a pretty woman before she'd realized why his name had felt so familiar, and she'd disappeared off with scarlet cheeks and an obvious sense of relief.

It had been delightful, in fact, to flirt and converse with Miss Edie Stewart without her disappearing off over the hills, heels flying.

But it would have it end now. The moment she heard his name, it would be all over.

"Mrs. Teagan, how pleasant to make your acquaintance," Frederick said aloud, remembering to bow low. "Frederick Chance, Viscount Pernrith, at your service."

Mrs. Teagan bobbed a curtsey and started muttering pleasantries along the lines of how agreeable it was to make his acquaintance. At least, he thought she did. Frederick wasn't listening.

His attention was fixed on the woman beside her.

Miss Stewart's lips had parted, eyes wide and glittering with curiosity, and…

And that was it.

Frederick could not understand it. He had given her his name, his full title. Anyone who was anyone in the *ton* knew the sordid history of the fourth Chance brother. They knew Viscount Pernrith was not the sort of person to invite to an intimate dinner—that if he had to be included on a guest list, it was best to make it as large as possible so he could be lost in a crowd.

It was only at Cothrom's insistence that he be included that he got out of the house as much as he did.

Yet Miss Stewart—she had not recoiled, or flushed and looked away. She did not appear astounded that he had the mettle to approach and speak to her. She did not even appear pained that he had kept the truth from her.

She was just... smiling.

Mrs. Teagan was not smiling. "Lord Pernrith! Oh, I say, I do not think—"

"Yes, my father and his lordship and I had a short conversation at Lady Romeril's ball," said Miss Stewart, as though it had been a pleasant chat. "Such a shame you were indisposed for that evening, Mrs. Teagan."

Mrs. Teagan halted speaking and glanced at Frederick with a discerning eye.

Frederick swallowed. *Well, it was not exactly a lie.* Miss Stewart had not said anything untrue—however, she had described the encounter far more positively than it perhaps deserved. And indicated to Mrs. Teagan, quite erroneously, that her father approved of the acquaintance.

Acquaintance? Could he call it an acquaintance if they had never been formally introduced? If Edie had not known his full name until minutes ago?

"I hope your father is well, Miss Stewart," Frederick said, out of habit to engage with others politely more than anything. What else could he say?

"Very well, I thank you," said Miss Stewart. "Mrs. Teagan, shall we continue?"

"Not certain I should permit... I mean, a conversation on the street." Mrs. Teagan was prattling along.

"Do not concern yourself, Mrs. Teagan," said Miss Stewart lightly, stepping forward and taking—taking his arm? "His lordship and I are acquainted. Walk with us a little, my lord."

It did not look like Frederick had much of a choice. Stunned into silence by the bold step she had taken—*taking his arm? In public!*—he allowed himself to be turned around and propelled forward.

He was walking in public with a woman. Arm in arm, with a woman, in public.

Dear God, the scandal sheets will have a field day...

They continued in silence, Mrs. Teagan behind them, until eventually Miss Stewart said softly, "Why on earth would you want to keep your title a secret from me?"

Frederick swallowed. Was it possible...

Surely, it was not possible she did not know. Everyone knew! It was impossible to walk into a room and for every single head *not* to turn toward the bastard viscount.

How could she not know?

"I..." Frederick cleared his throat, hardly able to believe what was happening. "I... I did not wish to presume."

It was the truth. Many a lady would have turned up her nose at an introduction to him, even if effected by his brother, the Marquess of Aylesbury. His brother William, Duke of Cothrom, was far too involved in his growing family to worry about such a thing. If a marquess was insufficient...

And Miss Stewart was beautiful. A lady, a member of the *ton*. The debutante of the year's Season. She should have recoiled in horror at the mention of his name. Perhaps gasped. Run off with muttered excuses about appointments needing to be kept.

Instead, they were walking arm in arm together down Oxford Street.

There was only one explanation: she had no idea of the scandal she was about to put herself through.

"I apologize for leaving you so swiftly, at St. James's Court," Miss Stewart said conversationally as they meandered along a pavement. "It was most rude of me. I am sorry."

Frederick intended to speak but discovered his throat was far too hoarse for such a thing.

He should step away. Now. A woman's reputation could be destroyed through the simplest of things, and walking with such intimacy with a bastard was hardly simple.

If he had any true honor, Frederick knew what he should do.

Yet he could not. Moving away from Miss Stewart would be like leaving the sun. One did not wish to, the warmth of the rays heartening one's soul in a manner that could not be replicated by anything else in the world.

"Far be it from me to monopolize this year's flourishing rose," Frederick found himself saying. "Did you bloom?"

She must have done. She was simply blossoming now. With just a hint of a flutter of a pulse in her neck—something Frederick immediately told himself he had not noticed—Miss Stewart smiled.

"I do not believe I stayed long enough to bloom properly," she said lightly as they turned a corner. Where they were going, Frederick did not know. He certainly wasn't steering. "But blooming is not something I do particularly well, I fear."

There was something more to Miss Edie Stewart than merely being a flourishing rose. Frederick could not put his finger precisely on why he was so sure of such a thing, but he must certainly was. There was an intangible power to this woman, one repressed, fought, subjugated.

As though the world could not contain her multitudes.

"Besides, my father is greatly disappointed."

Frederick stiffened. "He is?"

The baron certainly hadn't seemed impressed with his daughter's conversation with Viscount Pernrith. Not that he could blame Lord Stewart. What man would?

Miss Stewart nodded, the graceful arc of her neck only limited by the fur wrapped around her shoulders. "Yes, I did not receive a proposal this Season. Well… I could not say I received a serious proposal I would deign to entertain. Suggestions have been made in that general direction and I—well, to continue our gardening metaphor, I rather took a pair of loppers to their hopes and made it very clear that I was not willing to be picked and stuffed into a vase to be displayed on their mantelpiece. It is a great defeat to both my father, and to Mrs. Teagan, my chaperone."

Frederick glanced over his shoulder. He could have done so over his left, which was perhaps the most appropriate thing to do. But he did not. He glanced over his right, bringing his face closer to Miss Stewart's.

Oh, the scent of her. It was mesmerizing. It was fortunate his feet were steady, though he did not know how, for Frederick was almost certain he was going to trip over, his head giddy with the intoxication of Miss Edie Stewart.

Did she know she did this? How on earth had this woman enjoyed the entire Season without receiving a single proposal?

Mrs. Teagan was walking a few feet behind them, her attention fixed on Frederick's back.

He smiled weakly, then turned back in the direction they were walking again.

She was a chaperone, after all, he told himself. It would be most surprising if she just permitted him to wander off with her charge and not ensure that nothing untoward was happening.

Except be walking together at all, he thought bitterly. *Which most mamas would never permit.*

"Though I suppose my time will come."

Frederick blinked. It was all too easy to get dazzled by Miss Stewart's presence and forget she was speaking. "Your time?"

She shrugged lightly, as though she had not a care in the world. "For proposals."

Proposals.

Marriage.

Love.

Three things Frederick knew he would not experience. Oh, he wasn't a bad-looking chap, by all accounts. He wasn't as fashionably attired as his brothers, but then his coffers did not run to the same depths. He was rarely out of an evening, spending most of his time at home, and had gotten into no real mischief, as so many other men of the *ton* had.

No, his birth alone had been enough.

And so Frederick had always told himself he had no interest in matrimony, no time for love, and therefore no need for proposals.

It had all been very simple. Until it hadn't been.

He looked into Miss Stewart's clear, brown eyes, and wished to goodness his pulse would stop beating so frantically. It was starting to become impossible to hear his own thoughts over its thunderous pulse.

What in God's name was he supposed to say?

Miss Stewart was grinning. Leaning into him as they walked, she reached over to his shoulder and pretended to pick something off his greatcoat.

The sudden proximity was overwhelming. Frederick could hardly breathe, could see nothing but Miss Stewart—nothing but Edie, the closeness of her face, her scent wafting up his nose. The abrupt connection was more than he could bear, and the gesture—oh, one of intimacy and closeness, the sort of genteel movement a wife would impart on her husband.

One lover to another.

When she straightened up, there was a knowing look in Miss Stewart's brilliant eyes. "Do not worry about Mrs. Teagan. Her hearing is not good. She will be unable to hear our conversation."

Boiling heat was bubbling through Frederick, making it difficult to think.

This was unlike anything he had ever experienced before. Ladies did not converse with him in public. They did not walk arm in arm with him down any street, let alone Oxford Street. They did not murmur, lean close and brush his arm. They did none of those things.

And Miss Stewart did.

"Yet unfortunately, I did not choose a circuitous route," said Miss Stewart softly.

Frederick blinked. "Wh-What?"

"Ah, we are here," said Mrs. Teagan cheerfully, bustling up to them and somehow extricating her charge from his arm. "Your father will be wondering what took us so long, my dear—thank you, my lord, for the escort."

They were standing outside a tall townhouse with wide gables and a front door painted in a sky blue. And Edie was smiling—a hesitant, sad sort of smile.

"I am sorry to have arrived home so quickly," she said quietly. "Good day to you, Frederick Chance, Viscount Pernrith."

Chapter Five

November 8, 1812

"—THINK YOU'LL FIND Miss Stewart is far more interested in what I have to say, Mr. Thomson," said Mr. Peters, his fleshy chin stuck up in the air.

"Well, actually," Edie began softly.

"Poppycock! Your ego does you no credit, my good man," said Mr. Thomson proudly. He puffed out his sizable chest. "I think you will find Miss Stewart has been desperate to talk to me all evening."

"You truly believe that? You must be dull-witted indeed. Consider, after all, that my fortune is far greater than…"

Precisely what Miss Stewart thought, no one knew. That was because Edie had remained standing between the two men for nigh on ten minutes, and at no point had they bothered to ask her.

Edie sighed. It was wearying, enduring this sort of discussion day after day. It did not appear to matter where they went. Almack's, private balls, dinners, card parties…

This afternoon tea had proven most hopeful. The invitation had promised entertainment, which appeared only to be a singer by the pianoforte. She was very good, but it was nothing compared to what Edie had hoped for.

And she was once again being subjected to being the topic *du jour*. Or should that be *de l'année*?

"Miss Stewart has commented on how much she liked my carriage," said Mr. Thomson pompously.

"Ah, but Miss Stewart has remarked on how delightful she found my horse," countered Mr. Peters.

Edie pursed her lips but did not bother attempting to interrupt. This was not, it appeared, anything to do with her.

What she found most amusing was that she had made neither the comment nor the remark. Clearly, her polite acceptance of a carriage ride with one and a ride in Hyde Park with the other was sufficient for the gentlemen to presume her compliments.

Men!

"—such a beautiful woman as Miss Stewart would never—"

"I know full well the beauty of Miss Stewart—she is the year's flourishing rose—"

Edie sighed, a tad louder than perhaps was polite, but it did not appear to make any difference. Mr. Thomson and Mr. Peters continued to talk loudly about how much she admired them, without at any point requiring her participation in the conversation.

Oh, it was so dull. The whole afternoon tea was dull, in fact. There was hardly anyone here she did not know, and of those she knew, there was no one she wished to—

Frederick Chance, Viscount Pernrith.

Edie's heart skipped a beat. She had not realized he had been invited. Despite—or perhaps because of—the little she knew of him, and the very little Mrs. Teagan had been willing to discuss with her, the man intrigued her. There was something... something different about him.

While other gentlemen attempted to talk over her rather than at her, her few interactions with Frederick—with Lord Pernrith—had been most agreeable.

"Though I suppose my time will come."

"Your time?"

"For proposals."

Edie shivered, despite the temperature of the room.

Lord Pernrith was standing in a trio of gentlemen, though he appeared to be saying very little. Taking advantage of the fact that her conversational companions could not have cared a fig what she was saying, Edie examined the enthralling viscount.

He was dressed well, but then all gentlemen were. It was a Society event. One had to be dressed well.

And yet, now that she came to consider him more closely, she could see she was mistaken. Though Viscount Pernrith was dressed in an impressive jacket with a silk waistcoat, Edie realized both were of last year's fashion. Perhaps a few years older than that.

Or at least, what had passed for "this year's fashion" in Woodhurst, where the styles changed more slowly.

It was the same cravat, Edie spotted, that he had worn at St. James's Court. Not that there was anything wrong with that, but it was... unusual.

Oh, how she wished she had friends in London. She loved her home village of Woodhurst, of course, but the instant Edie, her father, and Mrs. Teagan had arrived in town, she had realized just what a disadvantage her long years in the country had proven.

There was so little she knew about... about gentlemen. About flirtation. About how one was supposed to go about getting a husband, something her father was most stringent about.

About what she was supposed to do with all these feelings for Frederick Chance...

He looked up and Edie's insides melted.

She looked away quickly, back to her companions, before remembering why she had stopped attending.

"No, it is Miss Stewart's eyes that are the most fine," said Mr. Peters confidently. A lock of dark, oily hair danced above his brow. "No one could disagree with—"

"Fie, it is her lips!" Mr. Thomson protested. His own lips were remarkably chapped. "To think otherwise is to denigrate—"

Edie ceased listening again. They had not noticed her inattention, she was certain. It was most rude of them, but it did give her an idea.

Why not simply... walk away?

It would have been the height of rudeness if the three of them were in a genuinely reciprocal conversation, but as they weren't, Edie thought it would be rude of them to not notice if she was suddenly gone. Which she couldn't do... could she?

Testing out the waters, Edie took a hesitant step backward, her cup of tea still in hand.

Neither of the men noticed.

"—more like the *Mona Lisa* with her ineffable—"

"You would compare Miss Stewart to that old trout?"

Edie took another step backward. She was now definitely not in their conversation, yet that did not appear to slow either man down.

"She complimented me when—"

"You fool, she was complimenting *me*!"

Taking a third step back, Edie gave a sigh of relief and meandered a few feet to the left—still within their hearing, but far enough that another person could approach her. If they wished.

And she caught the hazel gaze of the one man in the room who appeared to be looking at her eyes.

Edie smiled nervously, heat radiating through her as Viscount Pernrith's eyes glittered. Though she knew it was bold of her, she much preferred thinking of him as Frederick, but they were in public. They were supposed to keep to some sort of decorum.

But just when she was trying to convince herself to look away, that holding the steady eyes of a gentleman like Lord Pernrith—particularly when her father had wished her not to—was a bad idea...

He winked.

Edie's lips curled into an answering grin before she even had time to think about what she wished to do next. It was unthinkable. Grinning at a gentleman across a crowded room, and after such a rebellious, flirtatious act as a wink?

Heaven forbid!

And yet she did. He was... well, delightful. There was no other word for it.

The viscount jerked his head.

Edie turned, bemused, and saw he had indicated a door in the room that led, as far as she could recall, to a corridor.

He doesn't want me to—

But he did. Moving slowly and sedately as only a gentleman completely at ease with himself could, Lord Pernrith was moving through the room toward the door. He glanced back over his shoulder and jerked his head a second time.

There was no mistaking his meaning. Edie's gasp caught in her throat. It was outrageous, what he was silently requesting across a room. She could no more go with him than abscond to Gretna Green. It was an impossibility!

Still. There was no harm in gently placing her cup of tea on the sideboard and... meandering in that direction, was there?

I only wish to speak to him, Edie attempted to convince herself as she stepped farther away from Mr. Thomson and Mr. Peters, still arguing over whether she would be impressed by the former's golf swing or the latter's fencing stride more. She walked past Mrs. Teagan, having what appeared to be a very dull conversation with a Mrs. Marnion about linen, and her father, who was engaged in a vehement discussion with a gentleman she did not know.

"Absolutely preposterous," snapped Lord Stewart as she walked past. "Begonias, in a border like that? The planting would be all wrong!"

Edie's pulse quickened at the audaciousness of what she was about to do. Her father's obsession with gardening had shown no sign of lessening, even after they had left Woodhurst.

By the time she reached the door where Lord Pernrith was standing, her heart was thumping painfully, her fingers tingling.

"Yes?"

The viscount said nothing. He merely smiled—that delicious, enticing smile that surely had worked on hundreds of women before her—reached out to open the door, and stepped out.

And Edie hesitated.

He was asking a great deal of her. They had already been caught by her father in what had appeared to be a tête-à-tête. Moreover, they were both guests, and it would be indecent if they were to be discovered alone outside of the drawing room.

Afternoon tea was one thing. An assignation elsewhere was quite another...

Edie stepped through the door.

Lord Pernrith was nowhere to be found.

Glancing up and down the corridor in great confusion, she was almost ready to step back into the drawing room and hope no one had noticed her momentary absence.

Then a gentle voice said, "This way."

Edie turned hurriedly. Lord Pernrith's face had appeared in a doorway farther down the corridor, a tantalizing expression—his lips cocked into half a smile, his brows raised—on his face. Then he disappeared into the room.

Her footfalls sounded like elephant stomps as she moved along the corridor, but Edie did not hesitate. His conversation had to be at least better than that which she had suffered with Mr. Peters and Mr. Thomson.

A natural propriety, however, made her pause in the doorway of what was revealed to be a library. Lord Pernrith was peering at the books in a bookcase near a window, and he looked up as she waited for him to speak.

"Not coming in?"

"Not... Not yet," Edie said lightly.

It seemed impossible that he could not hear the hammering of her heart, and while he could have laughed at her indecision, the viscount merely nodded.

"Quite right too," he said quietly. "Scandal is a most terrible thing."

Now what on earth did he mean by that?

Edie halted herself from taking another step into the library and was about to ask why he had summoned her here—albeit silently—when Lord Pernrith spoke again.

"You were bored, weren't you?"

She sagged against the doorframe in a most unladylike manner, of which Mrs. Teagan would certainly not have approved. "So incredibly bored. I know it is uncouth to say—"

"I think it more uncouth to tire out a lady with nonsense," said the viscount. He had not turned to look at her and was instead examining the spines of books. Still, she could tell he was smiling. "What were those two men, Mr. Thomson and Mr. Peters, what were they talking about?"

Edie sighed. "They were... well. Arguing. Over me."

It felt a tad crass to admit to such a thing, but it was the truth.

At this response, Lord Pernrith did turn around. He crossed his arms in a languid manner that spoke of riches, and privilege, and an expensive education. Leaning against the bookcase, he looked her full in the face.

"Well," he said quietly. "Can you blame them? You are beautiful."

When she smiled, it was tight. Edie had hoped for... what, she was not exactly sure. More than that. Better than that.

Beauty was all very well, and she supposed she was meant to be glad of it. She certainly had not earned the symmetry of her features, nor the way her figure made men's heads turn, even if she purposefully wore an ill-fitting gown of last year's style.

But was that truly all she was? Was that all men saw? Could she not be more than—

Footfalls.

Edie jerked her head, then inclined it as gracefully as she could to the passing footman, who was holding a silver tray. The servant stared curiously, then seemed to remember himself. Cheeks red, he dropped his gaze to the floor until he slipped through a servants' door.

"You can't just keep standing there, you know."

She turned back to the room, into the library where Lord Pernrith was standing. He was still leaning against the bookcase. "What do you mean?"

The viscount hesitated. "You need to decide, I suppose. Come in here and talk with me, or return to the drawing room."

A simple decision, on the face of it.

Yet it wasn't. Edie knew what she wished to do—to know this man, this unusual man, better. There was a gentleness in him that belied every other trait, and yet there was fire, and spark, and laughter. And he held himself back all the time. She wanted to know why.

And why her father thought it so outrageous she would even consider speaking to him.

Edie swallowed, rent in half by indecision. Her whole body was quivering, unsure which direction to take. Somehow, she knew the choice she made would be far greater than standing in a library or in a drawing room.

Footfalls again.

This time, they came from inside the library. Lord Pernrith walked toward her slowly, without taking his eyes from her. He reached out a hand. Having accepted tea earlier, certainly, he wasn't wearing gloves.

Neither was she. Without taking her eyes from him, unable to, Edie took his hand and stepped into the library. Both of them reached for the door, their hands mingling as they pushed it. A resounding click of the catch sounded in the room.

They were alone.

Edie's lungs were tight, each inhale a struggle as she stood there with her hand still held by Lord Pernrith. It was the single most sensual thing that had ever happened to her.

Though that, she tried to think rationally, *isn't that impressive. But still.*

"We should lock the door," said Edie without thinking.

Her cheeks burned as the viscount arched an eyebrow. "We should?"

"Y-Yes," she said, as boldly as she could manage. Her hand fumbled at the lock behind her, unsure which way to turn it. She couldn't tear her eyes away from the man beside her to look, but she thought she'd managed the task. "I would hate to be discovered here and be forced to answer difficult questions. Wouldn't you?"

Lord Pernrith continued to hold her hand as he meandered back to the bookshelves, forcing her to follow him.

Not that it was much of a hardship.

There was something so intensely intimate about this, and Edie knew that from now on, she was just as culpable for what happened as he was. He had invited her in, to be sure. He had taken her hand.

But she had made the suggestion to lock the door.

Swallowing hard and wishing she were more experienced in the area of flirtation, Edie pointed at random to a bookcase. "I suppose you have read all of these."

"I've read a fair few," Lord Pernrith said, pulling her to the bookcase. "But I didn't have the impressive education that... that my brothers did. I've had to work on my studies in my own time."

His brothers?

He was a Chance. Edie had carefully prodded Mrs. Teagan for information on the Chance family, who were, as far as she could tell, one of the most prestigious in the land.

A duke, a marquess, an earl... and a viscount.

Most unusual in one family.

So what did he mean, he had a different education than that of his brothers? Why would that be?

"We... We shouldn't stay too long." Edie hated the nerves in her voice, but who could blame her?

At any moment, her father or Mrs. Teagan or someone else would notice she was missing. There would be delicate inquiries made at first, and more intense ones as it became increasingly apparent she was unaccompanied. Alone.

And then—

"You know being here with me is scandalous, don't you?" Lord Pernrith murmured.

Precisely how, she was not sure, but Edie somehow had her back to the bookcase. She could feel the spines pressing into her own, and there was something... something eager in the viscount's expression that she had not seen before.

He was standing before her, mere inches away.

Her breath hitched. "Y-Yes. I suppose it is."

"I don't know about that," said Lord Pernrith quietly. The intensity of his look was overwhelming. "We're in a library. It ought not to be so scandalous."

Flickers of desire, of needing to know what it was to touch Frederick Chance, Viscount Pernrith, were fluttering through Edie's mind.

Thoughts she most definitely should have suppressed. Shouldn't she? Wasn't it wild of her to be even *considering* such a thing?

She licked her lips, deliberating what to say next, and could not help but notice a glimmer of lust on the viscount's face.

Did he want to kiss her as much as she wanted him to?

"We are alone," Edie pointed out quietly.

He took another step forward. Now he was toe to toe with her, his chest mere inches from her breasts.

And that would have been enough. Edie was certain if they had been discovered in that stance, her back against the bookshelves and her way blocked by the sturdy presence of the tall viscount, there would be sufficient scandal.

Certainly enough for the *Whispers of the Ton*. More than enough for Mrs. Teagan. Cataclysmic for her father.

But Lord Pernrith—Frederick—did not halt there. Leaning forward ever so slightly, he placed both hands on the bookcase, either side of her shoulders.

Edie exhaled jerkily, her chest rising and falling with no discernable rhythm.

How—How did he do that? The man wasn't touching her, yet she was enclosed by him, caged by strong arms, muscles taut against the sleeves of his jacket.

"Yes, we are alone," said Frederick, his gaze dipping to her lips before swiftly returning to her eyes. "And I am close to you."

"Very close," Edie murmured.

It was neither benediction nor remonstrance. She didn't know what she wanted to happen, didn't know what was supposed to happen next.

That Frederick was a practiced seducer was obvious. No man, surely, could be acting on instinct alone and have her cornered here, pinned up against the books like a strumpet.

Yet Edie did not feel like a strumpet. She had always presumed that if—and it had once been a very large *if*—she was caught in a compromising position, she would immediately feel how wrong it was. She would flee, bolt from the danger, and feel no compunction in informing the gentleman just how out of order he was.

And here she was, in just such a position... and she wanted him to kiss her.

"Very close," Edie repeated, pulse thundering. "And yet... yet you could be closer."

It was the most outrageous thing she had ever said—and it sparked the response she'd wanted.

Frederick had not needed to move a great deal to place his lips on hers, but the sudden intake of breath and the fire of his passion startled Edie more than the movement. His lips were crushed on hers, and it was overwhelming and overpowering and—

And pleasurable.

Edie sank into the kiss. Somehow, her fingers had become entangled in his wild, blond hair, and she was tugging him closer, as if he could *be* any closer. His chest was pressed against her breasts, holding her in a vise between the shelves and his broad plane. As she squirmed against the delightful pressure, he moaned.

"Edie," Frederick whispered against her lips.

Just the mention of her name from his mouth was enough to tilt her head and welcome him in. Welcome him deeper.

His teasing tongue seared a tender ache across her lips as Frederick plundered the wet core of her mouth. Edie whimpered, unable to help it as sensual ripples flowed through her body.

How did he do it? How did he transform what ought to have been the simplest of movements into something that delighted her body so utterly?

"Frederick," she moaned, unable to prevent herself.

And that somehow increased the pace, her reciprocal passion pushing them forward. A book slipped to the floor as Frederick pulled at her gown, tugging it past her shoulder and revealing the cusp of her breasts, tightly pinned by her stays.

Edie gasped at the sudden intimacy.

And he stopped. Pressing his forehead against hers, Frederick muttered, "I'll... I'll stop. If you want to."

She knew what the correct response was. She knew she was not supposed to let such things happen—that such things did not happen, even within an engagement!

And she hardly knew this man—beyond his name and the suggestion he was an absolute rakehell, perhaps proven by this encounter. Frederick Chance was like any other man she could pass in the—

No, Edie could not believe that. She looked deep into his hazel eyes and saw not just lust, not just the base desire she saw in all men's eyes when they saw her… but something more.

And she trusted that.

"Don't stop," she whispered.

Frederick moaned as he pressed a hard, furious kiss on her lips—but his hands weren't idle.

Though she had believed her stays held her breasts tightly, it took but a moment for Frederick's hand to free one. His thumb raked across her nipple and a jolt of molten desire soared to her core.

Edie whimpered. "Again! Again, please, Frederick, please—"

"Put my daughter down!"

She froze. The whole library went cold.

Frederick broke the kiss, still panting, every rise and fall of his chest pinning her more tightly then less tightly to the bookcase. Very slowly, as though he were not quite moving, he slipped her breast back into her stay.

Edie could not move. The voice—she knew who that was. But it wasn't possible, it couldn't be. There was no likelihood he could have—

"I *said*, put my daughter down!" repeated Lord Stewart, his footsteps harsh as he strode toward them. "Dear God!"

Edie swallowed as Frederick stepped back from her. The loss of his presence was painful, a sudden chill in her bones, an unhappiness she had not known was there.

"I thought you locked the door," Frederick murmured, his eyes wide.

"I—no," Edie whispered weakly, realizing the mistake she had made as her shoulders slumped. "I… I thought I did, but I wasn't sure. I didn't check. I never thought we would be—"

"Discovered," said her father menacingly. "Well, damn."

Chapter Six

November 10, 1812

FREDERICK WAS FORTUNATE, really, not to be waking that morning for a duel.

He supposed he should have been grateful. He didn't *feel* particularly grateful, as he stretched out in his bed and stared at the ceiling, unwilling to get up.

Getting up would require him to face what he must that day. And it was going to be... awkward.

How had he managed this? After so many years of toeing the line, always ensuring he could never be accused of even the slightest misstep... of trying to earn his brothers' trust, of always attempting to show them he knew what was required of the Chance name... he'd done this?

"I'll... I'll stop. If you want to."

"Don't stop."

Frederick clenched his bedsheets into fists, but it didn't change what had happened yesterday. Nothing would.

Now he had a ten o'clock appointment with Lord Stewart to discuss the matter.

"It's not a duel," he muttered as he kicked his legs out of the side of the bed and sighed heavily. "You're not going to get shot in the head."

Probably.

Frederick dressed swiftly. It may only have been eight o'clock, or just past, but there was no reason to delay. With no valet—with no income to support paying a valet—he had learned to tie a cravat in three different ways before he had left the family's seat of Stanphrey Lacey and come to town. Three were all one needed.

Wild thoughts scattered through his mind as he stomped bad-temperedly down the stairs, but his mood was not improved as he stepped into his breakfast to discover—

"Ah," said Frederick weakly.

William Chance, Duke of Cothrom, carefully folded his half-brother's morning newspaper and placed it on the table. "Ah, indeed."

Despite all his intentions, Frederick felt his shoulders slump.

He should have guessed. He was a Chance, after all, even if he was only half a Chance. The name had to be maintained. It could not be permitted to be dragged into the dust, and that was precisely what he had done.

How his eldest brother had managed to hear about it so quickly...

"I'll leave the two of you to breakfast, shall I, Your Grace? My lord?" asked Mrs. Kinley, his stout and gray-haired housekeeper, who was bustling about putting the final touches to the table. Jams and preserves shone in their jars.

Frederick had never felt less hungry.

"Thank you, Mrs. Kinley," he managed to say. "That will be all."

His housekeeper gave him a look, as though she knew precisely what had happened last night, stepped smartly across the room, and shut the door behind her with a snap. He had to hope the footman who had seen them hadn't been so uncouth as to spread the gossip that quickly...

"I received an urgent letter from Baron Stewart at about six o'clock this morning," said William quietly, answering the unspoken question. "I think we need to have a little chat. Please, sit down."

Swallowing the irritation at being invited to sit at his own breakfast table, Frederick obliged. He fought the temptation to pour himself a cup of tea. It would be merely a distraction tactic—both to distract his brother, and himself from the mess he'd found himself in. It was strange; despite sharing a father, they looked very dissimilar. The three full brothers, of course, were occasionally mistaken for each other by a vague acquaintance in a dark light, but not him. No, he was fairer, and with a less angled jaw, and he held himself differently. Always different.

"Why?" asked William quietly.

And Frederick was back to being a child again.

It did not help that William looked so much like their father. Countless memories scattered through Frederick's mind of being called into the study at Stanphrey Lacey and having to look into those sky-blue eyes and give an account of himself.

It's usually Lindow's fault, he thought darkly. And he had known better, even then, than to admit to that fact.

"I don't know," he said aloud.

William raised a disbelieving eyebrow.

"She's beautiful," said Frederick, unable to deny that fact. "I desired her. I think any gentleman who came within ten feet of her would desire her. And I wanted... more."

William groaned. "You didn't—"

"I don't mean like that!" Frederick said hotly, wishing to goodness he had poured himself some tea. At least then he could have hidden his face from the judgmental glare of the Duke of Cothrom for a moment. "I meant... there is something more. Something between us. I can't explain it. I've met her a handful of times and yet Edie—Miss Stewart, I mean—there's something... Damned if I can explain it."

It sounded pathetic, even to his ears. What on earth had he been thinking? He hadn't really *been* thinking—he'd been acting on instinct. An instinct that had told him being close to Edie was preferable than being apart. That knowing her better was only going to enrich his life.

He'd been a fool.

"You know what you'll be asked," William said quietly. "What is required of you. As a Chance."

Frederick supposed he should have been grateful he was still considered a Chance, after what he'd done. Still, it did not prevent his stomach from lurching.

"I know."

"And I am disappointed in you," his half-brother continued. "I had expected better."

That was when his temper flared. *Better? Better?* Had he not spent his whole life being better, trying harder, restricting himself at every turn?

And some of the pain and hurt he had swallowed for so long finally burst to the surface.

"'Disappointed'?" Frederick repeated in a harsh voice. "I kiss one woman and am a disappointment, whereas to my knowledge, Lindow—"

"Our brother has nothing to do with this," William said in a warning tone.

It was a warning Frederick did not heed. George Chance, Earl of Lindow, had always been harsh on him, always loathed him, always attempted to convince the other two brothers to leave Frederick out in the cold.

"Lindow has bedded more women than I've had hot dinners," Frederick continued. "And—"

"He is married now."

"—you didn't tell him he was a disappointment every time!"

William's gaze was steady. "Actually, I did."

Frederick hesitated. Oh. He hadn't known that. "I have always sought to maintain this family's honor, always tried to be worthy of you—"

"It's not like that—"

"Isn't it?" Frederick gave a laugh. "Cothrom, you've spent most of the last five years bailing Aylesbury and Lindow out of every disaster they have found themselves in, and here I am, one mistake before me, and you wish to pressgang me into marriage?"

Marriage.

He had tried not to think about it all morning. Marriage, love, affection. The things other gentlemen could decide whether they wanted. Some did, some didn't. Some married without love, some gave in to their lust and never married.

But him? Frederick Chance, bastard of the late Duke of Cothrom, had few options and even less choice. Especially now.

"I've been good." Frederick hated how his voice cracked, but he could not prevent it. "I've tried so hard to be worthy of the Chance name. You know I have. And now—"

"It's different," said William, and there was a slight awkwardness in his tone. "You know it is."

He swallowed his retort. *Yes. Because I'm only half a Chance.*

His half-brother sighed. "I hope you are going over there."

Frederick forced himself to sink into the stiff, polite, restrained disguise he so often inhabited. That he had created purposefully to prevent such situations as this.

Much good that has done me.

"I have an appointment with the baron at ten o'clock," he said crisply.

William sighed, and Frederick tried not to see the slip of the man's shoulders as his brother was filled with relief. "Good. You had better eat up, then. I'll see myself out."

Perhaps he should have asked his brother to stay with him—to see if reconciliation beyond their trite conversation was possible.

But Frederick did not attempt it. William had been good to him, in the main, but he could not change the past. He could not make him something he was not. There was a divide between them, a gulf nothing could bridge.

And so he ate his breakfast alone, nothing but the ticking of a clock edging him closer and closer to the moment when he would have to leave his home.

By the time Frederick was standing outside the Stewart home, his feet were lead and his lungs were tight and painful.

The neat and tidy butler frowned as he opened the door. "Sir."

Frederick did not bother to correct him. "Good morning."

"That remains to be seen," said the butler archly as he stepped aside. "Come on in, my lord."

A presumptuous thing to say, Frederick thought as he entered the Stewart home and handed the nearest footman his hat and gloves. To think a servant would be so bold—

"There you are! We only have five minutes. Come on."

A hand grabbed his wrist.

Frederick hardly had time to think, to question what on earth was going on, before he had been pulled at great speed into a side room. The door slammed behind him and a voice spoke hurriedly.

"You know what we have to do, don't you?"

He blinked. Miss Edie Stewart swam into view, standing in what appeared to be a morning room.

If only she weren't so beautiful, he could not help but think. It was most distracting, a pretty woman like Edie before him when so much was at stake.

She could have at least *tried* to look unwelcoming. Attired in a soft-pink cotton gown that skimmed beautifully to her wrists and tucked delightfully under her breasts, the image was greatly accentuated by her heavy breathing. Breathing that lifted her bust closer to his tingling fingers—

Frederick hastily clasped his hands behind his back. "Good morning, Miss—"

"I think we're a mite beyond that, don't you?" Edie said with a hasty smile. "Now. I've thought it all through, and I have a plan."

He blinked. *A plan?*

"You must have thought of it too," she said, her eyes raking over his face. "Isn't it obvious?"

Well, yes. Frederick had known, from the moment Lord Stewart had demanded he call on him the following morning at ten o'clock sharp, that there was only one way out of a situation like this.

A woman had been compromised—a lady. Worse, she had been discovered. Far worse, discovered by her father.

There was only one outcome.

"Marriage," Frederick said stiffly.

Edie nodded. "And that is out of the question."

He had not expected the fire of resentment to course so strongly through his veins. She spoke so matter-of-factly, as though it were a clear disaster they were both desirous of avoiding.

And he... he hadn't been.

Frederick could not explain it, not even to himself, but the idea of marriage to Miss Edie Stewart... Well, it would not exactly be a hardship, would it? Waking every morning beside her, spending the day getting to know her, seeing more and more of her character, her spirit—

Then going to bed with her every night.

Frederick swallowed, hard. Then he swallowed again. He mustn't permit his mind to run away with itself. After all, had she not just said how impossible that would be?

"If you go in there, my father will force you to marry me," Edie was saying, her voice hushed. "So it's clear what we must do. We must pretend we are engaged."

Perhaps it was too early to follow such complexities of thought, but Frederick rather believed it ended the same way. "What difference is there if we pretend—"

"It's simple," she said quietly. "If my father demands marriage, then it will happen. If we pretend an engagement—"

"Absolutely not," Frederick said sharply.

The very idea! He was a gentleman, and though he may not have been the paragon of virtue at the time, he knew his responsibilities. He knew what was due Miss Stewart, and—

"I must save my reputation!" Edie's voice rose in both volume and pitch, and for the first time since entering, Frederick realized just how worried she looked. "Surely, you can see—if you don't walk out of his house engaged to me, one way or another..."

Her voice faded as she bit her lip, fingers twisting before her in clear concern.

Frederick swore quietly and turned away. He had been prepared to marry her—had even desired it, he would admit—but then she had come to him, urging him to allow her to escape such a fate. The blow had been swift—and devastating. But he could not walk away and leave her because she had no desire to spend her life with him. He had to think, and that was most definitely not something he could do while looking at such an attractive face.

Because she was right. As he stepped around the room navigating chairs, sofas, and numerous little tables with vases of flowers, Frederick could think of no other way around it. A woman's reputation was a delicate thing—so delicate, he had rarely bothered to converse long with a lady before now in case there was any hint of impropriety.

All that had disappeared when he had seen Edie step into the alcove at Lady Romeril's ball.

And now they had been discovered, and she was right—if there was no engagement...

"The only way to save my reputation is if that kiss was appropriate," said Edie firmly. "It is appropriate to kiss if you are engaged."

"Not the way we were doing it," Frederick said dryly before he could stop himself.

Her cheeks turned scarlet. "I... I suppose not."

Damn and blast it, but there wasn't much else to say. What they had shared had gone beyond kissing. Frederick had flattered himself that there had been a true connection there, something deeper than he had ever thought to experience before.

Why, in that library, he had been closer to Edie than any woman he had ever fumbled with in the dark.

Hesitating at asking the question, and knowing it was most uncouth of him to do so, Frederick pressed on. "You don't want to marry me."

"Obviously not," Edie said lightly. She cleared her throat, her eyes darting downward.

Her confirmation hurt Frederick far more than he had expected.

Oh, not just the rejection. He had known that there was no way a woman like that, as beautiful as that, would ever wish to have anything to do with him. She must surely know, by now, the sordid history of how he'd come to be. The complicated relationship he had with his brothers. The way the whole *ton* permitted him to be a part of Society but had never truly accepted him.

And she had followed him into that corridor, allowed him to pull her into the library, reciprocated his kisses.

But of course, she would not wish to be tied to him forever.

"We can pretend to fall out later," Edie was saying. "The engagement only has to last a few weeks—a month or two, perhaps. The exact timing is immaterial."

"Yes, I suppose it is," Frederick said faintly.

It was hard to believe this was happening. All his newfound hopes for affection and family were about to be upended by a pretend engagement to avoid a real marriage merely because he could not keep his hands off a woman who entirely enchanted him.

How had he managed to get this tangled?

"—you see?" Edie finished desperately. "Don't you care what people will think?"

"You care about what people think too much," Frederick said without thought.

Her eyes glittered. "And you don't care enough. So we are well matched. Do you not see that this is the only way?"

Frederick sighed. "This is a bad idea."

"You have a better one?" she countered in a low voice. "Because in less than a minute, my father is expecting you upstairs—and you'll have all the choice taken away from you. You *will* marry me."

And you'll marry me, Frederick could not help but think, raking his eyes over her beautiful features. *And you'll be stuck with me.*

She'd made it perfectly plain—painfully plain—that she had no wish to have him as a husband. This desperate plea, this grabbing him and pulling him into the morning room, it had come from a place of panic.

"There'll be a scandal," he said, mouth dry. "When we break it. The sham engagement, I mean."

Edie waved a nonchalant hand. "Not if you do it. You... well. Your reputation will weather it."

Frederick's stomach lurched. "Because...?"

She frowned, as if it were obvious. "You're a gentleman. Gentlemen can do whatever they like—it's only ladies who are frowned on. I know Society says it's only the lady's prerogative to end an engagement, but well, that hasn't stopped a few men before, surely. The Season's flourishing rose ought not to be seen as so capricious, even if a new one is named soon enough. My father wouldn't stand for it. Now, are you going to rescue me, or not?"

She did not wish to marry him, and only his agreement to go along with this sham would save her from such a fate.

Well, he was supposed to be a gentleman, after all.

Frederick drew himself up as he took a deep breath. "Fine."

Edie blinked. "You... You'll do it?"

"Far be it from me to disappoint a lady," he said as magnanimously as he could.

She pinched her lips. "You didn't disappoint me last night."

And before Frederick could ask what on earth that comment was supposed to mean, or wrap his head around the fact that he was now, to the world, engaged to be married, Edie pulled him out of the morning room and into the hall.

He was not permitted to get his breath back before Edie had dragged him into the room next to the morning room.

It was plainly a gentleman's study. Leather and wood, a patina of age across every piece of furniture. A few ink splatters on the desk demonstrated generations of use, and there was a splendid silver inkstand that held a variety of silver pens.

Behind that formidable desk was an equally formidable man.

"So," said Lord Stewart malevolently. "You are late."

The chiming of the clock on the mantelpiece was still going, but Frederick thought it would be gauche of him to argue. "My apologies, my lord."

"Hmmm," sniffed the older man. His dark eyes examined him closely, and Frederick forced himself not to shuffle his feet. "You may go, Edie."

"I will remain, Father," she said in quiet reply, moving to sit in a chair opposite.

"You will—"

"This affair is my business, and I will remain to discuss it," said Edie in a firm yet soft voice.

Frederick's admiration of her only rose as she elegantly swept her skirts around her and deposited herself in the chair.

She had pluck, that woman. Not every lady would speak so directly to her father, at least from the little he knew about such matters. And with such calm, such style. It was no wonder she had been named flourishing rose of the—

"I said, my lord, will you sit?" Lord Stewart said testily.

Frederick hastily stepped forward and sat in the chair beside Edie, cheeks burning. He really had to concentrate. He had his brother's comments ringing in his ears and his own honor to uphold.

"I hope you are going over there."

"Edie is my daughter. My only child, the flourishing rose of this year's Season," Lord Stewart said with a sharp look. "A woman to whom the whole of the *ton* looks for a display of elegance and delicacy and propriety."

Frederick winced. This was going to be just as awful as he had expected.

"The flourishing rose, as I am sure you are aware, is a title bestowed only to the—"

"He knows what the flourishing rose is, Father," came the pert voice beside Frederick. "May we move this along? I have a walk agreed with Mrs. Teagan."

Frederick could not help but smile. He had not expected that.

Her father did not look similarly amused. His glare was unchanged.

"So," said Lord Stewart threateningly, "I suppose you know what commitment I am going to expect from you."

"In fact, Father, I think you will be pleasantly surprised," said Edie before Frederick could open his mouth. "His lordship and I are engaged."

Her father snorted. "Damned straight you are! Now that I found you out—"

"If you had bothered to listen to us for more than a minute together last night, you would have been informed that we have been engaged this past week," Edie said, her voice not rushed, but each word spoken swiftly. "Engaged *to be married*," she added.

Frederick worked hard not to fiddle with the button of his jacket. He clasped his hands together instead and tried to look for all the world as though this were not brand-new information.

Lord Stewart's frown lessened, but only slightly. "Engaged. To be married."

"We had thought to tell you this week," Edie said. And then she did the strangest thing. She reached out and took one of Frederick's hands. "And ask for your blessing, naturally."

Her father did not look mollified. "It didn't look like this man was asking for anyone's blessing last night when he—"

"A momentary lapse of judgment, I assure you," said Frederick, sensing it was time he got involved in the conversation. "I consider your daughter to be most beautiful, most—"

"You and half the *ton*," growled Lord Stewart. "And you are Viscount Pernrith."

"Yes, I shall be Lady Pernrith," said Edie hastily. "Haven't you always wanted me to have a title and—"

"*The* Viscount Pernrith." Her father spoke over her and his eyes never left Frederick's face. "You know what I mean."

Frederick straightened his spine and tried to sit straighter. "I do, my lord."

Of course he did. Edie evidently did not, despite Frederick's certainty she'd have discovered the truth by now. She was looking between the two gentlemen with pinched brows and puckered lips, but Lord Stewart did not need to say any more. Frederick knew what he meant.

All Society thought it. They looked at him and saw nothing more than an interloper. A bastard. Someone of illegitimate blood who had usurped his way into one of the most noble houses of England.

On paper, they were right.

But by God, he hadn't asked to be born. To be loathed for the circumstances of one's birth! To be ostracized merely because one's eyes were not the same as all other Chances'. To know that no matter what he did, good or ill, he would always be reduced to half a Chance.

"Hmm," said Lord Stewart darkly.

If knowledge of his origins was not the cause behind Edie's insistence they not end up married, what was? Had she heard that, for a titled man of his stature, his fortune was far from impressive? Yet she had not heard of the circumstances of his birth? No, unlikely. Could he have been so mistaken about what he felt between them?

Frederick felt a squeeze on his hand and took it as a sign he needed to speak. "I am an honorable man, my lord. Edie will receive nothing but the utmost respect from me throughout our marriage and will be given all the power and prestige a viscountess deserves."

He saw, even though the older man attempted to hide it, the flicker of delight. Yes, a baron may well be delighted that his daughter would take a step up the social ladder. It was not a huge one—he was hardly a duke. But it was an improvement.

"And we shall have to announce the engagement soon, Father," Edie said swiftly. "In case... In case anyone else saw... saw us."

Her cheeks pinked prettily and Frederick tried not to think of the hand clasped in his. The soft hand. The soft hand mere inches away from his throbbing, aching—

"You know I don't like this," Lord Stewart said suddenly.

"I know, and I am sorry we did not come straight to you," Frederick said stiffly. "That I did not seek your permission. It was remiss of me."

"It was more than *remiss* of you, it was damned rude," came the sharp reply. A long breath escaped his lips. "But I cannot deny it is a relief to know you are of the same mind as I. That marriage is the only way to resolve this... this error."

This error. Frederick.

He did his best to keep his face impassive.

"There will be talk. There is always talk," said Edie's father heavily. "I will be relying on the two of you to attend as many Society events as possible—as an engaged couple. Make it clear you are planning a wedding. We shall scatter invitations far and wide, to as much nobility—"

"Father!" Edie chided.

Lord Stewart shrugged. "You think you have a better way to restore your reputation? To cease the whispers? To make absolute certain you are not snubbed for your... indiscretion?"

Indiscretion was putting it mildly, and Frederick knew it. On the other hand... This was supposed to be a fabricated engagement. Attending balls, card parties, dinners, as an engaged couple? With Edie?

"And there is nothing I can do now to stop it," Lord Stewart said, furthering the impression that if possible, he would have whisked Edie back to the country. "I suppose we'll just have to go ahead and announce it, then."

Edie beamed at her father. "Thank you."

"Yes, thank you," said Frederick, his mouth dry. "An announcement. Of our engagement. Oh, good."

Chapter Seven

November 15, 1812

"Another cake, Miss Stewart?" came the imperious voice.

Edie shook her head. Her stomach was fit to bursting. Her sweet tooth had always been a weakness, and these little pastries were absolutely—

"I insist!" said Lady Romeril aggressively, actually picking up the tray and thrusting it into Edie's face. "You would not wish to anger my cook, would you? Or offend me?"

It was on the tip of her tongue to say that consuming five of the small cakes already could hardly be constituted as an offense, to either cook or hostess.

But she said nothing, smiled vaguely, and took another cake to place on her plate.

Lady Romeril returned the tray of cakes to the console table beside them. "Excellent. Now, where was I?"

"You were enumerating the number of marriages that have occurred this year," said Edie, attempting to keep the weariness from her voice.

"Ah, yes, so I was." Lady Romeril beamed, leaning back in the wingback armchair within which she had been reposed from the moment Edie had arrived for tea. "Now, there is that young lady, what's her name…"

Edie had learned swiftly that when Lady Romeril trailed off like this, it was not—decidedly not—an invitation to interject. The older woman rather relished the own sound of her voice, it seemed, and so much preferred to be permitted to meander her way to the answer.

Leaving Edie free with her thoughts.

"—I must have met her a few times and she had that nasty habit of coughing. Can't abide a woman who coughs without cause," Lady Romeril said wistfully. "And she wore that horrendous concoction to the Duchess of Axwick's summer ball. That headdress—I thought she would collapse under the weight! Hennessy, that was her name. Her marriage was announced only last month…"

And despite all this talk of engagements, Edie could not help but think, *Lady Romeril has not yet congratulated me on my own.*

It was only a small fault. She certainly should not have been so irritated, considering that the engagement itself was a complete fabrication. Edie would not marry a man forced into making a proposal because of one evening's indiscretion. Barely an indiscretion. She had thought to save herself the shame of Frederick's indignation over how her own foolish mistake would result in everlasting consequences by assuring him of his freedom from such a match—if only he would grant her the right to exit gracefully.

So yes, though only she and Frederick knew it, their wedding would never happen. But still. It was galling. Sitting here and being forced to listen to the list of ladies who were being wed, and Lady Romeril did not even consider her?

"I *knew* they would marry. My instincts are never wrong about these things," Lady Romeril said expansively with a smile. "The moment I saw them at the Earl of Chester's party—you would not have been invited, as you were not in town then—but if you had seen them!"

Edie forced herself to return the smile and hoped to goodness the woman would not make her eat the sixth cake. "I wish I had."

"Oh, they were elegantly matched," said Lady Romeril with a nod.

"Far better than that young lady now, what was her name…"

Again, Edie did not attempt to interject. She could not even if she had wanted to. Lady Romeril had a far better grasp on the complexities of Society than she did—than she ever would.

And still Lady Romeril did not mention her engagement to Viscount Pernrith.

Edie could not help but feel offended. She was the year's flourishing rose. She thought the *ton* fawned over her. But still she was considered less impressive than her contemporaries? Was it because, come July when the Season had ended, she had not been engaged? Was it because she was merely a country girl, a daughter of a very minor noble, and from the village of Woodhurst, no less? A place that she was certain no one in London had ever heard of?

"I suppose your marriage preparations abound?"

"What—oh, yes," Edie amended hastily. "Yes, we have spoken to a florist and ordered a modiste to start preparations for the gown. The church is being selected."

They were, she and Frederick had agreed, the easiest wedding preparations to make, ones that could be swiftly canceled when needed. After all, some effort had to be made to make it appear as if they were actually planning the thing.

"Some marriages are better than others," Lady Romeril was saying blithely as she helped herself to what Edie believed was her eighth little cake. "And some… well. Delicate."

Edie blinked. "'Delicate'?"

Lady Romeril's beady eyes met hers. "Like your own, for example."

And it was only then that Edie realized her hostess, far from ignoring her engagement, had been slowly working her way to it. As though it were a most difficult conversation. As though there were something desperately wrong.

Edie swallowed. "My own, my lady?"

Yes, there was definitely something holding Lady Romeril back. She was silent at the moment, a rarity in and of itself. But Edie could also see something in the woman's expression, something akin to...

Her stomach lurched. *Pity?*

"You know something about my betrothed, don't you, Lady Romeril?" Edie said without thinking.

It was a good thing Mrs. Teagan had not accompanied her to Lady Romeril's invitation of tea, for her chaperone would have been mortified by the openness with which she spoke.

But how could she not?

Curiosity had been teasing at the edges of Edie's mind the instant she had met Frederick. That little alcove where they had both hidden from the masses at Lady Romeril's ball had been the beginning of something that would regrettably conclude with their false engagement coming to an end—but it had also begun a marvel that had never left her.

What was the reason for everyone's stiffness about this man? Why had her father been so outraged by the fact that she had been speaking with him? Whatever the cause, her father had at least overcome his objections now that he thought marriage a certainty, but...

Why, when Lady Romeril should have been congratulating her heartily on capturing a handsome, well-titled gentleman for a husband, did she look so... so uncomfortable?

"What do you know of Viscount Pernrith, Miss Stewart?" her hostess asked quietly.

Edie hesitated. Not much, as it turned out. Though she was loath to admit it. "I know a little—as much as any lady knows before a gentleman and her father agree to a match for her."

She had thought her response elegant, but Lady Romeril waved it aside with a blunt wave of her hand. "I meant his reputation, his background. His wealth—or should I say, lack thereof."

"*Lack thereof*"? Edie blinked, attempting to wrap her head around a viscount without wealth. Surely, Frederick was not penniless? Surely, she would have read about such a thing in the scandal sheets?

"His... His family."

"*Family*"? Edie racked her brain and tried to dredge up the little she knew about him. "He has three brothers, I think."

Family, that was what Lady Romeril had said. And a thought occurred to her that stunned Edie into silence.

Was it possible—was there any chance that Frederick had been married before?

What did she know about him? She had never even asked if he had children—hadn't thought to.

That guess was proven to be incorrect, however, as Lady Romeril said, "Yes. Yes, three brothers. Three estranged brothers—or should I say, one estranged brother and two brothers warming through an estrangement?"

Edie stared.

Estranged? These things happened, but to the best families? It was most unusual. What could have precipitated such a breach, and between four men who should surely be closer than any people in the world? In what other family did four brothers share the estate's titles, for example?

"Oh, those blue-eyed boys," said Lady Romeril on a heavy sigh, her mouth downturned. "It was quite the talk of the town when they arrived in London. You do not typically get so many handsome, titled, eligible men arriving so swiftly. And all from the same family."

Edie blinked. *Blue eyes?* "But Frederick—Frederick has hazel eyes."

She'd noticed them the very first moment she had seen them. Who wouldn't? They had the richness of the forest, the glint of gold, that shimmer that spoke of intelligence and power.

Lady Romeril was looking at her with a clenched half-smile. "The Chance family is... complicated."

Complicated? Now what on earth could she mean? The title sharing?

Edie carefully placed her plate, which still held the untouched sixth cake, onto the console table between them. Then she leaned forward.

"Complicated," she repeated, looking closely at Lady Romeril as she said the word.

Her hostess pursed her lips. "Yes, that is how I would describe the Chances in... in polite Society."

"Let's just pretend, for a moment, that we are not in polite Society," said Edie, knowing there was a high possibility she may regret this later. Her father certainly would not have sanctioned such directness. "Would you do me the honor, Lady Romeril, of explaining what you mean by 'complicated'?"

Lady Romeril's eyebrow arched imperiously. "You mean to tell me you don't know?"

Of course she didn't know! Everyone else seemed to—there were enough raised eyebrows and murmurs whenever she entered a room now for Edie to realize that something had happened, a long time ago, in the Chance family.

But no one would tell her. Not Mrs. Teagan, not her father, not... Well. There wasn't really anyone else she could ask. Frederick did not deserve such scrutiny from her, not after the position she'd put him in.

Which was why she was delicately accosting one of the most powerful women in the *ton* in the hope that she would reveal what her curiosity could no longer leave alone.

"I don't know," said Edie quietly. "But you do. And I wish you would tell me."

Lady Romeril held her gaze for a moment as though considering whether or not the younger woman could take the strain of the truth.

She gave a curt nod. "I suppose you should know, as you are about to marry him. The third brother."

Edie frowned. The third—no, that wasn't right. Frederick was the youngest. He had to be. He had the lesser title. "Frederick is the fourth brother."

"The third," said Lady Romeril, dropping her voice as though they could be overheard. "Only by a month or so, my sources tell me, but most definitely older than the Earl of Lindow."

Edie's frown deepened. How on earth could that be? Were they twins? But what twin was born a month after his brother?

"I don't understand," she said helplessly.

Lady Romeril rolled her eyes, as though she had made it perfectly clear. "My dear child, your betrothed was the late Duke of Cothrom's bastard. He's only half a Chance."

Half a Chance—a bastard?

Edie stared off into the distance, no longer hearing precisely what Lady Romeril was saying. If she was saying anything at all.

Frederick Chance... had been born illegitimate?

It would explain a few things. Why his eyes were not the same blue as his brothers'. Why her father had been so mortified to discover them together. Why Frederick and her father had exchanged that most surprising of phrases when the engagement—the false engagement—had been agreed.

"And you are Viscount Pernrith."

"Yes, I shall be Lady Pernrith. Haven't you always wanted me to have a title and—"

"The Viscount Pernrith. You know what I mean."

Lady Romeril was, Edie realized now that she'd come to concentrate, still talking. "And the current Duke of Cothrom, the eldest brother, William, he decided to give Frederick a title. No one else in the family was using it, and it was his right to give it. I suppose he felt emboldened after he broke from tradition and gave his other brothers titles as well. Still. It did not prove popular in all quarters..."

And something Frederick had said, only the second time they had met, blossomed in Edie's memory.

"I understand what you mean about titles unearned. It is a strange sort of burden, being asked to live up to a title you would not have necessarily chosen for yourself."

Oh, dear Lord—did he think that she knew?

"You do not appear to be mortified, Miss Stewart."

Edie gathered her senses together. "I am... I am astonished, certainly. But not mortified. These things happen."

Yes, there were always whispers about certain people being born on the wrong side of the blanket. Sometimes children were born slightly too soon after a wedding, and murmurs went around Woodhurst... but nothing came of it.

Though when it came to dukes and their mistresses, that was undeniably a different matter.

"They certainly do," said Lady Romeril imposingly. "I must say, I am impressed with your sanguine approach. Others would have been... less calm."

Edie could well imagine. She would just have to hope she did not make it obvious, the next time that she encountered Frederick, that she knew. She could not bear to have him think she'd treat him any differently upon learning the news. No, best to have him think she'd already known it and had acted as she would with any gentleman she'd put in such a position. They were still... friends, were they not?

Besides, he must not have wished to discuss it. He'd never brought it up himself, not even with all the talk about marriage.

How they had managed to keep it out of the scandal sheets—but then, it had all happened so long ago. He must be a few years older than her, so there was no reason why she would have read about it. No reason why it would have mattered to her.

Until now.

"Well, this has been a most pleasant encounter, Miss Stewart."

Edie blinked. Lady Romeril had risen, clearly indicating their time together had come to an end.

She rose hastily, brushing cake crumbs from her skirts. "Yes—Yes, very pleasant, thank you. Thank you, my lady."

Moving in a daze of confusion and too many thoughts, Edie curtseyed, allowed herself to be shepherded by the butler out of the morning room, along the corridor, through the hall—taking her bonnet, gloves, and pelisse from a silent footman—and out of the front door.

And still all her mind could think was, *"Your betrothed was the late Duke of Cothrom's bastard. He's only half a Chance."*

She should have waited there for Mrs. Teagan. Her chaperone had promised to meet here there precisely at midday, for she had presumed Lady Romeril would not wish to take tea for longer than an hour.

"She is, after all, a…a lady," Mrs. Teagan had said impressively just that morning.

Edie's stomach had lurched at that comment. *So would she be, once she married—*

Not that she was going to marry him. Obviously.

"You don't want to marry me."

"Obviously not."

It had been difficult to speak with such certainty, but the last thing she wished to do was put Frederick in any sort of delicate position. No, she had done precisely what was right. She had given him the opportunity to get out of marrying her, and he had taken it.

The fact that she had been sorely disappointed by his swift agreement to go along with her false engagement plan? That she had said the words "obviously not" only to pretend she was not wounded by the absence of any declaration that he'd happily wed her? Oh, that was by the by.

Edie should have remained just outside Lady Romeril's house waiting for Mrs. Teagan. And she would have done. If it had not been for—

"Ah, Miss Stewart," said a voice she did not recognize.

Turning, Edie had flushed to see Frederick walking toward her, accompanied by a gentleman she did not know. The stranger was the same height as him but with much darker hair and sky-blue eyes.

Her lungs tightened. *The Chance blue eyes.*

"Good afternoon," Edie said, curtseying, as was expected.

When she straightened, it was to see both Frederick and his brother—for who else could it have been?—bowing to her.

"May I be so bold as to demand a proper introduction?" asked the man with a teasing smile.

Try as she might, she could not help but flush. Why, if things had been different, this would have been a far more formal affair. To be introduced to a future brother-in-law...

But that wasn't her future, was it? Edie tried to remind herself that the entire engagement was a sham. A sham! This was nothing more than a coincidence, a chance of fate.

Frederick was so stiff, she wondered how he managed to speak. "Lord Aylesbury, Miss Edith Stewart. Miss Stewart, my brother John Chance, Marquess of Aylesbury."

"Delighted to make your acquaintance," said the Marquess of Aylesbury. "Can't wait to welcome you into the family!"

Edie smiled self-consciously.

Had... Had Frederick told him? How on earth was she supposed to reply to congratulations about an engagement that was in no way real?

"Thank you for a pleasant conversation, Aylesbury," Frederick said distantly. "I will see you tomorrow for lunch. Give my regards to your wife."

Edie glanced at the viscount. He looked... Well. Under a great deal of tension, now that she came to examine him. There was a tightness in his jaw, a formality about him she had not seen before.

The loose, relaxed, and charming man was gone, though they could have been twins. Instead, there was nothing but a man who appeared uncomfortable and most unhappy. What on earth could have happened?

The Marquess of Aylesbury nudged his half-brother on the shoulder. "Right you are. I'm sure Florence sends her best back to you.

Delighted, Miss Stewart."

He bowed and Edie hurriedly curtseyed again. By the time she had risen, the man had continued along the pavement whistling as though he had not a care in the world. Perhaps he had not.

She turned to the remaining Chance gentleman. "Your... Your brother?"

"One of them," said Frederick curtly.

Although she waited for him to continue, there appeared to be nothing more to say. It only piqued Edie's curiosity even further, and she could not help but think of what Lady Romeril had said to her mere minutes ago.

"And the current Duke of Cothrom, the eldest brother, William, he decided to give Frederick a title. No one else in the family was using it, and it was his right to give it. I suppose he felt emboldened after he broke from tradition and gave his other brothers titles as well. Still. It did not prove popular in all quarters..."

"Come with me," said Edie softly, slipping her hand into Frederick's arm before he could argue with her. "It is not so cold out today. St. James's Park is not too far, and any passersby might assume my chaperone is watching us from a park bench."

He did not disagree. True, he did not exactly agree, either. He merely allowed himself to be guided along the pavement, crossing the road carefully after a carriage rattled past at high speed, and through the gate that led to the delightful St. James's Park.

Winter was approaching rapidly, and Edie saw with sadness that most of the leaves had now descended to the well-kept lawns. A few shrubs battled on with their greenery, but the whole place was transformed from when she had first arrived in town.

The gentleman beside her was silent. They walked for a good five minutes as Edie wrestled with herself, attempting to decide what to say.

Or rather, what not to say.

After all, she could hardly just come out and say it, could she? It would be most uncouth of her to make demands of Frederick, expecting him to spill all his family's secrets. Even if she did want to know them.

Most gentlemen would not do half as much for a woman to whom they were truly engaged.

"He's only half a Chance."

Yet his family, his past, the complexity of the relationships, the way Frederick so utterly transformed when he was with them... Edie could not help but be curious. Who would not be?

"It is good to see you."

Edie glanced up and saw with relief that some of the stiffness around Frederick's mouth had softened. "It is?"

"You doubt me?" asked Frederick lightly, tightening his grip on her hand. "It feels as though it has been too long... too long, indeed, since we have seen each other."

"It has been but five days—"

"As I said. Too long."

Warmth flowed through her at the compliment. There was something about being spoken to like this. Quietly, intimately, as though they were close.

And they were, in a way. They were certainly walking close together. And they were engaged. Everyone who passed them, every couple who walked by or gaggle of people they passed, they knew she and Viscount Pernrith were engaged.

And, Edie realized with a strange twisting within her, they probably knew too that her future husband's parentage was not what Society believed it should be.

Was that why he sometimes became all stiff? Was Frederick as conscious as she now was of the eyes that fell upon them, of the potential whispers muttered behind their backs?

"I saw the announcement," he said.

"In the newspapers?"

"I even took a leaf out of your books and reviewed the scandal sheets," said Frederick, a slight smile curling his lips. "*Whispers of the Ton* was most complimentary."

She flushed. She had seen the announcement in the papers, and it had been written just as it ought to have been.

> *The engagement is announced between Frederick Chance, the Right Honorable Viscount Pernrith, younger son of the late Duke of Cothrom, Stanphrey Lacey, and the Honorable Miss Edith Stewart, only daughter of David Stewart, the Right Honorable Baron Stewart, and the late Lady Vanessa Stewart, Woodhurst.*

It had been very strange to read such a thing—but far more astonishing to read the gossip in the *Whispers of the Ton*.

> *An engagement has been announced between the scandalously titled Viscount Pernrith, and the flourishing rose of this year's Season! Precisely what Her Majesty thinks, after bestowing such an honor on a country bumpkin who could not, even with such an honor, secure a match before Season's end, this author does not know—but we shall follow the marriage preparations with interest.*

Country bumpkin, indeed! She was a daughter of a baron!

At the time, she had not comprehended quite what had been meant by "scandalously titled." Thanks to the gossiping Lady Romeril, she did now.

"We're the talk of the town," said Frederick.

And Edie relaxed. There was now an earnestness in his expression, a lightness to his tone, that returned him to her Frederick.

Well. Not my *Frederick, obviously*, she corrected herself hastily. More the Frederick she had thought she'd known. The jubilant one, the one with all the charm and the allure. Not the staid, stiff, unbending Frederick she had seen with his brother.

His half-brother...

"Yes, I suppose we are," she said as they meandered down a path. "But I suppose that is only because—"

Edie halted herself just in time.

She had only just been informed of the scandalous nature of Frederick's past—but he had not chosen to tell her. She had gone behind his back and inquired of so many people, it had only been a matter of time before someone like Lady Romeril had spilled his secrets.

And they had not been Lady Romeril's secrets to spill.

A twist of guilt encircled Edie's conscience. She had been wrong, she knew that now, to persist in attempting to discover what Frederick had not been telling her. It would have been different if she were truly to be his wife—he'd at least have owed her the courtesy of informing her so she could make an informed decision. But she was already asking too much of him. Now she knew the history of his parentage, she could quite easily see why he might wish to keep such a thing to himself.

She had intruded, and what had it gained her? Nothing.

"Because what?" Frederick asked, nudging her in a familiar way that made her stomach swoop.

Edie smiled weakly. "Oh, nothing. Nothing at all."

Chapter Eight

November 21, 1812

"Aᴸᴸ I'ᴍ sᴀʏɪɴɢ is—"

It was never just "all" and Frederick knew it. However, he kept his staid expression of mild interest fixed on his face, never faltering. He could never falter. Never let them see what was inside.

The plates were empty, the delicious food provided by the Duke of Cothrom's cook swiftly demolished, and the wives had meandered off to discuss... Frederick was hardly sure. What did his three sisters-in-law discuss?

"Alice and I do not need your advice on this matter," William said sternly to John, Marquess of Aylesbury. "We are raising Maude how we—"

"And I am saying, Florence and I would be more than happy to take her to the ballet, or something like that—when she's older, I suppose," said John with a shrug and a laughing grin. He was leaning back in his chair, obviously delighting in teasing the oldest Chance brother. "How old does a child have to be to appreciate the ballet, anyway? Four? Five?"

Frederick silently sipped his wine, watching the debate happening and trying not to smile. It was all too easy to tease William, and as long as he didn't get involved, he could amuse himself.

His focus accidently meandered in the same path as George Chance, Earl of Lindow.

The darker man's scowl became prominent instantly. Frederick looked away, lungs tight, hating how much his half-brother loathed him.

But there was nothing he could do. How did you get past twenty years of constant dislike?

"—and I met her," John was saying triumphantly. "I met Miss Stewart—and I must say, you have made an excellent choice, Penrith."

Frederick jolted in his seat. *Oh, hell, they weren't going to talk about—*

"I presumed I would be the first properly introduced to Miss Stewart," said William, pouting. "Yes, I've met her during the Season earlier this year, though I was interrupted by Lady Romeril and had little chance to converse—but once she became the prospective bride of my brother, there is more etiquette involved in such an introduction. I am the head of this family, after all."

Both John and George rolled their eyes, chuckling at the pompous nature of their eldest brother.

Frederick would have liked to do so, too. How pleasant it would have been to be a part of a family. To jest with them. To laugh, to tease, to know there was little he could do to overstep.

Not so, sadly. His place in this family, in the monthly family lunches—it was precarious.

Anything could break it.

"It was mere accident Aylesbury was with me when I happened upon Miss Stewart," Frederick said as formally as he could manage. "There was no disrespect intend—"

"As it happens, I have met her," William interjected with a sniff. "At Almack's earlier this year. Very beautiful, Frederick. The flourishing rose, indeed."

And just as Frederick knew he would, George snorted.

"Flourishing rose? How did he manage it, that's what I want to know." The Earl of Lindow pointed a fork across the table at Frederick, who worked hard to maintain his equilibrium. "A man like that, with a background like that—marry the flourishing rose?"

"She agreed to marry me and her father approved the match," Frederick said curtly. "That's all that—"

"I call it a farce," George snapped. His ire was evident, the tension in his brow only growing as the conversation continued. "I refuse to believe you—that someone like you—"

Frederick was doing his best to stay calm, to ignore the waves of irritation threatening to seep into his very core, but it was a challenging thing. He'd thought Lindow had changed—if only slightly—the past few weeks. He'd come to him—to Frederick, of all the brothers—shortly before securing his own match. They'd had... an evening of sorts.

But the man hadn't changed at all.

The monthly lunches between the four Chance brothers had been William's idea. Of course it had. He was nature's peacekeeper.

In the main, they were bearable. Sometimes, even mediocre. There had been one when George had been in Bath that Frederick had actually enjoyed.

But today?

George's eye gleamed with malice as he continued to wave about his fork. There was a pea stuck on one of the tines. "I wouldn't be surprised if she changed her mind, Pernrith. Realized she had made a mistake, that she would never wish to—"

"Thank you for your unsolicited advice," Frederick interrupted, knowing his voice was no longer exuding the calm, unfettered strength it should have been. "Perhaps if you were more involved in my life, I would take that advice."

Silence fell upon the dining room in Cothrom House.

Frederick was breathing more heavily than he ought to have been.

John shifted uneasily to his right. "Now then, men, there's no need to—"

"I think it's highly suspicious we're only hearing about this engagement now," George muttered. "I think—"

"Well, I don't care what you think." Frederick spoke over him as tranquilly as possible, but there was a bite to his tone he knew was audible. "You have never wished to know what was going on in my life until recently. I don't see why you would interest yourself now."

The man's words cut only deeper with the truth that Edie—Miss Stewart—would not actually marry him. How the earl would gloat in a few weeks' time.

"You're going to be married, and that makes Miss Stewart our future sister-in-law," William said stiffly. "It's only natural—"

"His anger is not natural," Frederick retorted, glancing at George.

The Earl of Lindow's cheeks were pink now, but his glare remained defiant. "So you're not going to introduce her to me, then?"

It was on the tip of his tongue to bite back that heaven and hell would have to move before he subjected Edie to George's vicious dislike, but he did not say that.

Besides, it was a relatively valid request. If the engagement between Edie and himself had been true, he would have been expected to make the introductions to the whole family. Perhaps even present Lord Stewart and Mrs. Teagan to them as well, God help them all.

But as it was…

As it was, the engagement was entirely false. A part of him had hoped she'd felt the same about him as he felt about her, but there was no requited affection between them—plenty of lust, but that was about it. They had mutually agreed to pretend the engagement to maintain her reputation.

He was under no illusions. Miss Edie Stewart would be escaping his engagement as soon as possible. Introducing her to the family formally—God above, introducing her to George—would be a disaster.

There was no point getting the other three Chance brothers involved.

"Well, that's how it is, is it?" George said into the silence. When Frederick looked up, he was glaring again. "I think you've got a lot of cheek, coming here and pretending to be a part of this family, when in truth—"

"It is not my fault how I was born, you idiot, and I am sick and tired of being treated differently because of it!"

Frederick clasped a hand over his mouth.

But it was too late. The words had left his mouth, making their escape and echoing around the impressive dining room.

George was staring, slack-jawed. William's lips were tightly pursed and he was looking straight ahead, neither at George nor Frederick. John was clearly deeply uncomfortable, his hands twisting his napkin around and around.

Oh, hell. Twenty years of holding his tongue, desperately trying to earn their respect when Frederick knew that if he had been a true born son, it would have just been given...

And he'd had to go and wreck it all.

"My compliments to Alice," he said gruffly, standing and throwing down his own napkin. "Good day, gentlemen."

Frederick did not even look at George as he left the dining room. His temper was so fractious, he was certain if he even met the blaggard's eye, he would say something unforgiveable.

Even more unforgiveable than he already had.

His bad mood followed him all afternoon. Rattling around Pernrith House, the small townhouse that had come with the gift of the title, Frederick had still felt his hackles raised and his temper frayed as he strode out in the evening air toward the Stewarts' house.

He had been invited to dinner. More's the pity.

It did not begin well.

"Ah," said the butler warningly. "You."

"'My lord,'" snapped Frederick, pushing past him and handing over greatcoat, hat, and gloves to the nearby footman. "And the family is?"

It looked like the butler was seriously considering whether or not to ask Viscount Pernrith to leave. Clearly, the servants knew his full history, even if the daughter of the house did not.

Guilt washed through Frederick, intermingling with his exasperation and sparking even more irascibility through his lungs.

He really should tell her. He couldn't just let Edie continue to waste her time, threaten her reputation, on a man like him. A bastard like him.

"The drawing room is over there, sir," said the butler eventually, not bothering to escort him to the door, but merely pointing to it.

"'My lord,'" ground out Frederick before striding over to the door the churlish man had indicated.

He managed to hold his tongue in the half an hour before dinner. This, in fact, was not as difficult as he had presumed it would be. Edie sat demure on a settee, quite unlike herself and not even meeting his eye. Lord Stewart explained Mrs. Teagan's absence by suggesting she had a headache, but he quickly changed topics, as he had a great deal he evidently wished to say about what the wedding would be like: flowers, cake, hosting the wedding reception, demanding Edie go to the best modiste…

It all washed over Frederick's head like water. What did it matter, anyway? They were not actually going to be married. It was all a lie—a farce.

And echoing in his mind, the cross words he had exchanged hours ago…

"I think you've got a lot of cheek, coming here and pretending to be a part of this family, when in truth—"

"It is not my fault how I was born, you idiot, and I am sick and tired of being treated differently because of it!"

Frederick almost forgot to lead Edie into the dining room when the gong rang out, but her father appeared to forgive that momentary lapse by chalking it up to good manners.

"No, no, it is your place to take her now," Lord Stewart said gruffly. "Lord knows I have led her in more than enough times."

Perhaps if Frederick had taken a second look at the older gentleman, he would have seen not gruffness, but sparkling tears in the man's eyes. Perhaps he would have seen the gruffness as a struggling acceptance of the next stage in his daughter's life. Perhaps then his heart would have softened.

As it was, Frederick marched Edie at a rapid pace through the door into the dining room and deposited her none too gently into her seat.

"What has gotten into you?" Edie hissed.

Frederick did not reply as he marched around the head of the table to sit on the other side of Lord Stewart, opposite his supposed intended. She was unable to repeat the question as her father took his seat between them.

"So, tell me," said Lord Stewart formally, "how are your brothers?"

Of all the damned questions that he could ask me…

Try as he might, Frederick could not keep his voice level as he replied, "Two of them are doing well, and the third is an absolute fool."

He glanced at Edie as he spoke. Her cheeks were pink and her eyes downcast, staring at the plate upon which a footman was serving the most delicate roasted quail and freshwater trout.

"Oh. I see." Lord Stewart had nothing more to add, it seemed.

Frederick's stomach churned. *Fine, it was an idiotic thing to say.* He should have known, better than anyone, how unfair it was to accuse a man of being a fool without any evidence—without the gentleman in question being present to defend himself.

But red-hot, bitter anger, the anger of years that had been repressed for so long, was pouring through his veins. Every pulse pushed it further through his body, taking over his reason and making it impossible to speak rationally.

He needed to calm down.

The dinner continued mostly quiet. It was only when dessert had been served—a luscious helping of pistachio and strawberry ices, the like of which Frederick had never seen—that Edie volunteered something herself.

"I had the pleasure of being introduced to the Marquess of Aylesbury a few days ago, Father."

Frederick groaned internally and was not surprised when he saw the man on his left perk up.

"Truly? The Marquess of Aylesbury?"

"My brother," Frederick said gloomily. "I think he was hoping for an introduction and so walked with me on just such an errand, Miss Stewart. You will have to forgive him."

"There is nothing to forgive," said Edie prettily.

But Frederick was still filled with the aggression that his interactions with George had wrought.

And that was why he could not halt his tongue from continuing, "My brother William, Duke of Cothrom, also wishes to formally meet you—but I won't subject you to the company of Lindow. You don't deserve that."

Edie's smile was tight. "I am sure I can decide whom I should and should not meet, my lord."

"I doubt it," snapped Frederick.

Cutlery clanged onto plates around the table. He swallowed.

Well, hang it all, that wasn't what he'd meant. He hadn't meant to suggest Edie could not make those decisions for herself—obviously, she could. He had just meant—Lindow was hardly a man to be trusted. God knew what he would say to Edie, the brute could be quite—

"I think I shall retire," Lord Stewart said. "Edie?" He rose from the table, his arm extended in Edie's direction. "Shall we see our guest out?"

The aggravatingly beautiful lady dabbed at her lips with a napkin.

"I'm not quite finished, Father. Neither is Lord Pernrith, by the looks of it." She glanced Frederick's way.

Yes, his ice was in danger of melting onto the table at this point. As delicious as it was, he couldn't quite stomach the sweetness at the moment.

Lord Stewart frowned, his elbow sinking back against his side. "Perhaps I shall see if Mrs. Teagan feels well enough to join you."

"No need." Edie set her napkin down and picked up her spoon. Her gaze flicked to the footmen standing behind Frederick. "I shan't be long, Father. And Jenkins will join me in seeing our guest out, I'm sure."

If Jenkins was the name of the butler, Frederick was certain the man would *love* to see him out the door.

Lord Stewart seemed to think over it, his eyes darting to the servants present, then nodded. "Only a few minutes more, mind you." Without another word, he strode out of the dining room.

The footman who'd held the door open for him snapped it shut behind him.

"That will be all, thank you," said Edie with flushing cheeks.

For a moment, Frederick had no idea what she was talking about, but then he saw the movement of the two footmen behind him. They followed their master out of the door that led into the main hall, and the snick of the door shutting behind them echoed painfully around the room.

He hoped the news of Edie's machinations to get the two of them alone wouldn't reach Lord Stewart or Jenkins before the woman had said her piece.

Or maybe he did hope they found out soon enough. Then he could be on his way and put this blasted day behind him.

"Right," said Edie, leaning her elbows on the dining table and examining him closely. "What is it?"

"What is what?" Frederick said petulantly.

He hated the way he had spoken the instant the words had been out of his mouth. Was this what he was reduced to? A mere child who threw a tantrum when he did not get his wish?

There was only so long a man could take always being criticized, always being on the edge, never feeling a true part of a family. Perhaps he had finally reached his limit. He had never known before today if there truly was a limit, or whether he would just allow Lindow to push him around for the rest of his life.

Frederick swallowed. "I am sorry. I… I apologize."

He managed to meet Edie's gaze. He had expected… sorrow. Empathy. Compassion.

Instead, he stared into golden-brown eyes of sharp fury.

"Just because this is not a true engagement," Edie said firmly, "that does not mean you can be so rude. To myself, or my father."

Frederick swallowed hard, his throat dry. "I said I was—"

"And did you mean it?" she countered before he could finish.

He instinctively started to say *yes*. Yes, he was sorry. He would not have said it if he had not meant it.

But Frederick halted and forced himself to do what he loathed. He inspected his heart.

There was sorrow there, to be sure—but it was primarily directed at himself. He felt a great deal of sorrow for his own position, for the frustration of being born illegitimate, for always being on the outside, looking in.

In truth, until she had challenged him on it, there had not been a great deal of regret for the way he had spoken to Edie.

Until now.

Frederick slumped in his seat. "I do apologize, Edie. I… I had no right to speak to either of you like that."

His eyes had fallen to his plate as he'd spoken, so he was not sure what Edie's expression was. The silence, however, lingered on for almost a full minute before he gained the bravery to look up.

Edie was leaning her chin on her hands, examining him thoughtfully. "You know," she said softly. "Just because I am—because Society considers me beautiful, that does not mean I am invulnerable. That I should be treated poorly or that anyone can just speak to me how they please."

Panic, a desperate need to explain poured through Frederick. "That wasn't—I would never treat you badly because you're beautiful!"

The very idea was astonishing. Why on earth would Edie think such a thing?

Was it—surely, it was impossible gentlemen in the past had spoken poorly to her merely because she was so handsome, they found her to be without feeling?

And Frederick took a slow and careful look at the woman before him.

Elegance personified. A delicacy of mouth and nose any artist would have wept over. If a bust were made of her and placed among those from Rome and Greece, Edie's face would not have been out of place.

And that was just her shoulders upward. Frederick could not deny that the suggestion of her form through her gowns made it clear Edie was the pinnacle of perfection—at least, in the eyes of the *ton*. The fashion for small, pert breasts and a waist over swelling hips had been personified in the woman before him.

And she was—

Clever.

There was a sparkle in those magnificent eyes. The color alone was not what made Edie beautiful—it was the intelligence that lingered there. The mouth, lips perfect for kissing, was pursed in a knowing smile. The fingers splayed under her chin were elegantly held as though... as though on purpose to frame her face.

She knew what she was doing. And Frederick had, ever since he had first met her, greatly underestimated Miss Edith Stewart.

"You weren't rude because I am beautiful?" Edie raised an eyebrow. "Well, in that case, you must have an explanation as to the insolence. We are supposed to be engaged to be married, after all."

Her imperious look was magnificent and Frederick's mouth went dry as he considered.

It wasn't as though he could actually explain.

Where would he start? Being abandoned on the doorsteps of Stanphrey Lacey? Being told, on an almost daily basis, he was not to disturb "the true sons of the house"? Watching them go off to Eton as he'd traipsed to the local school, where he'd been ostracized for not being a country boy and gawped at for being a bastard?

Frederick swallowed. Perhaps in another life, he could have tried to make Edie see just where this anger, this rage had come from.

But they weren't even truly engaged. It was all a farce, a pretense she had requested to salvage her reputation without actually going through with the honorable deed. She didn't want to marry him.

"*You don't want to marry me.*"

"*Obviously not.*"

There are no confidences expected between two people who are not engaged, Frederick told himself.

"I have no reason," he said quietly. "No excuse. I am sorry, Edie, truly."

For a moment, she examined him as though her gaze could pierce his very soul. As though her understanding were stronger than that of any gentleman he had ever encountered. As though she could read his thoughts and know he was lying to her.

A lie by omission, which felt less guilt-inducing than a bare-faced lie.

But still.

"You can talk to me, you know," Edie said softly. "I know we're not—that this isn't a true partnership. But I would like to be a... a friend to you, Frederick Chance. If you would let me."

Frederick hesitated.

It sounded wonderful—in theory.

A friend. He couldn't recall ever having a friend, not a true friend. There were those who had attempted to grow close to him upon discovering his wealthy and well-born half-brothers. There were those who had considered him a soft target for a little light beating, which Frederick had seen swiftly off.

But someone who truly wished to know him, for himself? To listen to his thoughts, answer his questions, laugh with him?

The idea of his first true friend being a woman was, naturally, ridiculous.

Frederick shook his head. "I thank you, but there are... there are no hidden depths to this, I assure you. Just a fractious man who should have known better."

Edie looked as though she were going to say something—perhaps refute his comment. But instead, she folded her hands in her lap. "Then your apology is accepted."

She smiled and the temperature of the room transformed. It was as though the sun itself had decided to come for dinner, the place becoming radiant. Frederick groaned as the warmth of her expression bathed his bones in much needed cordiality.

"My father likes you."

Frederick snorted. "It's very kind of you to say so, but—"

"I speak the truth—it's the only way I know," Edie said, a slight teasing twist creasing her lips. "Honestly, I think he is more impressed than he expected."

It was all he could do to keep a straight face. Yes, he supposed Lord Stewart had expected the worst of the bastard viscount. Perhaps he *had* displayed the worst of his character to the man this evening, but if he still liked him after this...

"After all, there is no reason why my father would not like you, is there?" said Edie lightly.

Frederick hesitated. This was it—the perfect moment to explain his history.

But she was so... so good. Beautiful, yes, but there was an innocence, a sweet naivety in Edie that he just could not bring himself to end.

Once a woman like that knew the world was a dangerous, sordid, double-crossing place, she would never be able to unsee it. He would have ruined that for her—and he wouldn't. He just couldn't.

"No reason at all," said Frederick as frivolously as he could manage. "Save for my terrible manners."

Edie paused a moment, pursing her lips. But then she chuckled.

And their laughter filled the dining room, and the sun shone.

Chapter Nine

November 23, 1812

THE SILENCE WOULD have been getting to Edie, if she hadn't been enjoying herself so much.

Most people promenading up and down Rotten Row did not appear to be having much fun. Perhaps it was the chilly, wintery breeze. Autumn had most definitely ended, temperatures dropping with every successive day and the nights drawing in. There were more scarves and fur-lined gloves being worn today than there had been last week. A few people strode along the path for ten minutes or so, then departed.

Not them.

Edie glanced at Frederick, who was walking alongside her in silence. She had attempted to slip her hand into his arm when they had first met there—partly for the closeness, but admittedly, partly for the warmth—but he had stepped aside.

And in truth, for probably good reason.

"Do we have to do this?" muttered Frederick.

Edie smiled, heat fluttering through her at his mock irritation. At least, she was almost certain it was pretend. "What, walk up and down?"

"That's not what I meant."

"You do not like to be viewed by all of Society as we promenade?" Edie asked gayly, as though this were one of her favorite activities.

In truth, as evidenced by all the stares, the whispers behind cupped hands, she loathed it herself. Though there was something extraordinarily strange today about the way passersby always seemed just far enough away to avoid a conversation... But she knew that wasn't what Frederick had meant.

He jerked his head over his shoulder. "You know precisely what I mean."

Edie's smile widened as she glanced over her own shoulder. There, about ten feet behind them but maintaining that distance at all times, was her father arm in arm with Mrs. Teagan.

Just out of earshot, so the newly engaged couple could have a modicum of privacy... but not too much.

"They don't trust us," said Edie with a wry look, turning back to Frederick. "And who can blame them?"

He snorted with a teasing grin, and molten-hot lava trickled from Edie's stomach to between her legs.

After all, it had been her father who had discovered them. Who had walked into the library and discovered them kissing. And not just kissing. Frederick had managed to pull down her gown and free her breast, teasing her nipple with his—

Edie swallowed, hoping the pink in her cheeks could be ascribed to the chilly wind.

It was certainly not a circumstance a polite and genteel young lady was supposed to find herself in. She was fortunate, indeed, that Frederick had agreed to this charade. If the truth had got out...

"I know it's the proper thing to do, but you would think Society could trust me to take you on a walk in public," muttered Frederick.

Edie looked at him, attempting to discern if he were truly irritated or just teasing. It was one of the things she was swiftly learning about this man—or rather, not learning.

His humor was different from hers. Not better, or worse, not necessarily. Just... different. He said things sometimes to plague her, and

Edie was learning it was not a personal slight, but merely how Frederick made jests.

She had never met anyone like him.

Nor had she met anyone with such wild and untamed hair. Honestly, there was nothing to be done, according to Frederick. It just flew about all over the place.

"Edie?"

Edie cleared her throat loudly and concentrated on the path before them. It wouldn't do for Frederick to know just how closely she had been watching him. "Father and Mrs. Teagan are protecting my reputation, that's all."

"And very soon, that will become my role, or so they think," Frederick said in a low voice.

Excitement thrummed through her. *If only that were true*, she found herself wondering wistfully. If only Frederick had been charmed by her and had instead of agreeing to this false engagement...

But there was no point in dwelling on such matters. The fact was, he clearly had not wished to be entrapped into a marriage by her father, and she had done the only honorable thing and offered him a way out. If he had been serious about marriage, he would have told her he'd had it in mind before dragging her off to the library...

"If they're not too careful, people will start to think that your father and Mrs. Teagan are themselves courting," added Frederick with a mischievous look.

Edie's lips parted. "Frederick—my lord! You cannot say such a thing!"

"Why not?" he quipped. "Stranger things have happened."

She closed her mouth hurriedly and took another swift glance over her shoulder. There did not appear to be any great cordiality between her father and her chaperone. They were walking in almost complete silence, arm in arm along Rotten Row behind her.

True, it was a silence that did not appear to be discomforting. Edie could well recall her father's discomfort in sitting with ladies long after his wife had died.

Something twisted painfully in her stomach. Surely, her father would not... Her mama had been so wonderful, the flourishing rose of her Season. He wouldn't—

"Careful," said Frederick softly as he swiftly reached out and grabbed her arm.

If he had not, Edie would have undoubtedly toppled to the ground. A stone that had been placed there by a rascal attempting to dislodge a horse's canter had been perfectly suited to entrap her foot. As she had not been facing forward, she would have fallen instantly.

Frederick's hand was strong, holding her arm safe. Edie gave into the temptation, slipping her hand into his arm and holding on tightly. This time, he did not pull away.

The warmth that flowed through her was entirely ridiculous. This was all pretense. All fake. The moment would come when it would be time for them to act out a disagreement, and the fabricated engagement would be unmade.

He would go his way, Edie thought with a sudden lump in her throat. *And I would go mine.*

"You are very pensive," said Frederick softly. His voice had lowered even further, now that they were walking arm in arm. "What are you thinking about? Not that ridiculous comment I made about my brothers, I hope."

Edie cleared her throat awkwardly. "No. No, not at all."

Not your ridiculous comment about your brothers, she could have said. *No, I have been dwelling far more on what Lady Romeril said about your brothers...*

"He's only half a Chance."

It had been impossible to dislodge the knowledge, once it had taken root in her mind. Still wondering whether she should have asked the doyenne of Society, Edie had gone back and forth in her internal arguments about whether to speak to Frederick about such a thing.

She had tried to encourage him to speak of it, but he had not.

It was... scandalous. The idea that his father—that the late Duke of Cothrom had taken a mistress, the result of which was the man beside her...

It happened, Edie knew. *But it does not happen to people you know.*

"There is something on your mind."

Her chin jerked up. "I assure you, there's—"

"You can't lie to me, Edie." Frederick spoke softly, not just in volume, but in tenderness too. "I can see right through you, and I suspect... I wonder whether it's something you think will harm me. Why else would you keep it from me?"

Edie swallowed. The tenderness was something she had not expected, and it was most welcome. The way he spoke to her, as though he really cared...

But what was it she had said at the dinner they had shared but a couple of days ago?

"I know we're not—that this isn't a true partnership. But I would like to be a... a friend to you, Frederick Chance. If you would let me."

Well, she had attempted to draw them nearer, had she not? It had been her instigation, and now she was reaping the reward of that.

Or the price.

Unsure whether this was a good idea or not, and knowing she could not take back the words once they had been uttered, Edie inhaled deeply.

"Oh, dear," said Frederick with a grin. "As bad as that?"

She gave him a crooked smile. "I am not sure. I had tea with Lady Romeril last week—"

He placed his free hand over his heart. "A disaster in and of itself!"

"Frederick!" Edie said, nudging him as she laughed.

He grinned back and there was a moment—

It was surely just in her imagination. The flirtation was not one of overt sensuality, after all. A brother and a sister could nudge like that, laugh like that, tease like that.

The sensations flowing through her body could not be further from that of siblings, of course, but there it was...

They stopped briefly to greet an acquaintance of her father's and Edie did her best to hurry the conversation along, taking note of the way the wizened gentleman's eyes kept cutting to the viscount beside her, over and over, as if he found her companion a strange species to encounter. Her father joined them and took over the conversation, and Edie used the excuse to guide Frederick forward, knowing her father wouldn't linger for long.

"I was speaking to Lady Romeril, and she was speaking about you, naturally," Edie continued once out of earshot.

Frederick groaned. "Naturally."

"And she said..." Edie hesitated. Did she truly have the bravery to speak openly about this? Did she even have the language to describe it?

Perhaps he guessed, merely from the hesitation. Maybe he saw the look on her face and immediately knew of which topic she wished to speak.

"She mentioned you were not wealthy," she blurted out, unsure whether she could bring herself to ask the question she truly wished to.

Frederick raised an imperious eyebrow. "Right. Well, Lady Romeril is correct, at least in part. I am not a wealthy man, not comparatively to some, I dare say. But I suppose that is relative. I own and maintain three homes—a country estate, a townhouse in Bath, and one here. I am hardly a pauper."

Her cheeks tinged. Oh, she should never have brought this up... or she should have started with the question that was uppermost in her mind...

A deep breath escaped Frederick's lips and he swallowed before speaking. "This is about my parentage, isn't it?"

Edie's shoulders sagged as guilt and relief mingled within her. "I am a cruel woman to bring it up."

"No, you're an honest woman. And a curious one, which I think is part of human nature," said Frederick quietly. "I didn't know if you knew. I didn't think you did, but if you just learned last week, that explains it."

They had reached the end of Rotten Row and Edie's heart twisted. This was the perfect excuse for him to put off having this conversation—perhaps forever. He was completely within his rights to beg off the walk. They had been promenading together for some time. If he did not wish to tell her—

"Come, let us take another turn," Frederick said softly. "If that is quite acceptable to you, my lord, Mrs. Teagan?"

Edie turned. Her father and chaperone had caught them up, but both expressed how content they would be to walk down Rotten Row again.

She stared at them curiously as she and Frederick began walking again, opening up the gap of ten feet. Could there be any truth to his guess, about her father and Mrs. Teagan? Surely, they wouldn't—

"So," said Frederick quietly, "I suppose you have a great deal of questions."

Edie turned back to him with flushed cheeks. "I suppose I do."

"What would be easier for you? I can explain the situation, if you would like, or you can ask me questions." He spoke with such nonchalance, Edie was quite sure it was a pretense.

No one, no matter how much they had ruminated on their own history, could have been that calm.

She squeezed his arm and said with true feeling, "What would be easier for you?"

Frederick's head jerked back as he met her eyes. "I beg your pardon?"

It had seemed a simple enough comment to Edie, but she explicated on her remark. "I mean, this is your story, your life, your family. I have no wish to pry, though I will own I am curious. So... So whatever you would like to tell me. However you would like to tell me."

Her arm lifted a few inches as Frederick took a deep breath, one that seemed to go to the very core of him.

He smiled, though there was little merriment in the expression. "You honor me with your patience."

"And you honor me by even considering talking about it," Edie said in a low voice. "I... I should not have listened to Lady Romeril."

Or asked her about it, she thought wretchedly.

It was not difficult to see the pain on Frederick's face, nor feel the tension in his arm. This was not a topic about which he liked to speak, and she had almost cornered him for the details.

"I do not imagine Lady Romeril has all the truth of the matter, no," Frederick said dryly, inclining his head to someone as they passed. The gentleman ignored him.

Edie frowned. "Why did he not return your bow—"

"Because I am but half a Chance," he said quietly. "Because my parentage makes it impossible for most people in the *ton* to accept me. You saw how your father reacted to me at Lady Romeril's ball."

She cast her mind back, attempting to recall the exact words.

"*—can't believe you would speak to such a man. Of all the people—*"

Her stomach swooped. "I... I see."

"My mother was a maid at Stanphrey Lacey," Frederick said quietly. "That's the family seat out in the country, the seat of the Duke of Cothrom. He was a kind man, but foolish, as far as I can tell. He should never have betrayed his wife, but there it was. My mother was dismissed the instant it was discovered she was with child, and for a time, she did not reveal who my father was. At least, that is what I have been told."

It would have been all too easy for Edie to step in and ask a question, but something told her to hold back. The words came stiffly from Frederick's lips, but they were coming—and now he had started, they became a torrent.

"My mother sickened. She was a maid at a local inn—my father had procured her the position, all the better for him to...to visit. But despite his money for medicine, she would get better at first, then the sickness would last longer, and longer, and I think—I suppose she knew her end was coming," said Frederick, his attention drifting off into a distance Edie could not see.

"She knew she... she was dying?"

He nodded. "That is what I have guessed. She took me back to Stanphrey Lacey, leaving me on the doorstep with a note, printed in her finest hand."

There was sorrow in his voice, but Edie could also hear pain, and regret, and disillusionment. What had it taken for that poor woman to leave the boy in the hands of another?

"I heard later my father admitted to the... the indiscretion the instant I arrived," Frederick said ruefully. "It broke his wife. Killed her, I think."

"No!"

"The duchess died not long after, leaving behind three boys. William, John, and George. George was but a month younger than I, and most unhappy that I was there. All three boys were devastated at their mother's death." Frederick spoke with a harshness now Edie had never heard. "And I was never made to forget it."

She squeezed his arm, hoping that through the small gesture, he could feel just how sorry she was. "Everyone seems to have suffered in this story. You, your father, the duchess, your brothers—"

"Half-brothers," Frederick interjected, and there was a steeliness to his tone now. "The differences between us were... were stark. Different food. I had their hand-me-down clothes, never anything new. They had the best education, the best opportunities, and I..."

Edie could well imagine—at least, she could try to imagine. Separate in that large house, without a mother, a father distant, grief-stricken...

"It was after my—our father died that William, the current Duke of Cothrom, gave me the title." Frederick chuckled dryly. "Our father had legitimized me before this death, but he had not let me know, had not treated me any differently. I thought at the time William's act was a gesture of pity, and perhaps it was. But it has enabled me to join Society. In a way."

"'In a way'?"

He nodded. "You'll soon notice, if you haven't already, how differently I am treated to the other gentlemen of the *ton*. A mere mister will receive greater respect than I, a viscount—though I suppose I am not truly a viscount by tradition."

There was such bitterness in his voice, and Edie wished for nothing more than to kiss away the pain.

Kiss it away? Where did that thought come from?

"It was difficult when you were a child, to be different," she ventured. "Set apart."

Frederick sighed as another pair of gentlemen passed them— passed them, Edie noticed, and studiously did not make eye contact with Viscount Pernrith.

"It's hard now," he said quietly. "I've been cheated at cards and called a liar merely because of my birth. The Dulverton Club puts up with me, but I'm never welcome. I am given the cut direct on a daily basis—you saw it, just now."

Edie bit her lip. She had, and it had been a most discomforting occurrence. To receive such a thing… she was the flourishing rose of Society. She knew those gentlemen, too, at least by name. Usually, they would have stopped to speak with her. Was her mere engagement to this man—a false engagement—enough to thrust her from the *ton*?

How awful for Frederick, to experience such a thing on a daily basis.

"I am sorry."

"For what? I cannot help my parentage. I am proud, in a way," said Frederick with a forced cheerfulness that tore at Edie. "I have a foot in both worlds, in a way. A mother who worked, a mere servant—"

"Don't say that," Edie said quietly. "No one is a 'mere' anything."

He looked at her curiously, and her cheeks burned. "Do you think so?"

Nodding softly, she said, "Your father was a nobleman who gave you less than he did his other sons, and your mother did everything she could for her child. Who was the better parent?"

For a moment, Edie was certain she had gone too far, but Frederick laughed gently at her words. "I suppose you are right. Yet that does not help me now, unfortunately. I am the outcast of Society, despite my name, but it is a name many believe is not my due. One of those people is my own half-brother."

"He's only half a Chance."

Edie's lungs tightened. *What must it be like, to grow up in a household where you are not wanted? More than not wanted, blamed for the death of an innocent woman, merely because of your existence?*

"I never had any siblings," she said quietly. "I cannot know what it is like to have them but not be wanted by them."

"Oh, Cothrom and Aylesbury do their best, I suppose," Frederick said brightly, though there was a forcedness to it that made Edie wince. "They were but children themselves, and... well. I know what it is to lose a mother. But I admit, it has been hard. To never be wanted."

"I, too, know what it is to lose a mother." The words came easily to Edie—but then, she had hardly known her mother, had she? "She died several years ago now. I nursed her until... until the end."

Frederick swallowed. "So you understand."

She hesitated, just for a moment. "I... I don't think so. Oh, my father and I miss her terribly, and I have certainly felt the lack of a mother now that I am in town—but with every day that passes, my recollection of her slips. Her face... Without the portrait at home, I am not sure..."

Edie bit her lip. It was a most indecorous thing to admit, forgetting one's mother.

Frederick's grip on her arm tightened. "There is no moral failing in being but a child when you suffered the loss. Another thing we share, I think."

Edie did not think about it. She merely acted on instinct, needing to be closer to him. Needing Frederick to know that she was alongside him, was with him—was not about to walk away merely because of an accident of birth.

And that was why her hand slipped from his arm, trailing down the forearm of his sleeve, her fingers entangling themselves in his.

Plainly startled, Frederick looked at his hand—at their hands, entwined together.

Almost holding her breath she was so nervous, Edie squeezed his hand. "No one should feel as though they are not wanted."

"It's the way of the world."

She shook her head impetuously. "It's outrageous—it simply should not happen!"

Frederick was smiling, and this time, there was delight in his eyes. As they continued to walk along Rotten Row, the winter breeze increasing in pace but not in temperature, he said quietly, "It happens every day."

"I don't want it to happen to you," Edie said vehemently.

She could not put into words just why this mattered so much, but it did. The idea that Frederick had spent so much of his life feeling alone... It was awful. It could not be allowed.

"No one should be treated as you have been," she said fiercely. "No matter their background."

Frederick shook his head. "You are rare, you know."

And her bravado, her proud defiance, melted away. Edie sighed, looking away to the path before them. "Yes. Yes, there's only one flourishing rose."

Yes, the conversation had to circle back to this.

"No, that's not what I—Edie, look at me."

There was such tenderness, such affection in his words, that she immediately glanced over at him.

That was when she realized that they had stopped walking.

Edie looked around herself for a moment. When had they ceased their movement? When had Frederick stopped? Had she been so absorbed by the conversation that she had not been conscious of her footsteps?

Her father and Mrs. Teagan had halted themselves and, clearly out of some deference for the younger couple, had remained about ten feet from them. They were in conversation now themselves and appeared most animated.

Surely, they would never—

"Edie Stewart, you are rare. And you are the Season's flourishing rose, which I am starting to realize is more punishment than pleasure," said Frederick softly.

Edie smiled ruefully. "Something like that."

"But I said that you are rare for quite another reason." He lifted his free hand, tilting her chin with his forefinger so she had no choice but to look him directly in the eyes.

She almost gasped with the intensity of the look within those liquid hazel eyes. No, they weren't the Chance blue. They were so much more interesting than that.

"Most people don't think like you," Frederick said softly. "Most people don't have the heart for people like you. Most... Almost no one I have ever met has been able to look past the labels the world has given me, and just see... me."

Edie swallowed.

She *did* just see him. And he was handsome, and charming, and vulnerable, and he ached to be loved.

And the trouble was, she was starting to—

"It's getting mightily cold," said Mrs. Teagan, who was suddenly at Edie's elbow.

Edie jumped. She released Frederick's hand and saw to her great disappointment, but no surprise, that he had taken a step back.

How close had they been?

"Time to go home, my dear," said her father with just a hint of sternness in his tone.

Edie nodded weakly as she exchanged a look with Frederick. Her stomach swooped. Swooped in that way it only did when she was with Frederick. "Yes. Right. Home."

Chapter Ten

November 27, 1812

FREDERICK SHOULD HAVE known, the instant that Edie rushed into the coffee house, Mrs. Teagan quite a few steps behind her, that something was wrong.

There were three clues.

Firstly, he was starting to learn the contours of her face. Looking beyond the beauty, there was a sharpness about her eyes when Edie truly was indignant, and he could see the crinkles on her forehead even from where he was sitting.

Secondly, there was the way she wrenched off her scarf with a terribly bad temper the instant the door closed behind her. A gust of snow fluttered in just in time. It was fortunate, indeed, that the gentleman who had come in behind her was at least three feet back, or he may have been accidentally garroted by the knitted implement.

And thirdly, and perhaps most obviously, there was the way Edie shouted across the coffee house—

"It's outrageous!"

Heads turned.

Frederick had never been one to be surprised at being looked at. It was part and parcel of being who he was, after all, and he had learned swiftly to ignore the pointed looks and muttering.

However, it did not appear that Edie had yet hardened herself to such an experience.

Eyes downcast and struggling out of her pelisse as she wove her way around the tables in Don Saltero's Chelsea Coffee House, Edie let her frown grow deeper, her cheeks even pinker, as she dropped into the chair opposite him.

Mrs. Teagan, her own face red from the cold, hastily sat two tables away at the nearest open seat, allowing them a modicum of privacy as she removed her gloves and pelisse. A modicum, anyway, though the tone of Edie's voice did nothing to dispel the staring of those around them.

"Absolutely outrageous!" Edie said firmly, as though continuing a conversation they had already started. "It shouldn't be allowed!"

Frederick waited for a moment for her to explain, but Edie was swiftly distracted by her gloves, which did not appear to wish to come off her hands, and the way her hat had slipped indecorously from her head.

"—can't believe it," Edie was muttering as she finally freed herself from her winter outerwear. "Can you?"

"Believe... what?" Frederick asked hesitantly.

She glared, then her expression softened. "It is pleasant to see you."

He grinned inanely like a fool, before he recalled himself and looked at his coffee cup. It wouldn't do for there to be even more gossip about him flowing about London. He didn't need to make a fool of himself in public.

"It is pleasant to see you, too," he said quietly.

His words were mainly lost in the long, heavy breath Edie exhaled. "I should have expected it."

Frederick was once again bewildered. "You should always expect me to be pleased to see you."

It was perhaps a little more open than he had expected, but he did not know why Edie appeared so confused. "I beg your pardon?"

"I think I need to beg *your* pardon," Frederick said with a laugh.

"Shall I order for you?"

"What?" Edie said, distraction mussing her voice.

He stifled a smile.

It had been her idea to meet here. She had suggested it only yesterday, when they had both been gawped at while they'd stood at the sidelines of Viscount Walden's ball. Lord Stewart had described it as the perfect place "to be seen," and they were most definitely seen.

Frederick had only been invited because of the engagement, he knew, and Edie had suddenly been aware of just how many people had been staring at them.

"Quite blatantly, too!" she had hissed last night.

"You'll have to get accustomed to it," Frederick had told her with a laugh, before adding hastily, "I mean... you know. Until this engagement is over."

It had been the perfect opportunity for her to say...

What, he did not quite know. Something deep and meaningful. Something about this attraction they felt, that they had felt from the moment they had first met. It was not as though they had held back...

"I'll... I'll stop. If you want to."

"Don't stop."

"We will simply have to find a place to meet where we aren't gawped at," Edie had said, elegantly applauding the musicians as a dance ended. "I like Don Saltero's Chelsea Coffee House—do you know it?"

Frederick had known it and had arranged to meet her there the following day at two o'clock. After lunch, he reasoned, but with enough daylight for them both to return home in the light. Respectably.

Apparently, however, this was not the right place. Edie was causing a great number of glances their way, which only increased as she spoke loudly once again, her voice trembling with feeling.

"It should be illegal!"

"It would be a lot easier for me to partake in this conversation,"

Frederick said hastily, taking her hand and lowering his own voice in the hope she would follow suit, "if I knew what we were talking about."

Edie went crimson. Why, he could not fathom. Then she looked at their hands.

Their hands. Or rather, his hand over hers, on the table. And neither of them was wearing gloves.

Frederick swallowed, hard. He could feel every inch of her hand, the throb of her pulse, the gentle shift of her fingers as they moved behind his own. Oh, this was intimacy. This was what he wanted, to touch her.

And she did not move away. Though Edie's face was pink, she had not removed her hand from his. She left it there, warm and ready for—

Edie removed her hand from the table, pulling it out from under his. For a moment, he thought he was going to attempt to catch it with his own, pull it back, make her touch him.

But he did not. He was hardly a rake.

"Here," Edie said quietly, rummaging for a moment in the reticule she had placed in her lap, then thrusting some paper at him. "Look at this."

Frederick unfolded the paper gingerly as though it were liable to catch fire if he were not careful. The way she had been handling it, it could very well have been dangerous.

"A coffee, three pastries, and as many sugar cubes as you can give me."

Startled, Frederick looked up. "I beg your—ah."

A lanky serving man of the Don Saltero's Chelsea Coffee House bowed, clearly startled by the demands of the lady, and swept away, stopping at Mrs. Teagan's table next.

"Look at it."

Frederick blinked. "I beg your—"

"What is distracting you this afternoon?" Edie asked, her frown finally softening as she examined him more closely. "You seem quite... preoccupied."

Distracted. Preoccupied. Yes, that's one way of describing it.

How could he tell her that with each passing interaction they shared, he was starting to wonder if this pretense could not be something... more?

More than false. More than a sham. More than a convenient way for Edie to save her reputation while escaping the bonds of matrimony with him?

For they would not have been bonds to him. Quite to the contrary, the idea of being tied to Edie for the rest of his life... it did not fill him with fear, or anything like what his brothers had complained about for years.

Complained, that was, until they had fallen in love.

Frederick pushed aside the thought and cleared his throat as he looked at the paper Edie had handed him.

It was today's copy of the *Whispers of the Ton*. He hadn't picked it up—newspapers were much more his style. His attention drifted over the paragraphs hinting at so-and-so's affair, or that Lord You Know who could no longer afford to send his son to Eton, until it settled on a paragraph Edie had circled, several times, with a pencil. With increasing vehemence, judging by the indentation on the paper.

> *Followers of this year's flourishing rose will be startled to know that it is still dangling off the arm of the scandalous Viscount P, a most undeserving man who nevertheless appears to be appreciating its petals. Though the flourishing rose looked stunning in a gown of cerise just two days ago, the possession of such a flower has done no favors for the ill-born gentleman. Is it possible that the shine of owning such a thing is already starting to fade? Has even he realized there must be some fault in a treasure that could not land a match by Season's end? It's hardly going to bloom any brighter as the years go*

on...

Frederick's jaw was tight by the time he'd reached the end of the paragraph.

It was hardly complimentary, but that was the nature of the scandal sheet, wasn't it? *Whispers of the Ton* was hardly known for its approving descriptions of anyone.

He looked up. Edie's expression was a glower.

"It's unpleasant," he said quietly.

"Unpleasant! It's—oh, thank you," Edie said hastily as the serving man returned with a tray. Upon it was a cup of steaming coffee, a plate of several pastries, some of which looked dusted in chocolate, and the largest bowl of sugar cubes Frederick had ever seen.

They halted their conversation as the man gently deposited his burden onto the table and looked expectantly at Edie.

"That will be all," she said lightly as she reached out to pop a sugar cube in her mouth.

Frederick grinned. "Sweet tooth?"

"Far too sweet," Edie said after swallowing the sugar cube almost, as far as he could tell, in one. "Now, aren't you outraged?"

"Outraged? I don't think so," he said reflectively. "I have a savory preference myself. My cook makes these delightful—"

"I don't mean the sugar cubes—I mean what they wrote about me, about us!"

Frederick shrugged. "You get used to it."

Not that he ever had done. The first week he had come to town—why, he must have only been about nineteen years of age—he had been astonished and hurt to discover that those with whom he had spoken so politely had turned to gossip about him the moment his back had turned.

That had been years ago. He was older now. Wiser. Harder.

But Edie, innocent as she was, had never endured such a thing until the Season had ended and she'd remained without a match. "It's contemptible!"

"You will get used to—"

"I don't think anyone should have to put up with such a torrid amount of drivel!" Edie sipped at her coffee, licking her lips and dislodging the last crumbs of sugar that had remained there.

Frederick shifted in his seat. He was most definitely not thinking about those crumbs that had clung so eagerly to those pink lips. Not at—

"You aren't offended, then?" Edie said, her voice hesitant as she selected another sugar cube.

He glanced again at the paper.

> ... *the scandalous Viscount P, a most undeserving man who nevertheless appears to be appreciating its petals... ill-born gentleman...*

His jaw was tight again, but he pushed past it. "It's nothing I haven't seen before."

Or heard before. Or had shouted at me across a crowded dinner table, when the ladies had departed and the men were in their cups.

Frederick did not bother to say it. There was no reason to upset Edie any further. In truth, she looked far more upset than he had expected.

"I have never been spoken of in such a manner," she said quietly, her voice finally dropping below the humdrum of the Don Saltero's Chelsea Coffee House.

And Frederick's stomach twisted.

Damn it to hell, why had he not thought of that? It was all very well for him, he was accustomed to such rudeness. Not that Society thought of it as rudeness—that was the trouble. They saw nothing wrong with casting aspersions on his character because they did not see their rudeness as aspersions. They merely assumed it was all true.

But Edie—she had surely never endured such cruelty. An engagement to him would have only amplified any gossip about her remaining unwed months after the Season's end. It was still a failure, in Society's eyes, to find oneself engaged to wed a bastard.

"You must have encountered rudeness before, in a small way," Frederick said quietly, empathy for her pouring through him. He would not point out the intended insult at her reaching November before she'd found a match. "The first time you entered Society, for example."

"I was judged then, to be sure, even with the eventual 'honor' of the title of flourishing rose. And, well, my first Season *was* later than most ladies'," said Edie, just a hint of pain in her voice.

"Truly?"

He had not thought to ask her age before, though she did not seem too young. He did not imagine he would have found a lady fresh from peeking behind her governess's skirts so captivating.

"My father kept me at home, at Woodhurst. We were out of the way of things there and I suppose..." Edie bit her lip. Frederick tried not to look at her lips, and failed miserably. "Listen to how they talk about me—it! It!"

"It is not complimentary—"

"I am not an object to be merely looked at, passed about to gawp at, treated like a thing! First, they say I have gone too long without a match, then they question the value of the match I—" She cut herself short.

A cup of coffee rising unsteadily to her lips, Mrs. Teagan grimaced as her eyes darted across the room at those all around them still looking at her charge, but she did not get up to tell Edie to calm herself.

Frederick stared at the woman in front of him. Edie's shoulders were shaking, actually *shaking* with the strength of feeling with which she had spoken.

Her voice had been clear, her intonation exact, and she'd spoken with such determination that she had accidently crumpled the pastry she had been holding into pieces.

He had very little experience with ladies.

Oh, not like that. He was hardly an innocent; even though his reputation had never really been intact and his title was, in some sense, perfunctory, there had always been a woman who would accept kisses and a swift tumbling. Frederick was not *that* inexperienced.

But he had no sisters, no mother since he had been three years of age. The women in his life were… well. Servants. His housekeeper, Mrs. Kinley, did for him very well, and Cook was a delight. The single housemaid at Pernrith House was polite and quiet and worked hard, and… and that was it.

There were his sisters-in-law, but he hardly knew Doris. Alice and Florence were polite, perhaps even kind, but neither engaged with him with any sense of warmth.

Precisely why a woman would not wish to be described as—what was it? Blossoming, and a flourishing rose, and all that—Frederick had no idea.

It was most confusing.

"You look muddled."

Frederick started. "How do you do that?"

"Do what?" Edie shot back as she helped herself to another pastry.

"I don't know how to describe it… look beyond my words into my true meaning, I suppose. Into the silences. Read my expression."

There was a strange sort of knowing look on the woman's face. "I just know you."

Forced to shift again in his seat, but this time because there was a most inconvenient pressure in his breeches, Frederick tried again. "It's not the most pleasant way to speak about someone, but you're not just an object, Edie."

"Really?" She arched an eyebrow. "What was your first opinion of me?"

Knowing it was a trap but not sure how to escape it, Frederick said simply, "That you were beautiful."

Edie leaned back in her chair with a sigh of disappointment.

"I don't see why that is so terrible!" he protested, shoulders tight. Why did it hurt so much to sadden her? "You *are* beautiful. It is hardly something I can avoid!"

"Yet I did not ask you what your first impression was of me, but your first *opinion*," Edie pointed out, eyebrow still arched. "Yes, many people's first impression of me is my beauty, and I cannot, will not begrudge them that. It is natural to see the surface at first glance. But I never get a second glance."

Frederick felt as though he was starting to see the shape of what she was trying to say. "You mean… that people do not get to know you."

"My beauty has always held me back," Edie said seriously.

He scoffed at first, an instinct he regretted the moment he saw her face. Taking a sip of coffee quickly to hide from the ferocity of her gaze, he found it was no less severe when he lifted his head.

"I am always discounted, always labeled as 'beautiful' and then never investigated further," Edie said quietly. Her hands were around her own coffee cup, twisting it round and around. "I can think of no one who has ever bothered to… to get to know me. For myself. Is it any wonder I did not secure a match before Season's end?"

Frederick stared, unable to help himself.

Dear God. It was perhaps unbelievable that someone like himself and someone like Miss Edith Stewart had so much in common—but they did.

"Yet here I am. With a title I did not earn, or even seek to receive."

Here he was, hating that people discovered his parentage and could therefore look no closer at his personality, his character, his true feelings… and here Edie was, experiencing much the same thing.

True, it was her beauty and not ill-repute that held people back from knowing the real person underneath. But that was surely a mere detail.

All the isolation he had felt, she felt too. From a different cause, but the consequences were much the same.

No wonder she felt so strongly about this.

Frederick could not help but grin. "I knew there was a reason I liked you."

Patently, that had not been what Edie had been expecting him to say. Slightly caught off-balance, the flare of her nostrils softening, her eyes rapidly blinking, she said, "I... What do you mean?"

"Well, I am hardly everyone's first choice of dinner guest," he said lightly. "If you looked around, you'd notice half the place is staring—your chaperone included—and half the place is attempting not to."

He watched as Edie's head turned from one way to the other. There was suddenly a great deal of clearing of throats about the place. A couple hastily left. One person coughed awkwardly. Mrs. Teagan quickly stared down at her cup, perhaps unable to think of a way to encourage Edie to handle the scene any more gracefully.

When Edie turned back to face him, her cheeks were pink. "I see what you mean."

"People do not bother to get to know us," Frederick said in an undertone, far more feeling in his words than he had expected. "For differing reasons, yes—but it still happens. We both feel alone, ostracized by things out of our control, not our choice. And you... you rail against it. I think it's been so long for me, I've quite forgotten that I should hate it."

Edie's flush did not disappear. "I had not considered it like that."

"I... I have never met anyone like you," Frederick admitted, his pulse skipping a beat. "Whom I could truly talk to."

God, how had he not noticed how lonely he had been? How had he not seen how alone he had become, solitude encircling him like a cloak?

And now... now he had Edie.

He had to tell her. Had to reveal that somehow, something was happening deep within him making it impossible to consider this as just a farce. He did not want to force her to wed him, but if she could only...

"Edie," he said, leaning forward. "Edie, I—"

"A letter for you, my lord."

Frederick started. The serving man had inexplicably appeared by their table, and was holding—dear God, was that a letter?

"Goodness, I never knew the postal service was so efficient," murmured Edie.

The serving man's ears reddened. "It was sent to your residence, my lord, and your housekeeper recognized the seal and requested it be brought to you here."

Frederick took the letter, completely bewildered. What on earth could be so urgent that Mrs. Kinley—

The moment he saw the seal, he knew why.

"Who is it from?" Edie asked curiously as the serving man from Don Saltero's Chelsea Coffee House disappeared. "A friend?"

"Something like that," Frederick said dryly.

The Lindow coat of arms was easy to make out, even through the smudging. So, George had sent him a letter. It was no surprise Mrs. Kinley had sent it on. This had never happened before.

"You don't mind if I—"

"Go ahead," said Edie, smiling as she leaned back. "I have my sugar cubes."

Frederick ripped open the letter and cast his eye swiftly over it.

It was an apology. Of sorts.

Penrith,

It was foolish of me to get into an argument at Cothrom's. Bad form all round, you as well as me. I am sorry for it.

You don't have to bother introducing me to Miss Stewart. I worked it out myself, and though I don't know how you compromised her, I suppose the swift engagement was a good enough cover. Will you go through with it? You don't have to tell me. Perhaps she will end the match soon enough, considering I haven't heard of any witnesses stepping forth claiming to have caught the two of you alone.

If marriage does still interest you, however, my wife, Dodo, has a new acquaintance, a Miss Quintrell. I can introduce you. If you wish.

Or not. I don't care much either way.
Lindow

Frederick could not help but chuckle ruefully as he folded the letter and placed it in his breast coat pocket.

Well, it was perhaps the nicest thing Lindow had ever said to him. Even then it was filled with ire, and irritation, and a clear wish not to write it in the first place.

Had Dodo, his wife, made him write it? Possibly.

The offer to introduce him to Miss Quintrell would, if Frederick had received it a month ago, been most intriguing. He wished to marry—he wanted a family. An introduction to a woman who might not mind his history would have been most welcome.

And now...

"Well?" Edie said promptly, curiosity finally overcoming her. "What did it say?"

Frederick smiled.

He was in too deep now. He couldn't precisely tell how, but the idea of being introduced to another woman was complete anathema to him. He simply did not wish it.

The woman he wanted to know was seated right opposite him.

"It was a pleasant letter, then?" Edie prodded.

He snorted. Yes, there was no other woman for him. He certainly couldn't tell her that, though, as there was no knowing what Edie Stewart might do. Run for the hills, probably. But until they had agreed on a time at which to end this sham of an engagement, he may as well enjoy the time they had.

"It is," he said shortly. "And I believe we have spent sufficient time here to ensure our engagement is believed for another day. I have even sent to the engravers for samples for our wedding invitations, so we are fulfilling your father's requirements."

"Yes, we are," she said quietly. "Aren't we?"

Frederick nodded. "In which case... Well. I am sure you have other calls on your time. If... If you wish to leave..."

Don't leave, he found himself willing her to say. Every moment with this woman was more and more precious.

Edie was smiling. "I'll stay if you tell me what, precisely, is in that letter."

"You are a very curious soul, aren't you?" Frederick countered, tingling with the anticipation of the flirtation.

There had been no malice in his voice, and it was clear Edie did not take it as such. She smiled, eyelashes fluttering as she looked demurely at her coffee cup—but not for long.

"Yes, very," she said openly with a light laugh. "I've never been able to stop myself from poking my nose where it's not wanted. At least, not since... Well. You won't want to hear about that."

Frederick leaned forward, every inch of him wishing to be closer to her. To know her. "Yes, I do."

"Well, it all began when our housekeeper decided..."

Chapter Eleven

November 30, 1812

"Y͟ou know that it's only right," said Edie with a teasing laugh that flittered through her.

Frederick groaned. "I don't want to."

"But you know I'm right."

"You don't need to be wrong for me not to want to go ahead with this," he said malevolently, though there was a mischievous glint in his eye.

Along with pain. Edie was not fooled by his overenthusiastic rolling of his eyes and clutching of his side, as though Viscount Pernrith had been mortally wounded.

What they were about to do... It was only right. It was what was expected. Indeed, she had heard muttered comments that had been most disconcerting wondering why they had not done so already.

Which was why, despite Frederick's protests, the two of them were standing in the drawing room at the Stewart house, both waiting.

Waiting for what was to come.

"I see your father has managed to avoid the whole debacle," Frederick said in a low voice, tugging at his cravat as he lingered by the window. Mrs. Teagan sat some distance behind him, working on needlework, though her gaze flicked up every so often, as if she might catch them in the act of something.

Edie was not sure why Frederick was so tense, standing by that window—the curtains were closed, night having fallen hours ago. Perhaps it made him feel as though he could escape at any moment? She certainly felt the flutter of excitement—panic—within her.

"He is about here somewhere," she said softly, reaching to cup Frederick's cheek.

What had possessed her to do such a thing, she did not know. Edie had moved on instinct alone, and though it was not an instinct she had felt before, it felt natural. His skin was soft, his cheek rough where he had not shaved today.

And though embarrassment shot through her at having done something so astonishingly bold, it did not appear to matter. Nor did Mrs. Teagan not-so-subtly clearing her throat.

Frederick placed a hand over her own and closed his eyes. "I'm just glad I have you by my side. That's all."

Edie's pulse fluttered painfully. "I'm not going to leave you."

"You mustn't because I can hardly talk to these people on my own," he said darkly. "You're all I need, Edie. Just stay with me."

Mrs. Teagan coughed, and yet neither moved.

The bleak intensity of his words was almost shocking, yet the intimacy felt precisely right. Edie leaned closer, hoping to bolster his nerves with her own presence.

They were standing close now. Very close. Edie could sense the heady scent of sandalwood, blackcurrant, and vanilla, the mixture she knew Frederick favored above all others.

It was what she smelled when she thought of him in the middle of the night.

Frederick was still holding her hand against his cheek. "Edie…"

She swallowed. Her hips were pressed against his now, his chest rising and falling against her own.

They had stood like this—well not exactly like this—when they had kissed.

"And yet… yet you could be closer."

Edie knew the last thing she should do was kiss the man. Mrs. Teagan was right there. Their guests would be arriving at any moment and they would have to be on their best behavior.

And yet... well, they were engaged. If they were to kiss in front of her chaperone, no one would be particularly shocked, would they?

And she *did* greatly want to kiss that mouth, taste the need with which she'd only had a swift encounter before. Know what it was to kiss him again, discover if the heat of the moment and the rose tint of nostalgia had made Frederick's kisses seem miraculous in her memory, or whether...

Whether he truly did curl her toes and make her want to rip all her clothes off.

Edie had just decided to lean forward and take the kiss she wanted when Frederick spoke in a low voice.

"I wish I hadn't agreed to this."

She leaned back.

There was such pain in his voice, such regret, that for a moment she wished the evening was not happening after all.

It had been her idea. She was the one who had suggested it to her father, and Lord Stewart had considered it a capital idea. In hindsight, she should have expected that. Naturally, he would wish to have people like that coming to his home for dinner. They were, after all—

"I think there is still time to cancel," said Frederick pensively. "Don't you think?"

"Not in the slightest," Edie said. "You know, you don't know how lucky you are to have them."

He scoffed just as Lord Stewart entered the drawing room. "You haven't even met them yet—ah. My lord."

They sprung apart, Frederick grimacing. And then the guilty expression was gone.

It was miraculous, it really was. Edie was still getting used to it: seeing Frederick laugh and tease, a confident looseness in his shoulders and a delightful looseness in his tongue...

The moment he remembered another person was in their sphere, it all changed.

Frederick straightened, all looseness gone. His spine would become a rod, the laughter would leave his eyes, and though the gentleness of his temperament would remain, there was little of the happiness she knew.

It was a protective gesture, Edie was starting to learn that. It was miraculous, the change that it wrought in him.

"My lord," said Mrs. Teagan, standing, dropping her needlework into a basket beside the sofa. "Miss Stewart was just... She and Lord Pernrith..."

Edie raised her brows at her.

"Ah, well, I... I do wonder if I might be excused," said the chaperone. "Another headache."

Lord Stewart frowned. "Oh, are you sure? We shall be sorry to see you go."

"Yes, I... Please give my excuses."

"Very well. I do hope you feel better." The baron nodded as Mrs. Teagan exited, then glanced at the viscount. "Lord Pernrith." He then swiftly stepped over to Edie and clasped her hands. "Now, I believe all preparations have been made. The footmen have been instructed—"

"I am sure they already know what to do, Father," Edie said smoothly.

His hands were wrinkled in hers, creased. How had she never noticed how old her father had become? Had the years just slipped by without her realizing, stealing away time with the one parent still remaining?

Lord Stewart's face was a picture of excitement. "I can't believe it. All of them, here!"

Frederick groaned by the window.

Edie shot him a look before saying smoothly to her father, "Yes, it's going to be a wonderful evening. Is it not, Lord Pernrith?"

She met his eye and saw with a sliver of pain to her chest that she had pushed too far. There was a haunted look in Frederick's face, one he could not hide from his host.

"This is what is expected of us, I suppose," she said hesitantly. "As... As an engaged couple."

Perhaps this was too much. Maybe she should not have suggested this—or as a matter of fact, perhaps she should not have sent the invitations before speaking to Frederick about it. The tension around his mouth, it was as she had never seen before.

"I don't feel well," Frederick said blandly, his eyes begging her for escape. "Perhaps what Mrs. Teagan has is catching..."

Edie swallowed. *There's still time.* "Father, Lord Pernrith does not feel well. And now Mrs. Teagan isn't going to join us, a shame. Perhaps the viscount should go home. We can have the dinner another—"

A loud, clanging bell interrupted her words and Lord Stewart squeezed his daughter's hands. "They're here!"

"Oh, good," Edie said weakly, regret already pouring through her.

This was a challenge of her own making, she supposed. It was only right that she was the one to attempt to fix it.

Slipping her hands from her father's, she strode over to Frederick. There was a definite nervousness in him now, something she should have noticed. The excitement that fluttered remained, however, as voices, many voices, started echoing around the hallway.

"It is remarkable how clear those voices are," Edie muttered, half to herself. "The walls must be made of paper."

She glanced at Frederick, expecting him to agree with her—but her face fell as she saw his quick, shallow breathing, his panicked expression.

"I am sorry you do not feel prepared," she whispered to Frederick, looking deep into his eyes. Behind her, her father moved to the door to welcome their guests. "I wish—"

"There's no more time for wishing, I suppose," Frederick said with a wry smile, and a flicker of the Frederick she knew appeared before sinking once more under the pressure of the evening. "But I will be glad when this is over."

"'Glad'?" repeated Edie, still slightly mystified as to his avoidance of the whole affair. "Frederick, they are your brothers!"

"His and Her Graces, the Duke and Duchess of Cothrom, the Most Honorable Marquess and Marchioness of Aylesbury, and the Right Honorable, the Earl and Countess of Lindow," intoned Jenkins the butler behind them.

Edie's heart skipped a beat. Well. This was it. This was the moment that she met her—

No. They weren't going to be her family, were they?

Whirling around and stepping over to her father so the Stewarts could respectfully welcome their guests, Edie was shocked at how similar all three Chance brothers looked.

Very different to the gentleman still lurking by the window.

"So pleased to have you, long overdue," Lord Stewart was saying.

The Duke of Cothrom had inclined his head politely but said nothing. His wife, however, appeared to realize something needed to be said.

"We are delighted to receive your invitation, Lord Stewart, and to such a delightful home," said the duchess effortlessly. "Tell me, you commissioned this painting yourself?"

Edie watched, fascinated, as the duchess expertly led the host away from the gaggle of visitors—leaving her alone to face them.

"Ah," she said aloud, somehow at a loss. "Welcome."

"Thank you, and how pleasant to see you again," said the Marquess of Aylesbury with a grin. "May I present my wife, Florence?"

Edie curtseyed before looking curiously at the woman.

So, this was the Bailey heiress. She had heard about the engagement and marriage—who had not? It had filled the pages of *Whispers of the Ton* for at least a week, which was a triumph for anyone who wished to be a little more well known.

"D-D-Delighted to m-make your... your..." The Marchioness of Aylesbury swallowed and looked to her husband.

"We'll avail ourselves of some drinks, if that is quite acceptable to you," said her husband, as though there had been no interruption.

Edie nodded. "Yes, please. There's a footman around here somewhere."

"Cothrom, you rascal. I knew you'd find the drinks cabinet," said the Marquess of Aylesbury with a snort of laughter as he pulled his wife off with him. "Which reminds me, you never did tell me..."

The noise in the drawing room was starting to become dazzling. Behind her, Edie's father was speaking loudly of the sculptor they had commissioned to create the busts that lined their drawing room. The two elder Chance brothers were chatting loudly about a shipment of brandy, or something, with interjections from the marchioness—who, Edie could not help but notice, appeared to be much calmer in speech now that she was talking to family.

And that left...

The Earl of Lindow smiled, but it was an expression of reserve. "Miss Stewart."

He inclined his head as his wife by his side curtseyed.

"Thank you for the invitation, Miss Stewart," said the Countess of Lindow. "I estimated it would take eleven days and made a small bet here with my husband—"

"A bet that I lost, as you'll see," said the earl, his smile becoming a tad more relaxed.

"Naturally, you did. You did not calculate the odds at all well," the countess pointed out seriously, as though this were a slight flaw of character but one that could be rectified. "Did you not think..."

Edie allowed their conversation about mathematics, of all things, to wash over her.

So many people. So much noise, so many conversations. It was a tad overwhelming—no, it was *greatly* overwhelming. She had never been someone who had lived in a loud, bustling house. For years, it had always been her father and herself—and the nanny, then the governess, then her chaperone—and the servants. Lord Stewart did not host house parties, and the Stewart household rarely hosted anything at all in town.

Not when there were so many other delightful invitations to accept.

Edie glanced over to Frederick. He had not joined them but was still standing by the window, ignoring his family.

And his family, she suddenly realized, was ignoring him.

None of his brothers had gone over to greet him. None had inquired how he was, or meandered over to him, or attempted to draw him into their conversations.

"All three boys were devastated at their mother's death. And I was never made to forget it."

Edie swallowed. She had always wished for a large family. For siblings, or at the very least, for friends so close in intimacy that they may as well have been siblings. And here was a family readymade—a family Frederick could have been enjoying.

But she should have recalled what he said only days ago.

"Half-brothers. The differences between us were... were stark. Different food. I had their hand-me-down clothes, never anything new. They had the best education, the best opportunities, and I..."

Always on the outside, looking in. Well, she could not have asked for a better example. All three Chance brothers and their wives had been invited by Lord Stewart to celebrate the upcoming marriage of the fourth Chance brother to his daughter... yet Frederick stood on the outside of his own celebration.

It was easy to be envious of something you believed someone had—to think that Frederick Chance, Viscount Pernrith, did not know what he was missing.

But perhaps he had been missing it all along.

"Now, I'm going to borrow Miss Stewart."

Edie's head jerked back to the Earl and Countess of Lindow. "You-You are?"

The countess nodded firmly. "I am. Come on."

There was no possibility of disagreeing with her. Edie had never met a more decisive woman—nor one who would so confidently take her by the hand and lead her over to her own sofa.

The moment Edie sat down—or was placed down—she saw what it was.

An ambush.

"Wonderful, an opportunity to talk with you," said the countess as she sat beside Edie on the sofa.

"It's what we've wanted to do since the moment the engagement was announced," said the duchess, who had somehow contrived to be seated on a stool opposite them.

The marchioness was seated beside her in an armchair. "Y-Yes. The m-moment we heard."

Edie smiled weakly and turned ever so slightly to see what the men were up to.

Her father was discussing something clearly riveting with the earl and the marquess, while the duke had—*finally*, she could not help but think bitterly—gone over to speak to Frederick. The two of them looked awkward together.

Though not, she thought, stomach churning as she turned back to face the three ladies, *as awkward as I feel.*

The duchess beamed. "You must call me 'Alice,' of course."

"Alice," Edie repeated in a slight daze.

What would her father say, if he knew she was speaking so lightly to a duchess?

"You must call me 'Dodo,' and this is Florence," said the countess decisively. "As we are all about to be your sisters, it is only right that you know our first names. Don't you think, Edith? May I call you 'Edith'?"

"Oh, I hear she prefers Edie, don't you, Edie?" offered the duchess.

Edie smiled weakly. They could have called her "Your Majesty" and Edie wouldn't have had the courage to correct them.

They were all so different, the three Chance wives. Alice Chance, Duchess of Cothrom, had that elegant and almost ethereal beauty that one did not believe could be found in real life—yet there was a very real charm about her that had already won over her father, Edie could see that.

Florence Chance, Marchioness of Aylesbury, had none of the confidence, but a great deal of elegance. She sat like an empress, regal and refined with red hair pinned with emeralds. There was a sparkle of true intelligence in her eye that made Edie wonder just what the woman would say if she felt comfortable.

The third, Dodo Chance, Countess of Lindow—and Edie was certain Dodo was not a real name—had the boldness of a woman twice her age, and a delicate power to her presence that made Edie like her, even though she knew so little of her.

And then there was her.

Edie swallowed. It was all very well being declared the flourishing rose of the Season, but amongst these women, she felt nothing but eglantine.

"Your father speaks very highly of you," said Alice in a low voice, though her eyes sparkled mischief. "He seems to be under the impression that you are the sunshine that lights the world."

It was impossible not to laugh weakly at that. "I suppose most fathers are like that."

"William certainly is with our Maudy," Alice confided. "But as she is three years of age, I am not certain she has truly earned that accolade yet. You, on the other hand, are clearly a very kind woman.

Gentle hearted."

"Not always an easy thing—I have a father much like yours, and they can be trying," said Dodo with a raised eyebrow.

Edie was not sure whether to agree or disagree. To agree would be her honest approach, but it would hardly do to tease her father.

Her indecision must have played on her face. "A l-loyal d-daughter, too," said Florence, her shyness seemingly overcome by her forced words. "Now that is a good s-sign."

"Yes, I believe Pernrith needs a loyal wife." Alice's words were even lower this time, and they struck a chord within Edie. "Given... everything."

Edie swallowed and looked over her shoulder at her future husband.

The man everyone thinks I'm going to marry, she corrected silently, heat burning her cheeks. Obviously, everyone here was under the impression that she and Frederick—that they wished to marry.

Which was a complete sham.

At the other end of the room, still by the window, stood Frederick. He was talking with the Duke of Cothrom—William, though it was strange to think of him that way. The second Chance brother, the Marquess of Aylesbury—John—had joined them.

In fact, it was only the third Chance brother, George, the Earl of Lindow, who had refused to speak to Frederick since their arrival.

"I won't subject you to the company of Lindow. You don't deserve that."

Edie's pulse skipped a painful beat as she turned back to the wives.

Dodo was looking at her closely, and when their eyes met, she nodded. "You are an intelligent woman, Edie. Yes, my husband is avoiding yours. At least, yours-to-be. It is something we will have to work on together."

It did not seem possible for her cheeks to flush any pinker, yet the burning sensation of her face certainly suggested that.

Yes, they would have to work together. If, that was, she were actually going to marry Frederick Chance, Viscount Pernrith.

Something strange was occurring and she could not quite put her finger on it. Something had been happening ever since she had sat with the Chance ladies, and Edie's mind struggled to try to understand what it was.

"Wonderful, an opportunity to talk with you."

"Your father speaks very highly of you…"

"A l-loyal d-daughter, too. Now that is a good s-sign."

Edie sat, stunned, as the conversation meandered around her.

"—never thought he would ever marry—"

"But until he found the right woman—"

"—not seen him like this before—"

Each of the women had complimented her. Which was not shocking in and of itself. It was polite to compliment one's hostess.

But they had not mentioned her sparkling eyes, or her pretty gown, or even the fact that she had been named this year's flourishing rose of the Season.

On the contrary, their remarks about her had been about… her. Herself. Her person, her character, her intelligence—the person she was, not the beauty everyone else saw.

Edie had never known anything like it. *Was this… Was this what it was like, having friends?*

"You are fortunate indeed, Edie."

She blinked. Goodness, she had become so lost in her thoughts, she had barely noticed what was going on around her. "I am?"

Dodo nodded, her eyes dancing with mischief. "Indeed. It is rare indeed in the *ton*, after all, to find someone to marry whom you love so deeply."

"'Love'?"

Try as she might, Edie could not help but glance over her shoulder at the man whom everyone in this room presumed she would soon be marrying.

Frederick appeared to have loosened up. The Marquess of Aylesbury had clearly said something amusing, for the three brothers were laughing together. The Duke of Cothrom had even put a hand on Frederick's arm.

Viscount Pernrith looked up—and caught Edie's eye.

And a heat, the like of which she had never known, poured through her whole body, roaring through her veins, tingling along her arms, overwhelming all other senses. The room faded away. There was no drawing room, no other guests, no need to look at anything except him.

No need to *think* of anyone but him. The way he made her feel. The smile he gave her that was entirely her own. The kisses they had shared, yes, but also the intimacies. The conversations they'd had, the way Frederick had bared himself to her as he never had before. Never had to anyone.

Edie swallowed, hard, but it did not slow her heart rate or make it any easier to breathe.

Frederick grinned, winking at her across the room. And that was when she knew—perhaps she should have known earlier, but it was impossible to tell until this very instant.

She loved him. Despite all her plans, for Frederick's sake, for a swift end to this false engagement, she had fallen completely in love with the man.

It was most inconvenient.

"How fortunate you have found each other," Alice was saying in a quiet voice. "How fortunate that, in all the world, you two know you can be happy together."

"Yes," said Edie weakly, not looking away from Frederick as she spoke. "Very fortunate."

Chapter Twelve

December 4, 1812

FREDERICK HAD AGONIZED over every line of the note. It had to be perfect. It had to be—

Well. It had to be convincing.

There was not a study at Pernrith House in London. The place wasn't big enough, so he used a writing desk in the corner of his cramped drawing room when it came to his correspondence. He had not expected to be writing something of this nature in his life—had never thought he would have the chance.

And if he got this phrasing wrong—or God forbid, if Lord Stewart saw it first...

The first two attempts were now balled-up paper just shy of the wastepaper basket. The third attempt was currently on the writing desk before him. Frederick examined it, eyes narrowed, trying to guess what Edie would think when she received it.

Dear Miss Stewart,

As our engagement progresses, I am certain you have felt the weight of the London Season upon you. With both of those factors in mind, I wondered whether you would accept my invitation to visit Wickacre Hall, my place in the country.

This will give you the opportunity to survey the country estate of which you will soon be mistress and escape the crowds for a few days.

Your father and Mrs. Teagan are, naturally, included in this in-

vitation.

Yours faithfully, I remain your loyal servant,
Penrith

Frederick tilted his head as he tried to guess what Lord Stewart would think of the letter if he happened upon it. He had been as polite as he could manage, and had even added in the sentence about her father and the chaperone just in case.

It was, all things considered, a polite request. An invitation.

Why his stomach was therefore lurching painfully whenever he thought about Edie's response to such a letter was quite another matter.

"It is just an invitation," Frederick muttered as he leaned back in his chair and read through the single piece of paper again. "Just an invitation."

Why it mattered so much, he could not tell. The idea had come to him at the dinner Lord Stewart had hosted on their behalf, inviting all the Chance brothers and their wives. There had been a moment when he had looked over at the women sat together, and Edie had looked at him, and—

Well. Something had changed in that moment.

Precisely what, Frederick did not know. He had not had the opportunity to speak to Edie that whole evening. Not properly. They had been sat together at the dining table but with Alice on his other side and John on Edie's left, it had been difficult to speak at all.

"It's natural," Frederick said aloud. It was a foolish habit, one he had got into when he had first moved to London and realized he was not going to be receiving many invitations. *Talking to himself. How pathetic.* "Completely natural. The world thinks we are engaged, so what could be more genuine than inviting my betrothed and her father to my country estate?"

Nothing, a small voice muttered in the back of his head. *Except that you are not engaged. So why does this matter so much?*

Edie's opinion on Wickacre Hall itself was relatively immaterial. Frederick had been given the place—it came with the title. It wasn't as though he had chosen it.

But he hadn't chosen Edie, either, he tried to remind himself. He had not properly courted her as she'd deserved, had not set out to wed her. They were not actually engaged. And though it was starting to become remarkably pleasant, meandering about town with her on his arm, attending gatherings and feeling, *knowing*, there was at least one person there who wished to see him...

It wasn't real.

Heaving a sigh, Frederick folded the letter, sealed it with wax and his signet ring, then went looking for Mrs. Kinley.

She was, as ever, helping Cook.

"We need a kitchen maid," said Mrs. Kinley firmly, looking beadily at her master with no hint of restraint. "And soon, if my elbows aren't going to fall off!"

"It's only a bit of dough!" called Cook from the oven. "Put your back into it, Mrs. Kinley!"

Frederick stifled a grin as Mrs. Kinley glared at the broad back of the cook. "Mrs. Kinley, if you would be so kind—"

"If you want me to polish anything or lift anything heavier than a feather, you've got another—"

"Just a letter," Frederick said hastily, proffering the note he'd written. "For... For Miss Stewart."

The ire disappeared from Mrs. Kinley's eyes as she wiped her hands on her apron, glanced at them, then wiped them again. "Ah, well, that's different. It'll be wonderful to have a woman in the house—a mistress who understands the challenges of a home."

Frederick nodded, swallowing hard.

It wasn't that he didn't trust Mrs. Kinley. It was more that her loose tongue adored gossip—she read more of the scandal sheets than perhaps even Edie did. The last thing he needed was the truth to get out. No one could know—

Well. Lindow knew. Suspected.

His stomach twisted as Mrs. Kinley babbled on about how the future Viscountess Pernrith would quite understand the need for a kitchen maid.

Lindow wouldn't... Well. He wouldn't do anything rash, would he?

Surely not.

"—take it right along to be franked," Mrs. Kinley was saying.

"Yes, good, excellent," said Frederick hastily, seeing his escape. "I'll be in the drawing room, Mrs. Kinley."

His housekeeper raised an eyebrow. "You're expecting a reply soon, then, my lord?"

Frederick grinned. "Today, if I'm lucky."

He was. The hastily scrawled note that returned to him not three hours later was short, but there was all the excitement in the quickly written letter that he had hoped.

Frederick—

A visit to the country sounds wonderful, thank you. Shall we come to your house tomorrow at eleven o'clock, to depart at midday?
Edie

His pulse quickened. Frederick. Edie. Their names together on the small scrap of paper incited something deep within him.

Names that belonged together.

"Mrs. Kinley!" he called out.

The whole of Pernrith House was aflutter the rest of that day, and all the inhabitants rose early the following morning to get the last few things ready.

"—expense, hiring coaches," Mrs. Kinley fussed as she checked his trunk sitting by the front door.

Frederick shrugged as he stared into a looking glass, adjusting his cravat. "I do not keep a coach, Mrs. Kinley. You know the expense is too great," he pointed out. "And I could hardly ask Lord Stewart to bring his own."

No, that would never do.

A knock at the door startled Frederick, his torso tightening with—what was it? Excitement? Anticipation?

"I'll get it," he said quickly, striding past his housekeeper. "You're late, I was starting to—oh. Mrs. Teagan."

Mrs. Teagan was blinking owlishly on his step. "Good morning, my lord."

Frederick opened his mouth, then closed it again. Where was the baron?

"I am afraid my father is feeling a little indisposed," said Edie, stepping around the figure of Mrs. Teagan to give him a bashful look. "I did not wish to postpone the visit to Wickacre Hall, so I thought... Well. Mrs. Teagan is an excellent chaperone."

Mrs. Teagan's cheeks pinked. "Oh, my dear, you are too kind—"

"And we are ready to depart," said Edie, her focus never leaving Frederick's. "If you are?"

Frederick beamed, leaning to take the handle of his trunk. "I'll have the carriages brought around directly."

It had been necessary, he had realized, to hire two. Though he himself kept no manservant, no valet, it was ridiculous to presume that Miss Edie Stewart would travel without a servant. And he was correct. A lady's maid appeared with a quiet expression, and Frederick argued over Mrs. Kinley to take their housemaid with them, to help the minimal staff at the country estate and as company for the serving girl in the second carriage.

And in the first carriage, himself, Edie... and Mrs. Teagan.

The distance from London to Wickacre Hall was not so very large. Eleven miles had sometimes felt like a great ocean of time, of course, but then Frederick had never traveled with Edie before.

Edie was a delight. Her light chatter, combined with the rocking of the carriage, soon lulled Mrs. Teagan to sleep, and they were able to have more of an open conversation.

"I hope you liked the dinner," said Edie quietly, staring out of the window as the carriage rattled along the country lanes.

Frederick forced himself not to snort. It would never do to wake Mrs. Teagan. "Something like that."

In truth, he had liked it. It was always pleasant to spend time with his two elder brothers, and Lindow had been so curtailed by politeness—thanks to the presence of the Stewarts, and in part, the wives—that Frederick had barely been forced to interact with him.

"In fact, I thought it went well," he confessed, jolted by the carriage as it turned a corner. "Thank you. You were an excellent hostess."

Edie's cheeks flushed. "Your sisters-in-law were very kind to me."

"I saw they apprehended you the moment they could." Frederick chuckled.

"They did, indeed! But thankfully, it was a relatively benevolent act. They... They think a great deal of their husbands."

He supposed there was some hidden meaning in that phrase, though he could not for the life of him understand what it was. "Oh?"

Edie nodded, opened her mouth, appeared to think better of it, then closed it again.

Frederick waited. He knew Edie better than that, knew she was attempting to formulate the phrase in her mind, testing it out before she spoke.

And five minutes later—

"It felt like I was truly a part of your family," she said in a rush.

Frederick's jaw tightened, but only for a moment. "Odd. I don't often think about them as my family."

"They like you," Edie said simply. "The wives, I mean."

He snorted. "It's easy for them."

"They could easily have absorbed their husbands' views," she pointed out quietly, a quick glance at the still-sleeping Mrs. Teagan. "And yet they chose to think differently. I liked them. I... I would wish to know them better."

Tension rippled across Frederick's back.

Edie had spoken, though only slightly, of the loneliness she had felt in Woodhurst. How strange it was to step into Society and suddenly become its focus—and still feel alone.

Alice, Florence, and Doris were fine women, and they would make fine friends for her. Fine sisters.

Except it was all a lie, wasn't it?

Frederick had not considered it before, but it would be nigh on impossible for Edie to meet socially with the Chance wives after their sham engagement was ended. The discomfort they would all feel... It would separate them as potential friends, perhaps forever.

But Edie wanted her freedom. Had practically begged him for it. If only he hadn't been so foolish as to rush into their entanglement. If he'd properly courted her...

"I think we're slowing down."

Frederick blinked. Then he glanced out of the window. "Yes, we are—we're pulling into the drive."

It was not a long drive. After a few minutes, the carriage came to a stop and Mrs. Teagan was jolted awake.

"David?"

Both the ladies flushed.

That had certainly confirmed some ideas he'd had.

"Let me help you out of the carriage," Frederick said quietly, stepping out and giving both of them a moment to collect themselves.

By the time he turned back to them, Edie and Mrs. Teagan were calmer, though the latter was still pink. Offering his hand, Frederick helped the elder, then the younger, of his guests out of the carriage. They stood and stared.

"Heavens above," muttered Mrs. Teagan.

"My goodness," whispered Edie as she stepped out of the carriage.

Frederick turned to see what they were looking at. "Ah. Yes. Wickacre Hall."

It was a pretty, little place, he supposed. Nothing to Stanphrey Lacey—no Tudor turrets, spiraling chimneys, and elegant oriel windows. The grounds of Wickacre Hall were also nothing to Stanphrey Lacey—there was no deer park, no knot garden, and the lake that had been attempted by an earlier Viscount Pernrith had been filled in eventually due to expense.

But it was not a place to be sniffed at. The yellow stone appeared brilliant in the winter sun, and the windows glinted in a sort of welcoming way. The portico over the door was a relatively new addition. Frederick thought it suited the place rather well.

Though judging by the responses of the two ladies gawping at the place, it was far more impressive than he had given it credit for.

"This is yours?"

Frederick spoke before he thought. "Yours as well, soon."

His cheeks burned, and he hoped to goodness Mrs. Teagan would prescribe it to the excitement of a future newlywed.

Not the shame of a man playing a trick on the world.

Edie seemed to guess what he was thinking, for she flushed too. "And will you... will you show it to me?"

"Of course."

"My lord!" Mrs. Watkins, Wickacre Hall's housekeeper, came to the door, a lock of her coiled silver hair escaping from her cap. "Welcome." She beamed at his guests. She'd never seen him having any guests. "We got everything ready for you, my lord."

"Thank you, Mrs. Watkins. Please welcome Miss Edith Stewart, and her companion, Mrs. Teagan." Frederick gestured to each in turn. The door to the servants' carriage opened up behind their own, the driver taking the place of footmen to help the young women out.

"We'd just asked for a tour," said Edie, offering a slight head nod to his housekeeper.

Mrs. Watkins practically bounced on her feet at being addressed so civilly by a lady.

"I thought perhaps *I* could give them the tour," Frederick said. "If you could help the maids inside?"

"Of course, of course," said Mrs. Watkins, who had the grace to duck her head and curtsey despite the task taken from her. "Cook has a grand meal planned for this evening. I shall check to make sure it is all going smoothly."

The tour ended up being far longer than Frederick expected. What appeared to him to be a humdrum design for the house, and mediocre or even dull furnishings, was apparently the latest style and most elegant taste. Mrs. Teagan did not cease to sing its praises, but to Frederick's disappointment, Edie was silent.

That was, until they reached the last room of the house, the library.

"And this is where you read *Whispers of the Ton*, I suppose," she said shyly, looking up through brown, almost-black, lashes.

Frederick's stomach lurched. "No. But I do read here."

"I suppose we could read here together," Edie said softly as Mrs. Teagan exclaimed at the number of botany books in his collection.

The charade was getting a little too real. Frederick could just picture the two of them here, reading quietly in armchairs side by side. Holding hands, perhaps. Or kissing—

"Well, then," said Mrs. Teagan cheerfully, interrupting some definitely delicious thoughts Frederick was certain he was not permitted to have. "Shall we see the grounds?"

After a long meander through the hibernating gardens and what other land could be described as "grounds," there was little daylight left. The three of them had afternoon tea, conversed lightly for a few hours, then retired to change for dinner.

Dinner itself must have happened. Frederick was certain of it but could not remember a single mouthful. All he could recall was the shimmering candlelight, making Edie sparkle.

She wore no jewels. She had no need for them. The simple, elegant, green silk gown was more than enough to set her off.

Frederick missed putting his fork in his mouth at least twice from staring.

It still did not feel real. What was a woman like that doing here?

Pretending to be your betrothed, he reminded himself. *And 'pretending' is the operative word here. You may have the world fooled—you may even have the father fooled. But you mustn't fool yourself.*

And so before he knew it, the three of them were seated in the drawing room and time was flying and—

"Well, I think I am for bed."

Frederick started. He had been so engrossed in conversation with Edie, a fire blazing merrily in the grate, he had almost clean forgotten there was anyone else in the room.

Most ungentlemanly of him. And a terrible move for a host.

He hurried to his feet. "Mrs. Teagan, you are tired?"

"Far too tired to remain here, I am afraid," said the chaperone with a breezy laugh. "I am not as young as I look!"

Panic flowed through Frederick's veins. *What on earth was the correct response to that?*

"Nonsense, Mrs. Teagan, we know you're secretly one and twenty," said Edie compassionately. "Though I understand if you wish to retire. It has been a long day."

"It has, indeed," nodded Mrs. Teagan, eyelids drooping. "Good night, my lord."

"Good night, Mrs. Teagan," Frederick said with a bow.

"Miss Stewart?" Mrs. Teagan clasped her hands together, staring down at her charge.

"Good night, Mrs. Teagan," she said sweetly. Yawning with great—perhaps overexaggerated—effect and stretching her arms above her head, she added, "I shall join you shortly in retiring."

Mrs. Teagan hesitated, her eyes going back and forth between her charge and Frederick.

"I shall ring for Evans to accompany me," said Edie sweetly, referring, it seemed, to her lady's maid. "After just a moment more. I'd like to warm up by the fire."

Mrs. Teagan cleared her throat. She locked eyes with Frederick and frowned, as if warning him, then nodded and crossed the drawing room.

Perhaps the woman knew better. But she, like Edie's father, assumed the two would indeed be married in the weeks to come.

What was the worst that could happen?

Frederick remained standing as the woman closed the door behind her. When he slowly lowered himself back onto the sofa he and Edie were sharing, his pulse was at least treble what it had been.

They were alone. Truly alone—for perhaps the first time since he had last kissed her...

"The only way to save my reputation is if that kiss was appropriate. It is appropriate to kiss if you are engaged."

"Not the way we were doing it..."

Frederick attempted to force the memory from his mind, but by God, he was only human. Edie was sitting there, radiant as ever, smiling like—

Like she trusted him. Like she liked him.

"It's a beautiful home, Frederick," she said hesitantly.

"It's a little more homely when decorated for Christmas—properly, I mean, not just the greenery." He gestured at the boughs of holly and ivy that festooned the paintings in the room.

"I suppose it will be," said Edie warmly. "I would love to see it."

And she wouldn't.

Because this couldn't continue, could it?

"I hope your chaperone is not too tired," Frederick said, venturing out on what he hoped was neutral territory. Need he remark that she had not, so far, called for her lady's maid to take the chaperone's place?

He knew Edie. She was never going to do that.

"She gets headaches, sometimes, but she brought her tonic with her," said Edie quietly. "She'll be as right as rain in the morning, as long as you have a copy of *The Times* for her to read at breakfast."

Frederick chuckled. "Well, thankfully, Mrs. Teagan and I share a taste in reading."

"Unlike me. I don't suppose you have *Whispers of the Ton* delivered from London, do you?"

"Even if I did, I very much doubt it would arrive here before breakfast!" he retorted. "I can't believe you read that rubbish!"

"'Rubbish'? I will have you know that *Whispers of the Ton* is one of the most preeminent scandal sheets in the country," Edie said with mock haughtiness.

Happiness poured through Frederick. "Well, that's censure in and of itself. Whatever happened to you being furious at what they wrote about you?"

"I was furious about what they wrote about *us*," she said flatly. But then a smile cracked her impassive face. She tapped him playfully and something shifted between them. Something that made Frederick's heart skip a beat.

"I suppose you only read that dull newspaper."

"I read the factual events of the day around the world, yes."

Edie rolled her eyes. "I'd rather have the excitement of the scandal sheets, if you ask me. Yes, I don't particularly care to be written about myself, but they're still usually quite fun. I've never had much adventure in my life. Not until... until you."

Frederick swallowed and shifted on the sofa.

Only slightly. Only to get comfortable. It was mere coincidence that the movement brought him closer to Edie Stewart.

His hand brushed against hers. For a moment, Frederick thought she would pull away, flush, then declare she was also tired and wished to retire to her bedchamber.

But she didn't. Quite to the contrary, Edie moved on the sofa toward him, eyes never leaving him.

"It's all been a bit of a whirlwind, hasn't it?" she said lightly.

Frederick swallowed. "I suppose my invitation to visit Wickacre Hall was not—"

"That's not what I meant," Edie said. "And you know it."

She had spoken with a delicate voice that belied the certainty in her eyes.

Attempting not to read too much into the line of conversation, Frederick nodded. "Yes. Yes, I do not think I could have supposed, when we were sitting there in your father's study, that all... all this would have occurred."

All this closeness. This sense that Edie was the one person in the world with whom he could be truly open. The happiness he gained whenever in her company.

None of that could have been predicted.

"You probably only wished for a kiss."

Frederick's look sharpened. Though her cheeks were pink, Edie looked at him steadily. "Only a kiss?"

"In that library, I mean," she said, her voice hushed. "You could not have known all this would have followed what... what was the most intensely pleasurable moment of my life."

Had she really said such a thing?

"I-I suppose not," said Frederick, hating how his voice quavered. "But I would do it again."

"You would?"

He nodded. By God, he would. Who could stay away from this woman?

Edie did not look away, though her cheeks reddened. "Would you do it again... now?"

Frederick needed no other invitation.

For invitation it was—and his instinct was proven right as he pulled Edie into his arms and brought his mouth upon hers.

In truth, he hardly needed to pull. Edie moved into his embrace, lifting up her lips to be kissed, and their intermingled moans of delight as their kiss deepened filled the spacious room.

Oh, God, this was what he had wanted for so long. The feeling of her body quivering against his, the taste of her mouth, all sweetness and heady promise, the way she melted against him, lips parting to welcome him deeper.

Try as he might, Frederick could not keep his hands idle. As one swept to her waist, pulling her as tightly to him as he could, the other had somehow managed to cup her buttocks.

Edie squirmed against his touch, and for a moment, he thought she was attempting to move away—but the whimper of sensual sensations that broke from her lips told him quite another story.

"Edie…"

Frederick had not meant to whisper her name, but he couldn't help it. It seemed to provoke a response that matched his own.

Twisting her fingers into his hair, Edie kissed him furiously, as though all the pent-up desire he had felt himself was mirrored in her. "Frederick…"

How long they were there, he did not know. He did know how his jacket and cravat mysteriously ended up on the carpet, and Edie's gown certainly would need a good going over again with the hot irons before it was presentable.

Even worse—or better—Frederick was throbbing with need. He was lying on the sofa now, covering Edie's body with his own and wishing to goodness he'd thought about this earlier.

He only came alive when he was with her.

Frederick ended the searing kiss and stared deeply into Edie's eyes.

She had no hint of shame or embarrassment. "Frederick."

He hesitated.

Because in that moment, it was all so difficult. He loved her. Of course he did. How could anyone not love her, once they had grown to know the woman behind the title of "flourishing rose"?

Every day, he awoke looking forward to their next encounter. Every minute with her was one that he wanted to last forever.

And though he very much wanted to get under her skirts—his fingers itching to do that very thing—he also wished to get inside her affections. To know what she thought of him.

"Frederick?"

Edie sounded concerned, and no wonder. He was staring at her like a dolt.

But how could he speak? Frederick had never known such emotions pouring through him, thoughts and feelings getting entangled as he attempted to put them in order.

This wasn't real.

But it could be—couldn't it? Frederick wanted her, wanted Edie, wanted all of her.

Precisely how this had happened, he did not know. There was no moment other than now that he could pinpoint as to a greater understanding of his affection.

And now it could not be denied.

Frederick sat up and was delighted to hear a moan of disappointment. "I... I should stop."

"Why?" Edie asked in a rustle of silk as she righted herself on the sofa. Her eyes were wide, her hands reaching for his. "Why?"

"Because..." Inhaling deeply did not help. It did not give him the courage he so desperately needed to carry on. "Because otherwise, I'll want things... things you can't give me. I can't do this."

Frederick forced himself to meet Edie's eyes, expecting censure, shock, perhaps even the decision to depart from his embrace and his drawing room immediately.

Edie held his gaze with one just as lust-filled as his own. "Can't... or won't?"

Chapter Thirteen

EDIE KNEW SHE should not be so bold as she attempted to catch her breath. But how could she not speak, when Frederick was threatening not to touch her? Her hands still reached for his.

His eyes still met her gaze.

They were fiery. Edie's gasp caught in her throat as she saw the unhindered desire flood through him.

"I'll want things."

Well, she knew what that meant. She did not need to be an experienced harlot to understand what Frederick wanted.

And she should have felt scandalized. She should be outraged he was even thinking it, horrified that he would suggest it. She should stand up, march out of here—adjusting her gown first, naturally—and resolve never to permit herself to be left alone with the viscount again.

But she didn't.

How could she, when what he clearly wanted was… what she craved?

"Because otherwise I'll want things… things you can't give me."

"Can't or won't?" she repeated.

Quite what had come over her, she did not know. It was not the sort of statement a young lady should be making, let alone twice—quite the contrary. She should have fled the instant it had become clear just what Frederick Chance wanted from her.

Everything.

But she could hardly deny the desire within—desire that had been awakened the first moment he had kissed her.

In that library, there had been no right and wrong. There had been no rules, no *ton*—no flourishing rose. All there had been was a person who'd enjoyed the touch of another.

Besides, Edie hardly knew how to control herself around this man. It was nigh on impossible for her to hold back when she knew how delectable he tasted, the blast of agonizing heat that flooded her when he touched her like...

Like he did.

Edie swallowed. "You... You still don't say anything."

Frederick had remained still as all these thoughts had hurried through her mind, but he finally spoke. "I... I am surprised."

Heat blossomed across her collarbone. *No polite young lady should admit to even knowing about such things, much less wanting them!*

Yet though Edie was certain what Society demanded of her—not that anyone could ever, ever find out about this conversation—she was minded to do the exact opposite.

She was a lady. And he was a gentleman.

And London seemed a very, very long way away.

"Frederick," Edie said softly, squeezing his hand. His fingers were entwined with hers now, and she had to take a deep breath before there was enough air in her lungs to continue. "We went into this by accident—"

"Oh, I don't know," he said dryly. "I most definitely wanted to kiss you in that library."

Her skin tingled at the revelation, but she managed to continue. "I mean, we sort of... well, *fell into* this pretend engagement—"

"It was your idea in the first place, as I recall," Frederick said, lip curling into a grin.

"You know what I mean!"

"I most certainly do."

"And so I thought... Well." Edie hesitated. There was still time enough to retreat, to prevent herself from saying what she wished to.

Then she and Frederick could return to being pretend betrotheds, and no one would be any the wiser.

But she would. And she would regret not attempting to take this opportunity, she knew. With every fiber of her being.

"And as we are in this situation, more or less accidentally," she continued, "I think... I think we should get as much pleasure as possible. As we can. As you'll give me."

Frederick's eyes flashed with desire. "You have no idea what you do to me when you speak like that."

"Oh, I think I do," Edie whispered. "Let me show you."

She lifted his hand that was entangled with her own, and for an instant, there was a flash of shock in his widening eyes—but whatever Frederick had thought she was going to do, it was different from what actually happened.

Pressing his hand against her heart, Edie smiled nervously as she felt her pulse throb in his fingers. Her rapid heart rate. Her rapidly increasing heart rate.

"Desire is one thing," Frederick said, his voice halting. His hand did not leave her breast. "But—"

"We have one night—for I doubt we shall ever find ourselves in such a situation again," said Edie. "Though now I think about it, I am not sure what we will do about Mrs. Teagan. If she hears—"

"You had to bring a chaperone," Frederick muttered.

Edie tapped him on the shoulder with her free hand, glorifying in the intimacy. "You invited her! You know there was no possibility that I could have come here alone!"

"I suppose not," he said, eyes glinting. "And by complete coincidence, it turns out that Mrs. Teagan's guest bedchamber is on the east side of the house... and mine is on the west. As is yours, as chance would have it."

There was such a look of twinkling innocence in his eyes that Edie could do nothing but laugh. "You planned this!"

"Oh, I hoped," said Frederick, finally removing his hand from her chest but using the opportunity to pull her closer to him. "Goodness, I hoped."

A thrill of anticipation trilled up her spine.

He had hoped? He had thought of this—thought of her, wanted her... wished to lie with her as one?

For that was what they were speaking of. She could finally articulate it within herself, though she did not yet have the bravery to say it aloud.

She wanted to enjoy amorous congress with Frederick Chance, Viscount Pernrith. And he wanted to enjoy it with her. And there was nothing to stop them—no father to interrupt them, no brothers or their wives likely to visit, no Mrs. Teagan close enough to overhear...

Edie stiffened. "I... You must understand..."

Frederick frowned as she faltered. "Yes?"

How was one supposed to say this? It was hardly as though she had much experience. "I... It's just, I don't want to have to read about this in the scandal sheets. I mean, the whole point of this engagement pretense was so my reputation as the flourishing rose—"

"And I don't want to read about it in the newspapers, either," Frederick said dryly. He lifted her hand to his lips, delicately kissing the very tips of her fingers. Bliss rippled down her arm. "You don't have to worry, Edie. I can be careful—I can take precautions. You'll be safe."

Edie's stomach squirmed.

Because she was safe. Frederick made her feel safe, and cared for, and as though she could be her absolute honest self.

And he made her feel in danger. In danger, on the edge of an indulgent precipice she had never jumped off before, but could do soon.

Perhaps that was why there was this aching feeling between her thighs.

"So... So, we are agreed?" she whispered.

Frederick examined her closely for a moment and her lungs tightened. If he said *no*... and he was within his rights to do so. She would not wish to have to argue with a man to lie with her.

Perish the thought.

Then he swallowed, his throat bobbing, and she knew before he had said the words.

"Let me take you to bed, Edie."

He did not need to say anything more. Edie leaned into him, claiming the lips she knew were her own, and tried not to whimper as Frederick's fingers clutched her to him.

How could she ever go back to a normal life after this? Seek a different husband, go through a new Season on the marriage market? How, after sharing such intimacies, could they ever be parted?

But she could not think of parting now. Not as Frederick's tongue was sparking shivers of elation through her body, his tongue twisting in the velvet warmth of her mouth.

Edie gasped with disappointment as he broke the kiss, and he seemed to know precisely why as he chuckled.

"Patience," Frederick said softly as he started to trail kisses down her jaw to that delicate spot below her ear. "Patience..."

Patience? She was melting—that was what she was doing. Edie could feel herself slowly softening into the sofa with every kiss he delicately placed on her skin. His cheeks were rough—he hadn't shaved again—and the friction between stubble and her neck only heightened the indulgence.

By the time Frederick had kissed down her neck and reached her collarbone, Edie was fairly certain her bones were nothing more than honey.

"Frederick." She moaned, hardly knowing what she was asking but knowing he would have the answer.

He most certainly did. His fingers moved lightly at first, then slightly more firmly over her breasts, teasing a sensation from them that Edie had never known before. Her back arched without her having to instruct it, and Frederick's groan in response told her that whatever she had done had to be right.

Just as her mind was spinning and her body was tingling and she was wondering what on earth could happen next—

"Oh!"

Frederick's thumb had grazed her nipple through her stays and gown. Oh, it harkened back to that ecstatic moment when he had managed to free that same breast in the library. The sensations then, the shocking intimacy of the moment—

"More."

It did not take anything else to encourage him. Frederick's breathing was heavy, blossoming over her skin as one hand gently caressed her breast, while the other...

Edie's eyes snapped open—when they had shut, she could not recall. "No!"

Immediately, Frederick froze. Then he leaned back, placing his hands above his shoulders. "I've stopped—I am sorry, did I hurt... I was rushed, but dear God, the things you do to me, Edi—"

"It's not that. It's just..." Edie struggled to right herself. It wasn't just that her bones were still liquids, but every inch of her seemed weighed down, throbbing with an ache that had still not been satisfied.

But she couldn't let him think he had offended her. "It is only—I did not mean 'no.' I meant, not here."

The concern in Frederick's eyes immediately died away. "Ah. Right, then. My lady."

Offering her his hand, he gave her a deep and penetrating look that spoke of heat and need and craving.

Edie swallowed. There was still time, she knew, to tell him she had changed her mind. He would think none the worse of her, she knew. Frederick would never countenance the idea of forcing a woman, even if she had consented most freely only minutes before.

And nothing had happened.

Nothing yet.

Edie reached out and took his hand. "Let's go."

Wickacre Hall was strange in the gloom. She had only seen it once in the light, and shadows appeared to leap from every corner as they stepped silently into the hallway, hand in hand. The staircase creaked under their steps, and Edie was certain the gentleman beside her could hear her pulse thundering painfully.

The guest bedchamber in which Frederick's driver had placed her small trunk was the first door on the left. Edie paused by it when they reached it, but Frederick tugged her arm as he kept walking.

"Where are you going?" she hissed, tightening her grip on his hand but still being pulled forward.

"To bed," Frederick teased, casting a look over his shoulder. "Where did you think we were going?"

"But..." Edie looked back at the guest bedchamber. *Where on earth were they—*

"Don't you want to see your future bed?" said Frederick softly as he opened a different door and pulled her through. "Well, the viscount's. But the viscountess would always be welcome there."

Her mouth fell open as they stepped out of the corridor and into the room.

Firstly, because it was not real, and she so desperately wished it could be. There would undoubtedly be a different tenor to the comment if this... if all of this had been real.

A real engagement. A real affection. A real courting that led to a real conversation with her father. A real growing of knowledge, of intimacy. Real wedding planning. A real wedding, and afterward, a real wedding night in which two people who loved each other could come together.

Edie swallowed. *And none of it is real, is it? It couldn't be.*

And the second reason her mouth fell open was the room itself.

"It's a tad more opulent than my taste," said Frederick ruefully as he closed the door behind them, not letting go of her hand. "It's not the sort of thing I would have chosen."

It wasn't the sort of thing most people would choose, as far as Edie was concerned, but that did not make it any less spectacular.

The person who had ordered the furnishings and ornamentation had evidently been to Rome. And Greece. And Venice, and perhaps Marseilles, and a whole host of other European cities that had culture and beauty on every street corner.

There were paintings everywhere. Landscapes, and details of statues—and real statues. Three plinths held more carved miniatures than Edie had ever seen. There was brocade, and gold leaf, and the ceiling had been adorned with a geometric pattern painted in reds and blues and golds. Candles had been lit in candelabras on every available flat surface, and a roaring fire flickered in the grate. The curtains were a thick velvet, flowing all the way to the carpet, which appeared to be made of the same fabric. And the bed—

Edie swallowed.

The bed was quite magnificent. And large. Most definitely large enough for two.

Well. She was doing this, then.

"You can stop at any point, you know."

Edie looked around and saw Frederick watching her closely with a lilting smile.

"I hope I have proven that by what happened downstairs," he said quietly. "I would never—I want you to come to me freely, Edie."

There was no other response to that than stepping back into his embrace and pressing, for the first time, a kiss upon his lips that came from her own instigation.

Edie allowed herself to be lost in the kiss just for a moment before she pulled back. "I want you, Frederick."

The growl in his throat spoke of a passion she had never seen in him before, and his rough tugging at the ties of her gown were matched only by the eagerness with which she attempted to undo his buttons.

As it turned out, it was far more difficult than Edie had expected to unclothe a man while his lips were dragging across your nipples and your knees felt like they were about to collapse.

"Frederick." Edie gasped.

That only seemed to egg him on further. As her gown slipped to the floor in piles of silk, she clung to his shoulders, hardly knowing how she was still standing up, such tremors of passion were pouring through her.

Frederick lifted his head from her breasts, but only, it seemed, to concentrate better on the ties of her stays. "How do you get out of these damned things?"

"With great difficulty." Edie gasped, finally able to reach his shirt buttons. "Whoops!"

Her frantic need to get the man she craved out of the shirt that was keeping her from seeing more of him had led to an inconvenient tug. Buttons flew all over the room as the shirt fell limply from his shoulders.

But she could hardly formulate a true apology. Not when the distraction of Frederick Chance, Viscount Pernrith, without a shirt was before her.

Edie trailed a finger along his collarbone. Strange, how sensual a throat and clavicle could be on a man when it was so often hidden by a cravat. As her finger meandered farther down, wiry hair brushed against the softness, lower and lower until—

"Oh," she gasped, eyes wide.

How he had managed it, she did not know. Somehow, while she had been occupied by the delights of his chest, Frederick had managed to remove—

Well. Everything.

And there it was. She may have been an innocent, but she was not uneducated. Her father, perhaps in an effort to protect his beautiful daughter, had encouraged her governess to be more edifying than most, but there were also books on art in the library and some of the classical statues reprinted in the engravings had been most instructive. Edie had had a theoretical understanding of what lay—or in this case, what stood—underneath a man's breeches, but seeing it as it were, in the flesh…

His manhood was magnificent. Thicker than she had expected, and dripping at the end. And somehow so… enticing.

"You're naked," Edie whispered.

"And you're not," said Frederick, a wolfish, hungry grin on his face. "But I can soon solve that."

He was as good—or as bad—as his word. Before she could say a thing, his fingers had made light work of the final tie of her stay, allowing both stays and undershift to fall to the floor.

And there they were. Utterly naked.

Edie swallowed. "N-Now what?"

Though she hated how her voice shook, Frederick did not appear much concerned. To the contrary, he smiled and once again offered her his hand.

"To bed."

The coverlet was a delicately embroidered soft silk, and it caressed every inch of her skin it encountered as Edie carefully lay down. Pulse thumping, hardly believing she was doing this, she found it a great comfort when Frederick joined her on the bed and pulled her close, lying next to her on his side.

"Ready?"

Edie nodded, though precisely for what, she did not—

"Oh!"

Frederick's hand had gently flickered over her waist, up over her hip, but had then slid gently to the area between her legs. Tilting her slightly so she rolled onto her back, Edie looked deeply into his hazel eyes as he slowly, slowly inched her legs apart.

Revealing... Well. The most intimate part of her.

"Kiss me."

Frederick obeyed at once, and she squirmed against the bed as his tongue delved deeply within her mouth, sparking the pleasure she was coming to expect from—

"Frederick!" Edie moaned in his mouth.

His tongue was no longer the only part of him that was delving into her. Gently, very gently, he had slipped a finger along her slick folds, and then tenderly inside her.

The aching need that blossomed between her legs made Edie's eyelashes flutter. How could anyone keep their eyes open at such an intrusion—at such exquisite sensations?

"Again?" Frederick breathed against her neck, nuzzling her as his finger stilled.

Edie swallowed. "Again—ohhh..."

It was impossible to speak from that moment onward. While his lips worshiped her own, sometimes darting down to kiss her neck, blossoming heat onto her skin, his fingers were not idle.

The stroking was flawless. Every fraction of an inch that he moved, bliss washed through Edie, not merely fading away but building on the last wave of delight.

It was all she could do to cling on to the coverlet as the scalding ache built, building and building until there was nothing she could do but surrender to the budding ecstasy.

"Yes, yes, so close," she whimpered, hardly knowing what she was close to, but knowing she needed it.

Desperately.

Frederick slipped a second finger inside her and twisted his thumb over the nub right in her core, and Edie cried out.

"Frederick!"

She was undone. Every part of her was cascading over the precipice of ecstasy, her body coming apart with every limb quivering. She wanted to ride this crest forever, her core pulsating around Frederick's fingers as he mercilessly kept up the rhythm that had gotten her here.

When Edie was finally able to open her eyes, it was to see a delighted Frederick Chance above her.

"God, that was sweet."

She squirmed on the bed as he slipped his fingers from her. "You... but you—I mean, you did not gain any—"

"Any man who brings their partner to pleasure should take pleasure in that," Frederick said softly. "And you're prepared for me now. Ready to go again?"

Again? Was it possible, then, to achieve such heights of ecstasy twice in one night?

Edie could hardly believe it, but she nodded eagerly, hungry for another taste of the decadence she had only just sampled.

For a moment, there was such a terrible absence of Frederick that she cried out.

"I'm here," he said, swiftly returning. "I just had to get—fortunate I had some, in truth."

She looked blearily at what he had in his hand, and saw a strange sort of...

"Oh," she said, understanding dawning. She flushed. "And that is—"

"A preventative. A French letter. It... It prevents—"

"Ah. Good." Well, what else was she supposed to say?

"Just let me—there." Frederick groaned as he moved on the bed, nestling between her legs. "You are everything, Edie. Everything."

Warmth flooded her cheeks as she reached out for him, her fingers splayed across his shoulders. "You're everything, Frederick. It's not me, it's—"

They both moaned at the same time, just as the tip of his manhood pressed against her wet entrance.

"And I want you," Edie said, emboldened by the sudden need that filled her. "Now. P-Please, Frederick."

Leaning down, he kissed her long and hard and passionately, as only a husband would do to a wife—and at the same time, he slid his manhood slowly into her welcoming body.

And it *was* welcoming. Though Edie had not entirely worked out how something as large as *that* would fit into something like *her*, her body appeared to acclimatize well, swelling and opening for him.

More, the sensation was... pleasant. Very pleasant. Flickers of the sensual decadence she had only just experienced started to shimmer again through her body.

Edie arched her back, lifting her hips to meet his, and Frederick groaned as he fully sheathed himself.

"God, you feel—"

"Don't tell me," said Edie, flushing at how boldly she was speaking. "Show me."

And he did. Though Frederick gritted his teeth at times and was obviously holding back, he once again began to build the sweet rhythm he had already proven he knew with his fingers.

It was all Edie could do to hold on. Waves upon waves were starting to pour through her now, and when Frederick shifted his angle, she gasped as he sank deeper. With every movement, he sparked bliss through her body—and unless she was very much mistaken, he was taking as much delight in their coupling as she was.

"Come for me." Frederick growled, fixing his eyes on hers as he slowly increased the pace. "Come, Edie."

"I'm not—not there yet." She gasped, writhing against the coverlet underneath him, desperate to get there.

Perhaps he understood her need, for Frederick slipped a hand between them, his thumb somehow finding her nub, and—

"Frederick!" Edie cried, her body pulsating with ecstasy.

And that was enough to push Frederick over the edge. Pumping furiously into her, then shuddering heavily, he managed a cry of, "Edie, Edie—oh, God!"

And then he collapsed into her waiting, willing, and welcoming arms.

Eventually, Edie said softly, "I should return to my room."

She hated to say it, but she could not deny the veracity of the statement. If she were found here—

Frederick did not open his eyes as he pulled her close, tucking her into his broad strength as though she belonged there. "This is your room."

And that was when she sighed slowly, slowly, and allowed every inch of herself to relax.

Because he was right. This was her room.

Chapter Fourteen

December 5, 1812

THE CARRIAGE ROCKED along the roads—but slowly. Frederick had given the order that the horses were not to be pushed, and thankfully, both drivers had taken him at his word.

They had also taken the crowns he had pressed hurriedly into their hands, requesting their silence and their acquiescence.

And it wasn't as though he had requested anything so terrible. Just a slower journey back to London. Just to dawdle at every turn, to not push the horses too hard when they were on the road, to slow whenever possible, and to give him as much time on the journey as could be managed.

"I often forget how far London is from everywhere else," said Edie quietly, glancing out of the window.

Frederick's smile was as natural as he could make it. Goodness, he'd gone soft. "Yes, it often surprises me."

She was pressed against him in the carriage, something Frederick was delighted with. He had offered to sit facing backward, but she had made such a song and dance of him potentially becoming seasick—all under the beady eye of Mrs. Teagan—that Frederick had been unable to overcome her objections.

And what a delight it was. Edie's hip pressed into his, the warmth of her body pouring through her gown and pelisse, through his greatcoat, coat, waistcoat, and shirt.

If he weren't careful, he was sure to combust.

Edie shifted in the carriage and Frederick's stomach lurched. It prompted him to do something without invitation, but the movement was swiftly welcomed.

He took Edie's hand in his.

They had both discarded their gloves the instant they had clambered into the carriage. Not because it was overly heated, but because…

Frederick did not know Edie's reasons for it, but he knew his own. Any opportunity he could have for touching her, feeling her skin beneath his own, claiming the closeness that would have to stop when they reached London—it was worth slightly chilly hands.

She squeezed his fingers, then pulled his hand into her lap.

They hadn't enjoyed this closeness the entire rest of his guests' stay. They had conversed, yes, and walked along the grounds, but they hadn't been alone. Mrs. Teagan had been more careful last night to accompany Edie to the guest room assigned to her, and though Frederick had meant to knock a few hours later, he had fallen asleep, dreams of Edie still floating in his mind.

Frederick swallowed hard as memories from the other night floated into his mind.

"You are everything, Edie. Everything."

"You're everything, Frederick. It's not me, it's—"

In a way, the whole encounter was like a delicious dream. It did not seem possible, could not be real, that he and Edie had shared one of the most intimate things a person could ever experience.

Three times.

It was a wonder, really, that they had managed to stay awake all the next morning…

"You're very quiet."

Frederick blinked. Edie was examining him with a wry expression, one he now knew well. One that he wanted to see every day of his—

But he couldn't permit those sort of nonsensical thoughts to overcome him. He wasn't about to admit just how deeply the other night had touched his soul, was he? No, that was for green-gilled fools of twenty who had just entered Society.

Not men like himself.

"I just can't—" He didn't manage to catch himself in time, and he burned with the indignity of letting his tongue wag.

"Can't what?"

Frederick hesitated, then permitted himself another hint of honesty. Well, it was hardly going to hurt him, was it? "Can't believe how happy I am."

For a moment, a painful moment, he thought he had gone too far. Exposed himself too readily, made himself ridiculous in the eyes of the woman whose opinion truly mattered.

Then there was another squeeze of his hand. "Neither can I."

They slipped into companionable silence as the road—slowly—eked out before them.

That was another thing that was so unusual about Edie. Frederick had never known it before—the ability to sit silently and for there to be no awkwardness whatsoever. He had never encountered such a quality, yet here it was.

"*God, you feel—*"

"*Don't tell me. Show me.*"

Frederick swallowed. They had been careful. Using a preventative had been an excellent idea and would preclude anyone from ever being any the wiser. Miss Edith Stewart's reputation was maintained, and no one could impugn his honor.

Still, his eyes slipped over the elegant face down the buttoned-up pelisse to the soft swell of Edie's stomach.

A stomach where, but for a single change of decision the other night, there could have been a growing child.

Sadness mingled with the relief. They had made the right decision, he was absolutely certain. But still. It did not prevent the mind from wondering. Imagining what the world could be. Wondering what could have been…

And unbidden, though not entirely, an image burst through Frederick's unsuspecting mind. An image of a child. His hazel eyes, hair just like Edie's, a quizzical expression as he peered at a newspaper, trying to make out the letters. They were seated around a fire—the fireplace at Wickacre Hall. Edie had a babe in her arms, and—

Frederick cleared his throat.

"Did you say something?" asked Edie quietly.

"No," he said, perhaps a little too hurriedly.

It took longer than he had expected for the image to fade. His mind had enjoyed the picture too much. A small Chance, partly himself, partly Edie. Her laughter and wit with his solid dependability and sense of honor.

Not a half Chance, brought into a family where he could not be loved as he ought. A full Chance, a boy who could grow up in a home where he knew he was loved. Wanted.

Frederick's eyes glistened, but he managed to control himself. He was not about to start crying in a carriage about a child who did not exist!

"You are very quiet."

He cleared his throat again. Perhaps some light conversation would do him good. Distract him from nonsense.

"I suppose I am," Frederick said lightly. "I suppose there is no need to be, with Mrs. Teagan in the other carriage."

Edie's eyes glittered. "Yes, I wondered about that."

"The woman's megrim is something terrible. I thought the other carriage had a smoother ride, would aid in her recovery," Frederick protested—perhaps too quickly. "I know she asked your maid to sit with us in her stead, but as we were all concerned about Mrs. Teagan's health…"

"Yes, stopping the carriage after just ten minutes and sending Evans back to the other one to 'check' on my chaperone. Who must have been—must still be—sleeping." There was a knowing look in his companion's expression as the carriage jolted to the left. "I am sure my maid appreciates not having to sit facing backward. Still. It is rather convenient."

Try as he might, he could not raise an imperious eyebrow like his brother William. Still, Frederick tried. "I have no idea what you—"

"I think you do," said Edie softly, leaning forward and pressing a kiss on his cheek.

It was a simple gesture. Frederick was almost certain grandmothers would do such a thing for their grandchildren, though never having met any of his grandparents, he was not sure.

It was not a grandmotherly kiss that the lithe, young woman pressed against him in the carriage placed on his cheek. It spoke of hunger and desire and need and—

Frederick hastily crossed his legs. *Damn and blast it!* "Well, I will admit the decision to hire two carriages was not entirely selfless."

Edie's giggle filled their own carriage. "And what you mean by that is that you designed the whole visit to your country home merely to give us the opportunity to lie together, didn't you? That was the purpose for your concoction!"

Lie together. As a man and a woman, as one.

There was no other way to describe it. When Frederick had awoken that morning, sprawled out completely naked in his bed with, to his delight, the naked form of Edie curled up in his arms, he had known from that moment.

This wasn't just bed sport, though it offered greater delights and gratification than any bed sport he had ever engaged in.

No, this was most definitely deeper than that. There was an intimacy in the way they had dressed each other silently that morning, in the way he had helped Edie creep back to her room so her maid could find her in the bed she was supposed to be in.

They'd shared something more.

Still. That did not mean aspersions could be cast against his character.

"I will have you know there were no expectations of you lying in bed with me, or any other such thing," Frederick said aloud as haughtily as he could.

Edie was not convinced. The slight frown across her forehead did not diminish her beauty, but rather highlighted her delightful character.

His shoulders slumped, just a few inches. "Well, to tell the complete truth—"

"Aha!"

"—I did not design the visit for that sole purpose, absolutely not," Frederick continued, his fingers tightening around Edie's fingers as his breeches grew tighter in turn. "But I will admit, I am delighted it ended up that way. It was… It was perfect. You are—"

It was perhaps a good thing he was unable to finish his sentence. Lord knew, if his tongue had continued speaking, he may have done something disgraceful.

Like admit his love for Edie Stewart.

As it was, she forestalled his confession. Moving swiftly forward and giving no heed to the cramped conditions of the carriage, Edie kissed him hard on the mouth, her lips parting almost immediately, coaxing him in deeper.

Frederick needed no further invitation. His free hand moved across Edie to the window, penning her in and forcing her to move closer into his embrace. His tongue slowly slid across her lips, teasing her and leaving both of them breathless until he finally gave into the desires of his heart and plunged into her mouth.

Oh, it was heaven. He knew he would never cease to find sweet release in these perfect lips, this willing mouth. The achingly sweet core of her was surely throbbing, and Frederick was just about to test that theory by slipping a hand under her skirts to find her secret place when Edie pulled away.

"We... We have to stop," she said, panting.

Frederick halted his movements, but he did not return to his side of the carriage. "Why the devil do we have to—"

"If we don't, we'll end up lying together in this carriage," Edie said softly with desire-filled eyes.

It was all he could do not to take her at her word and start unbuttoning his breeches. "Don't tempt me."

The words came out as more of a growl than a sentence, but she apparently understood his meaning. Pink tinged Edie's cheeks and her mouth became an 'O' of shock—two consequences that made her all the more kissable.

Groaning painfully against the hard manhood pressing in his breeches, which Frederick now knew would not find satisfaction, he leaned back. "Dear God, I would have you if I could."

The momentary lapse of control was but for a sentence, but it was enough for Edie to swallow hard. Did she despise him for being so open with his desire? Or was she flattered? Was there a chance she could change her mind and let him—

"I wish you could," Edie whispered.

And Frederick was clutching her again, pulling her closer, but she was laughing and pushing him away with splayed fingers.

"Frederick, no! We need to discuss—"

"There's nothing to discuss," Frederick muttered, pressing a hasty kiss on her neck.

It had the desired effect. When Edie spoke again, which was several kisses later, her voice had lost all its pert energy and she was instead panting. "We... We have to agree what will happen—"

"Oh, I know precisely what's going to happen," said Frederick, his pulse racing.

Dear God, he had never experienced anything like this before—and never would again.

Though Society may consider ladies to be those who were impressionable, who would be tainted once they had known the loving touch of a gentleman, Frederick now knew the opposite to be just as true.

Edie had touched him, and his affections, and he was now ruined for any other woman. How could he kiss someone else when there was Edie in the world? How could he countenance the betrayal if Edie was not the woman under his fingertips?

She most certainly was now. She was quivering, clearly aching with need, and he wanted to—

"I meant"—Edie's voice was ragged—" what we are going to do after."

Frederick froze. *After?*

Though the desire that had just seconds before been hurtling through his veins did not exactly stop, it simmered rather than raged.

Dear God—was it possible Edie had noticed something he had not? Had the preventative... split?

He had heard such things could occur. It would be damned bad luck for a gentleman who had attempted to do the right thing and take precautions. Was it possible it had happened to them?

Was there going to be a small Chance, someone he could love and care for all his days, after all?

He had unconsciously pulled back, his gaze searching hers, and Edie flushed. Perhaps the intensity of his thoughts showed on his face, but Frederick could not think of a way to articulate them.

Not with the image of that child flickering in his mind and—

"I meant," said Edie, seeing further clarification was necessary, "what are we going to do about this... this fake engagement?"

And just like that, the dream was over. The delusion he had managed to convince himself of, that he and Edie would simply ride about in this carriage forever, uninterrupted, never having to face the future, shattered into a thousand pieces.

Fake engagement.

Yes, it was all a sham. So lost had Frederick become in the sensations of Edie's body, in the laughter and wit of her personality, in the openness of her character, in how easily she slotted in with the family he had struggled to understand for so many years...

It had clouded his mind and made it impossible to remember this was all a pretense.

It wasn't real. And that meant it had to come to an end.

"We can pretend to fall out later. The engagement only has to last a few weeks—a month or two, perhaps. The exact timing is immaterial."

"Right," said Frederick unnecessarily.

Edie's expression was... He could not quite understand it. Her brows furrowed, but her lip trembled. There was sorrow there, and a little frustration—though whether that was of a physical nature or an emotional one, Frederick could not tell.

Both, perhaps. That was certainly how he felt.

"It's just... Well, we have done an excellent job at convincing the *ton* we are engaged," Edie said awkwardly.

"We have done an excellent job," Frederick said softly, "of convincing them we are in love."

In love.

The words echoed about them in the confined carriage, making his heart skip a beat and his attention focus on Edie.

For that skipped heartbeat, his whole being was attuned to her. Would she say... Would she say anything? Would she triumph at their deceit, would she scoff that such a thing could have occurred, or would she instead...

Frederick swallowed as Edie dropped her eyes to her hands—hands that were now free and unencumbered by his own.

What was she thinking? Oh, if only he could see the thoughts clearly whirling through her mind. Was it possible she felt... something for him? *Anything. I would take anything at this point,* Frederick thought feverishly. Just to know her affections had in some way been touched by their time together.

It was perhaps too much to hope that she felt as deeply as he did. He was not certain whether anyone had ever felt as deeply as he did for this woman before him.

A tingle of anticipation curled around him. Edie was opening her mouth. She was going to say—

"Indeed, we have done well," she said lightly. "But with all the wedding preparations we and Father have done, we have yet to set a date. If we do not start making actual wedding plans soon, people in Society will start to get suspicious. We cannot have that."

And all the hope which had risen died away.

He was being a fool—and if he were not careful, he would be making a fool of himself. Of course Edie Stewart did not love him. It had been her idea to create this pretense of an engagement in the first place.

"If my father demands marriage, then it will happen. If we pretend an engagement..."

No, he was being an idiot, and he would have to snap out of it swiftly if he was to prevent Edie from getting a whiff of desperation from him.

Frederick straightened his back as he always did when ready to face the world. It was not so different, really, to facing his family and keeping his heart protected.

Except it was completely different.

"The question is, therefore," Edie said into the silence, as though she could not wait about for him to speak, "how... how to end it."

End it.

End this. This closeness, this intimacy on which Frederick was starting to rely. End the laughter they shared, end the walks in Hyde Park and the coffee they shared at Don Saltero's Chelsea Coffee House. End the hopes and dreams he'd had of a child with this wonderful, spectacular woman. End the light touch of her hand on his arm, end the possibility he could kiss her with all the fire of longing erupting from his—

He needed to say something. This could not be allowed to happen. Edie needed to know how he felt about her.

His gaze met hers, and his whole body responded.

How he felt about her, and what he wanted from her. Nothing but her love.

"Well, I suppose there is one way to end this pretense of an engagement," he said, as nonchalantly as he could.

Edie nodded. "Excellent. I am all ears."

Frederick mirrored her nod, but his words did not appear to be coming, which was most inconvenient.

All he had to do was say he loved her. He loved her. *Edie, I love you. I love you—marry me. Be a part of my family. Make a family with me.*

How hard could it be?

"There's... There's a ball in four days' time," Frederick said, his voice painfully hoarse. He cleared his throat. "I believe you and your father are due to attend."

"We are, and Mrs. Teagan too. The whole family," Edie said dryly.

Frederick tried to smile as the carriage rattled along and took a right. Did every gentleman attempting to reveal his feelings get so tongue-tied—or was this just him?

"Good, good," he said vaguely. "Well, I thought, at that ball…"

His voice trailed away, unable to bear the burden, the weight of his import.

How was one supposed to say it? Was this, in truth, a proposal?

What he wanted to say was they could announce their wedding date at the ball. Actually choose one, choose each other. That the engagement that had been created to rectify an error in judgment—his, mostly—could become so much more.

That in fact, the ball could be the beginning of a true engagement, though the *ton* would not have to know that.

Frederick's pulse was thundering, hope rising and making him soar. Yes, he was going to do it. He was going to ask her.

Edie spoke nervously into his silence. "Yes? The ball? It will be quite an important one. I hear a great number of people have been invited. And that is important because—"

"I thought, at this ball," Frederick said slowly.

"—because naturally, as I am the flourishing rose of this year's Season, and there is the fact that the new Season is almost upon us, I need to ensure I make a good match, and fast," Edie said hurriedly, her words mingling together.

And his heart broke.

Oh, he'd been a damned fool to forget it.

Miss Edith Stewart was this year's flourishing rose.

And that meant she wished to make the most impressive match she could, to the best gentleman, with the most extraordinary title, and with an income that far outstripped his own. Her father, too, would have wished such a thing had he not caught them in that library.

In truth, her father probably still wishes she was not engaged to me, he thought darkly.

He was being selfish.

It was not a pleasant thought, but it was no longer one he could deny. By keeping her locked in this pretend engagement, Frederick was preventing Edie from finding a true match. A match worthy of her. Since no one else seemed to have witnessed that scene in the library, surely even her father would be willing to overlook the wound to Edie's honor and pretend the whole thing had never happened.

Which left him but one choice.

The carriage was starting to trundle down London streets. It would not be long before they would arrive at the Stewart house, and Edie would step out of the carriage... leaving Frederick alone to lick his wounds.

His jaw tightened. "In that case, let us falsify an argument at this upcoming ball and initiate the end of this charade."

Edie looked up, her breath shallow, a strange and unfathomable look in her eyes. "If... If you think that is best—"

"Most definitely," said Frederick, pulling his heart behind stone walls and lowering the portcullis. He couldn't—wouldn't allow himself to feel the pain of this moment. "Our engagement will end on December eighth."

Chapter Fifteen

December 8, 1812

"And the feather should be—"

"Don't fuss, please, it's quite all right—"

"—more to the left, I think. I mean your left, my right," muttered Mrs. Teagan, attempting to adjust the careful hairpiece Evans had spent more than an hour perfecting.

Edie tried to step delicately away from the fussing chaperone, but the pavement along the street was not that wide. "Please, I assure you—"

"—just need to—"

"It really is fine—"

"—one moment and I'll have it perfect—oh!"

Edie did not need a looking glass to tell her what had happened. In the cold, night air, the most inexplicable was happening.

Feathers were raining down past her shoulders.

"Oh, my dear!" Mrs. Teagan had clasped her hands to her mouth with a look of abject horror. "I do apologize. Oh, no! Oh, dear—they're falling!"

"Yes, they are," Edie said wryly, brushing a white feather from the shoulder of her pelisse.

"I cannot apologize enough. Your beautiful headdress, the feathers, they're all coming out. Oh, dear, oh—"

Lord Stewart turned around. He had continued walking steadily along the pavement and so was several feet away from the two ladies who had halted.

Edie was amused to see a smirk on his face.

"Ah, you decided to go without the headdress?" he called to them. His voice was almost lost in the growing chatter, the street filling with people making their way to the Duke of Sharnwick's Christmas ball. "Excellent idea. I never liked those feathers."

Stifling a laugh as Mrs. Teagan turned to soundly berate Lord Stewart for not understanding ladies' fashion, Edie pulled the last few feathers from the ribbon in her hair and allowed their white softness to fall to the ground.

She wasn't nearly so worried as Mrs. Teagan. In truth, she actually agreed with her father. Feathers were not something she particularly preferred, though they were, as Mrs. Teagan said, the height of fashion.

Some heights were higher than others. Why, she had seen Lady Romeril at Almack's only last week wearing what could only be peacock feathers, rising several feet from her head. Most curious, it had made her look, too.

"—and I wanted this ball to be perfect," Mrs. Teagan was saying, wringing her hands as she looked at the feathers now dirtying on the London road. "It was difficult enough to keep your gown clean. It's far too busy for a carriage, and now the feathers—"

"Please, Mrs. Teagan, I do not mind." Edie attempted to convince her to let it go as they started walking to catch her father, who was waiting for them. "I am not attending this ball so Society can see me wearing feathers."

No, she thought with a painful twist of her stomach as they reached the portico of the Duke of Sharnwick's home and were welcomed up the steps by a serious-looking footman. *No, I'm attending this ball so the man to whom everyone thinks I'm engaged to be married can start a mock argument with me, and break off that engagement, scandalizing the* ton *but avoiding my reputation being damaged as that of a capricious woman.*

The anticipation which had been thrumming through her took a lurch as they stepped into the entrance hall, where their pelisses, wraps, and greatcoat were taken by equally serious footmen in the same livery. Standing in a corner, without greatcoat or top hat but with a wide grin on his face, was—

Edie swallowed. *Frederick.*

Frederick Chance, Viscount Pernrith. The man to whom she had given everything. The only man in the whole of London who made her feel—

But she could not permit herself to get lost in those thoughts, particularly as they were matched by feelings Frederick evidently did not feel himself. After all, had it not been his idea to break the engagement here?

"In that case, let us falsify an argument at this upcoming ball and initiate the end of this charade."

Edie's smile blossomed, however, despite her nerves, as Frederick stepped toward them. She had thought for a few minutes in the carriage, days ago, that he had been about to say something completely different. Indeed, her foolish hopes had allowed her to believe he had been about to ask her to…

Well. Make the sham of an engagement a true one.

"Well, I thought, at that ball…"

It had been a foolish hope, indeed, and had been swiftly dashed. Just when Edie had hinted she wished to become engaged in truth, to find a husband before the end of the year from amongst the best of Society…

"—because naturally, as I am the flourishing rose of this year's Season, and there is the fact that the new Season is almost upon us, I need to ensure I make a good match."

She had been idiotic to say such a thing. Edie had seen the calm in Frederick's face, heard the serenity in his voice. He had merely been considering the best way to break their fabricated engagement—he had not been thinking of anything else.

And now...

"Good evening, Lord Stewart, Mrs. Teagan, Miss Stewart," said Frederick, bowing low to all three of them. "I trust you are all well this evening?"

Edie allowed Mrs. Teagan to twitter on, as she always did. It gave her a few moments to collect herself.

As though she could calm the raging fire of need within her. Need for him. Not just his touch, but also his closeness—

"Are you ready, Miss Stewart?" came Frederick's soft voice as he offered his arm.

Edie met his eyes steadily and saw within them a mirror of the many emotions rippling through herself.

Anticipation at the argument they would have to somehow create. A thrill, somehow, that their pretense had managed to convince so many in the *ton*. And... sadness.

It would soon all be over. The intimacy they had invented to convince the world had so easily convinced her. Edie knew nothing would be the same again after this evening, but a part of her—a growing part—could not help but hope...

"I am ready, my lord," she said aloud, taking Frederick's arm.

Edie almost cried out with delight as her gloved hand slipped onto the fine fabric of his coat. This was where she belonged. Could he not see that? Did he not know how desperately she wanted to remain here?

Thankfully, any hint of sound that may have escaped her lips was swiftly overcome by the playing of the musicians in the ballroom they were entering. The place was packed, the Duke of Sharnwick being a popular person in the *ton* and his Christmas ball apparently not one to miss, and the musicians were working hard to ensure their tune could be heard by the dancers over the loud chatter of the onlookers.

Vaguely aware of her father behind her with Mrs. Teagan on his arm, Edie allowed herself to be guided by Frederick to a corner of the room where there was space to breathe. It just so happened that it was on the opposite side of the room to the musicians, which meant they could also converse.

"—sorry I could not join you," her father was saying to Frederick with a genuinely contrite expression. "Though I hear from Mrs. Teagan that the grounds and gardens of Wickacre Hall are truly lovely."

"Oh, Father, they were magnificent," said Edie warmly, forgetting herself in the surge of affection for the place where she and Frederick had shared so much. "You will have to see it for yourself soon, before—"

She caught herself just in time.

Or rather, not quite in time.

"Before what, my dear?" asked Lord Stewart curiously.

Edie bit her lip as she met Frederick's eye.

She had been about to say, as clearly her "betrothed" had guessed, *before the engagement comes to an end.*

But that was foolish. Wasn't it due to come to an end tonight?

"Before Christmas, I believe Miss Stewart was going to say," said Frederick smoothly, rescuing her from her own folly. "The decorations are just spectacular."

"I admit, I had wondered what to do this Christmas," Edie's father mused quietly. "I even considered…"

Quite unlike him, his voice trailed away. Then his cheeks reddened to a crimson shade and his attention dropped—dropped to the woman's hand on his arm.

Edie stared between her father and Mrs. Teagan. *No. No, surely not. Though she had considered it once, that had been a jest! Her father was older, to be certain, but he was still a baron. If he'd wanted a second wife, he could have had his pick. Surely, Lord Stewart and her chaperone were not—*

"Well, consider this your invitation," said Frederick.

Stiffening immediately, Edie stared in wonder and confusion.

What on earth did he think he was doing, issuing Christmas invitations to her father—had he forgotten their plan?

"That is, if the place can be made ready in time for so many guests," Frederick added, his throat clearing as he appeared to recollect himself. "I am afraid Wickacre Hall is not suitably designed for a long stay of people of your caliber, my lord. I would hate you to—"

"And I would not wish to impose, not at all," said Lord Stewart just as stiffly. "I am sure we will be more than comfortable in London. Won't we, my dear—my dear Mrs.—I mean, Mrs. Teagan?"

Edie stared between the three of them in wonder, watching as Mrs. Teagan's cheeks joined her father's in turning pink.

What had got into everyone tonight? Was there something in the air, perhaps, that was leading them all to act so strangely?

Perhaps her father had remembered the charming young man he was conversing with was no other than the scandalous Lord Pernrith—but why had Frederick offered in the first place? And by God, what was going on between Mrs. Teagan and her father?

Edie had an inkling. It had been a great number of years since her mother had died, and she would not wish her father to become lonely when she married Frederick, but—

She was not going to marry Frederick.

The thought weighed on her like a stone. She was not going to marry Frederick. It was easy, standing in this ballroom in a soft, silk gown and Frederick's arm strong and dependable beneath her hand, to forget that.

"Ah, the flourishing rose of the year's Season," came a genteel voice.

Edie turned and curtseyed low as she recognized—

"The Countess of Dalmerlington," she murmured. "What an honor—"

"Yes, but it is most provoking," said the exquisitely beautiful Countess of Dalmerlington. "I had intended to introduce you to my brother, the Duke of Aynor—he was traveling abroad last Season—and now I am to discover you are already engaged."

Edie glanced up at Frederick before responding.

Yes, she was. Engaged. Though he had not demanded her pledge, her heart was more engaged than it had ever been.

Strange, to think she had missed the chance of being a duchess...

"You are a fortunate man, my lord," the Countess of Dalmerlington was saying cordially. "To have the flourishing rose of the year's Season as your bride."

Frederick's warmth was pouring through him to her side. Try as she might, knowing it would only bring her pain, Edie looked up.

She laughed, unable to help herself, as he grinned.

"Very fortunate," Frederick said with a charm all his own. "Though you do not appear to be short of flourishing roses yourself."

The Countess of Dalmerlington glittered as she tilted her tiaraed head indulgently. "Indeed, my lord."

She wandered away with a curtsey to Lord Stewart, and Edie was left grinning at her supposed betrothed.

Oh, this man. She had shared so much with him, so much of herself. In turn, Frederick had been more open with her than anyone in the world, she was starting to realize. And through their conversations, she had discovered not only more of herself, but what she wanted.

Could they really walk away from each other? After all they had done, all they had shared? She would not dare use it to force his hand, but he had taken from her something her future husband might consider his own right. She had thought that meant... But no. She had encouraged him. Had wanted it herself, whatever the consequences.

"Now then, Edie," said her father fondly. "It looks as though they are creating a set for the next dance. It's a country dance, your favorite."

If it had been any other situation, any other gentleman, she would have sent daggers to her father for his blatant solicitation of a dance on her behalf.

But this was Frederick—and they had not come here to dance.

What should they do? Have the argument now, make a clean break before they got lost in the evening? Or was there time to have a dance—a final dance—before the inevitable argument cost them the engagement the *ton* was convinced was true?

Just get it over and done with, part of her pleaded, gazing into Frederick's hazel eyes. *I can't live in this limbo space much longer. And yet... And yet...*

Edie could see he understood her. That was one of the many wonderful things about Frederick. He just seemed to know what she was thinking, without her having to say a word.

At least most of the time.

"Miss Stewart," said Frederick lightly, inclining his head. "Will you give me the honor of this dance?"

This dance, and the rest of my life. "Of course, Lord Pernrith."

Heads turned as they stepped through the crowded ballroom to where, as her father had said, a set was being created by couples. Try as she might, Edie could not entirely forget they were being gawped at—and neither could she ignore the whispers reaching her ears.

"Yes, that's her, the flourishing rose—"

"She is remarkably pretty, isn't—"

"—and Viscount Pernrith? Does she not know?"

Edie allowed herself to smile as Frederick carefully placed her in the line of ladies, then removed his arm to stand opposite her with the other gentlemen.

Yes, she did know. She knew all about Lord Frederick Chance's sordid past, though none of it was his fault.

She also knew about his kindness. The pain he had endured as half a Chance, always on the outside, never feeling truly part of a family. The way his eyes lit up when he was discussing something that animated him. The soft warmth of his chest as she had curled up against it just a few nights ago.

Edie swallowed. And yet there was still so much she did not know. How, precisely, he was planning on breaking her heart, for instance.

The music started and Edie obeyed the pull of the music. In concert with the other ladies, she stepped forward and curtseyed, returning to her place as Frederick and the gentlemen mirrored her.

"So," Edie said as lightly as she could manage as she stepped forward to take Frederick's hands. "What about the plan?"

"The plan?"

"I did not think our... our plan for this evening necessitated a dance," she said, trying to keep her tone unconcerned.

Which was very difficult. Dancing with Frederick was like amorous congress with Frederick. Highly intense, causing shivers of pleasure to roar up her spine, and making Edie wish to take all her clothes off.

Not ideal, in the middle of a ballroom.

If only he didn't have those wolfishly hungry eyes. If only he weren't looking at her like... like he wished very much she would oblige him by taking off all her clothes.

Edie swallowed. *Concentrate!*

"The plan does not prevent us from dancing," Frederick said easily. "Besides, I like dancing with you."

She tried to laugh carelessly as he slipped a hand on her waist—as the dance dictated. But there was something intensely sensual about the way he did it. "You do?"

"I do," he breathed, his mouth mere inches from her ear.

It was fortunate, indeed, his hand was keeping her upright, for Edie could have melted there and then.

Does he have any idea—

But he did. She could see the same desire reflected in his eyes. Frederick wanted to kiss her, right now, right here. Perhaps if they had not been planning to end the farce that was this engagement, he would do so, Society be damned.

"Move," Frederick whispered.

A shiver rushed through her body, peaking at her breasts and between her thighs. *What does he—*

"Move," he repeated, louder this time. "You need to take a step to the—"

"Oh," Edie said hastily, heat flushing her.

The dance. Of course.

It was all too easy to lose herself in the presence of Frederick Chance. The dance was not particularly complicated, and her mind could hardly concentrate on anything.

Just him.

When Frederick placed a hand on Edie's lower back, perhaps lower than the dance truly required, her gasp caught in her throat. Oh, how she wished his searing hand could travel just a little lower. The memory of him cupping her buttocks against him, of feeling his hardness pressing against her hip—

"What are you thinking about?"

Edie laughed uncomfortably. "Nothing."

Frederick raised an eyebrow as he slid his hand an inch lower on her back. "Nothing?"

Forcing herself not to bite her lip, she said, "Just... what we shared at Wickacre Hall."

She met his gaze as a throb pulsed in her folds.

Oh, he understood precisely what she meant. Those moments they had shared together, the intense intimacy, the ecstasy he had eked out of her body...

Kissing every inch of her. Touching her, showing her what pleasure could be found in the parts of her body she had ignored until that night.

Frederick's expression burned. "I would repeat that time at Wickacre Hall again, if I could."

"You would?"

"Every night," he murmured as they promenaded down the set. "And every morning."

It was all she could do to stop herself from moaning. The sensuality of the dance was heightened by Frederick's presence, by his words, by the way his fingers trailed longer than they should have with every touch, his heat burning even through his gloves.

The ache she knew was all his doing was building between her legs, and Edie knew only one person could satisfy it. The one person she knew she could ever love.

Frederick took her hands in his and she fought against the instinct to throw herself into his arms. Ball be damned, Society be damned, Lord Stewart and Mrs. Teagan be damned...

All she wanted was him.

And suddenly, she was not moving.

Edie stood, heart racing, shoulders rising and falling with every hurried breath. It took her a moment to realize that not only had the musicians ceased their playing, but that the other dancers in the line had reclaimed their partners and were returning to their parties around the ballroom.

Except themselves. She and Frederick were just standing there, staring into each other's eyes and thinking...

Oh, she hardly knew what *she* was thinking. There was no point in attempting to guess his own thoughts.

Was it possible they were thinking the same thing?

Edie's pulse was beating so rapidly, she was almost certain Frederick could hear it. Perhaps even her father could—perhaps the whole ballroom heard the frantic *thud, thud, thud* and was wondering if there was a water pump somewhere that had malfunctioned.

Suddenly, he was before her, Frederick, his chest mere inches from her own, and he gazed at her with such a blazing expression that Edie knew it meant that this was the moment.

This was it.

"I think," Frederick said softly, so softly, she was surely the only one who could hear him. "I think we should argue now."

Yes, that had been the agreement, hadn't it? An argument in public, one Frederick would start so he would be at fault. Edie would be the injured party, but the *ton* would not force her to go through with the betrothal after such a display.

Being caught kissing in a library was one thing—but scandalously insulting a lady before her father, before her chaperone, and in public?

No, no one would force the flourishing rose of the year's Season to endure such a thing.

And in that moment, in the certain knowledge that everything she had held dear for the last month was about to be wrenched from her, Edie slipped into a moment of clarity.

She did not want this to end.

Why would she? Frederick was everything she had ever hoped to discover in a suitor. Handsome, charming, kind—and so devastatingly agreeable, she was starting to find everyone who wasn't Frederick completely dull.

Edie slowly shook her head.

An expression of puzzlement slipped across Frederick's face. "But—why not?"

"I... I don't know," she admitted, hardly sure if this was the right decision but knowing she could not make any other.

Whispers were starting to rise around them. They needed to move, Edie knew they were attracting attention, but she could not shift a step.

"I want to be engaged for another day," Edie whispered, looking deep into Frederick's eyes.

And she saw the answering gleam of delight.

Frederick beamed. "So... So do I."

A shuddering breath rushed through Edie as relief coursed through her. They were not breaking their engagement. Their pretend engagement, that was. For another evening, she could walk about at Viscount Pernrith's side, and shoulder all the gossip, all the slander, the slanted looks and the pursed lips.

One more day with Frederick.

If only he wished to have her not just as his lover, but as his wife, it could be days, months, years, decades more.

"Well, in that case," he said quietly, his voice humming with evident desire. "Shall we dance again?"

Chapter Sixteen

December 9, 1812

FREDERICK WISHED HE could describe what he was feeling. *Nervous* did not quite cut it.

"You're being a damned fool, Pernrith," he muttered as he paced up and down his drawing room.

A damned fool, but one who was finally about to make the right decision.

How he had managed to get this far without spilling his affections to Edie, he did not know. He had been sure at the ball last night that all his emotions would tumble from his lips and he would be unable to stop himself from declaring himself right in the middle of the ballroom.

I love you.

I need you.

I crave you.

I can't live without you…

But this was most definitely the right decision. The invitation had been most clear, him asking his supposed betrothed over for afternoon tea, and Frederick had added a postscript to the note he had sent that morning that perhaps he should not have written.

PS. If you could perhaps leave Mrs. Teagan at home, I would be most grateful.

He had asked Edie to take a risk, to concoct another of her impressive schemes to allow herself to leave home without the company of her chaperone. The whole point of Mrs. Teagan was to act as chaperone, preventing any hint of scandal from following the flourishing rose of the year's Season.

Frederick snorted as he lowered his head to peer out of the window, looking for the carriage that would at any moment pull up outside Pernrith House. *Flourishing rose of the Season, indeed.* Edie would be relieved, he was sure, to escape that stifling title.

Besides, he reasoned as he resumed his pacing, Edie was only doing what was natural. As their supposed wedding grew closer, it was to be expected that they would meet occasionally to discuss things like... oh, he didn't know. Flowers. Canapes. Travel locations they might consider visiting during their honeymoon.

Why not do so at Pernrith House, where Edie would one day be mistress?

A jolt to Frederick's stomach forced him to halt and put a hand out to the wall. *Edie, mistress of Pernrith House. Well, why not hope? Why not dream?*

If all things went well in the next hour or so, it would be more than a dream...

"Lord, you look half done in for," came a conversational voice behind him. "I knew you stayed too late at that ball, my lord."

Frederick could not help but smile as he turned to see the concerned expression of his housekeeper. "I am well, I assure you, Mrs. Kinley."

"Hmm," said his housekeeper, plainly not convinced. "What you young things think you're doing, gallivanting about all over the place, exhausting yourself half to death—"

"It was just one ball," he pointed out.

Mrs. Kinley sniffed. "You came home at three in the morning!"

That he had. Frederick had stayed far later at the ball last night than he had at... at any other ball in his recollection.

There were probably stares. He had never stepped out into Society without attracting a few looks askance. Muttering, there had undoubtedly been. It was impossible to be Viscount Pernrith without it.

And yet Frederick had not noticed anything of the sort. His attention had been all too agreeably distracted elsewhere...

"And now you're hosting the young Miss Stewart, are you?" Mrs. Kinley's voice cut through his pleasant remembrances. "Fond of her, aren't you?"

There was no point in attempting to deceive Mrs. Kinley. Not only because his housekeeper had a sharper wit then most of the gentlemen at the Dulverton Club, but because Frederick knew the deception was coming to an end.

This false engagement, it would be made true, made right within the next sixty minutes. It would all be real.

"I am fond of Miss Stewart, yes."

"So long as she appreciates you," his housekeeper said, more stiffly than he had expected. "Sick and tired, I am, of seeing you underappreciated by those brothers of yours."

It was the most out of turn his senior servant had ever spoken, and Frederick would have reprimanded her for speaking so boldly if he had not heard the real care in her voice.

His heart softened. He was fortunate, indeed, to have a housekeeper like Mrs. Kinley. "Thank you. I believe she... Edie and I, we... we understand each other..."

Frederick's voice trailed away.

They understood each other. Well, it was true. He had never encountered a woman who looked past the indignity of his past and saw only himself. He had certainly never conversed with a woman so openly about his thoughts, his opinions, his... his fears.

And she would be here at any moment.

"Is the cake ready, Mrs. Kinley?" Frederick asked, forcing his mind to more practical matters.

Her eyes gleamed. "Only the very best for my master and my future mistress, naturally. I'll bring it through now."

His housekeeper bustled away.

Frederick did not have time to think of anything else before she was back, holding a tray upon which lay—

"Mrs. Kinley, you have outdone yourself again," he said in wonder.

And well he might. Alongside the steaming pot of tea, two cups on saucers, milk and sugar, stood—

It was magnificent. The cake had three tiers, each smothered in what appeared to be sugared violets. Fresh flowers—goodness knew where she had managed to get them—adorned the very top, along with peels of icing that curled and swept across the cake in cascades of delicious sugar.

Frederick's mouth watered just looking at it.

"I thought, show the mistress just what we can do," Mrs. Kinley puffed, laying down the tray on the small table just to the right of the fire.

The mention of "the mistress" did not pass Frederick's attention, and his chest swelled at the phrasing. Yes, Edie would soon be the mistress of this house—and his wife.

All he had to do was ask her.

It was the decision they should have made at the very beginning, when it had been clear Lord Stewart was going to demand an honorable act from him. He *had* resigned himself to it—even looked forward to it, despite the circumstances. But would Frederick have come to adore Edie as she deserved if she had not asked for her freedom? Would he have appreciated her, realized what a gift she was, if neither of them had been given a choice?

He would never know. *However we got here*, Frederick thought as his stomach twisted, *we have gotten here.*

And in mere moments—

"Ah, there's the Stewart carriage," Mrs. Kinley said, bobbing a curtsey before turning to the door. "I'll show her in, shall I?"

"I'll get the door, Mrs. Kinley," Frederick said hastily.

The thought of anyone else talking to her... No. He wanted to be the only person in Edie's world today.

His housekeeper gave him what could be considered a very knowing look. Then she was gone.

Frederick inhaled deeply as he strode across the hall.

This was it. This was the day he would remember for the rest of his life: the day Edie promised to be his wife. *Actually* his wife.

When the door opened, it was to discover Edie, alone as he'd hoped she'd be, raising her hand to the knocker.

"Oh!"

"Edie," Frederick said impulsively, desperate to say her name aloud.

She beamed, and he knew everything would go according to plan. "I received your note and managed to leave the house without Mrs. Teagan knowing. She had just gone to lie down again, you see."

"Another headache?"

"Yes."

"Excellent—that is, not for poor Mrs. Teagan's sake. But come on in," said Frederick, stepping back and encouraging her to enter.

She allowed him to take her pelisse, and he had to work hard not to allow his fingertips to linger along the embroidered hem of her gown. Her hair was piled up in a chestnut heap on her head, held together by more pins than Frederick thought could be in London, let alone on a single woman's head.

But he knew how rich and full those curls were. Had seen her hair fanned out over a pillow. Had seen it move as she cried out—

"I hope you have cake at the ready," Edie teased as she stepped across the hall to the open drawing room door. "Ah, I see that you have—my goodness."

"It is rather spectacular, isn't it?" Frederick followed her, shutting the door behind him for privacy.

A conversation as delicate as this required privacy.

Edie was standing beside the cake, examining it with wide eyes. "Where on earth did you purchase such a thing?"

"My housekeeper and my cook, they—"

"Goodness gracious, they could open a bakery and put Don Saltero's Chelsea Coffee House out of business within a week," she said with a tinkling laugh. "Is this why Mrs. Teagan could not accompany me? You were concerned we would have to share it?"

Frederick grinned but did not answer her immediately.

How could he? He wanted to drink her in first, and as usual, Edie offered a particularly delectable sight.

She was attired in a light-green gown, a muslin of the sort with a delicate, woven pattern within it. He could not quite make it out at this distance, and so Frederick took advantage of the moment and moved closer.

Little hearts. There were little hearts woven into the print.

Frederick swallowed. She must know, mustn't she? After their agreement to remain engaged for one further day, Edie must know what he wished to ask. What he had to ask.

"I want to be engaged for another day."

"So... So do I."

"Shall I cut, or do you wish to?"

Frederick blinked. "I... I beg your pardon?"

Cut? What on earth is she talking about?

Edie was pointing at the cake. "This spectacular affair—I am a tad concerned if I cut into it, the whole thing will fall apart. What do you think?"

Think? He would much rather take the cake knife, slit it up the ties of her gown, and watch it fall to the—

"I'll cut," Frederick said, mouth dry. "But first—first, I want to ask you something."

With doe-like eyes, Edie stared up at him. "What is it?"

It was not in his nature to hesitate, but in this moment, he simply could not barrel forward. He had to think.

Not that he hadn't given the matter a great deal of thought already. In fact, Frederick was conscious his eyes were a little weary and his skin a little pallid because he had done so much thinking.

Mrs. Kinley had been correct—he had returned home from the ball at around three o'clock in the morning. But he had not slept. He had stayed awake attempting to think of the best, the most impressive way he could offer marriage, true marriage, to Miss Edith Stewart.

She deserved something incredible. A flotilla of boats across the Thames, fireworks, a display of exotic animals, and perhaps even a juggler or three.

But Frederick couldn't offer that, and a part of him knew Edie did not require it. She knew him, knew his means, or lack thereof. He was far from the wealthiest suitor, though his two thousand a year meant he was hardly penniless.

Creating such a ridiculous, extravagant proposal would not endear him to Edie.

No. She already knew him, already cared for him.

He was enough.

"Frederick?" prompted Edie quietly.

Frederick started. "I beg your pardon?"

"You were going to ask me something," she reminded him with a sweetness in her expression that made him want to tangle his hands in her hair and ask the question through quite other means.

If only he did not feel so inadequate. She was the flourishing rose of the year's Season, and he was the reprehensible Viscount Pernrith, whom the whole of Society enjoyed shunning. Did she not know how above him she was? How desperately he would work to deserve her?

Frederick loved her. Would that be enough?

"Edie, I..." He swallowed. "I know our entire acquaintance has been—well, unusual."

Her eyes glittered. "It has, indeed."

"I never expected you to slip into that alcove and discover me at Lady Romeril's ball," Frederick continued, his voice growing stronger as his confidence rose. "And I never expected to feel such—such a connection with you. Such a desire for you."

There was pink in her cheeks and Edie's gasp had caught for just a moment, but she was breathing steadily now and looking with such trust, such open adoration, Frederick was heartened.

It was all going to go to plan.

"This engagement is false. It's not true, and you and I are the only ones who know that," Frederick said softly. He reached out and took Edie's hands in his, and his whole body vibrated at the connection. "It's been... well, damned wonderful to be gadding about London with you on my arm. You are... You know how precious you are to me."

Still, Edie did not speak, though there was an answering glitter in her expression.

Well, this was it. It was now or never. "And I... Well, I want to make this engagement true. I want to marry you, Edie. I don't want this to end. I... Marry me."

There. It was said.

And nothing else was said in the drawing room. The silence was natural at first—any woman would be stunned to receive such a declaration, Frederick knew.

But as the silence continued, growing and spreading around the room, highlighting the echoing thud of his pulse and the strained breathing, something started to prickle around his mind.

Edie hadn't said yes.

She hadn't said anything. Her hands were still in his, and she had not moved away—but she had not accepted him. She had not rejected him. She was just... standing there.

Frederick licked his lips a tad uncertainly. He had never proposed matrimony before. Was he supposed to just wait until the lady in question gained her equilibrium? Was that when she would launch herself into his arms and kiss him?

Oh, blast. Was he supposed to be one knee?

And then he saw it. The fear in her eyes.

Frederick dropped Edie's hands as if they burned and staggered backward. "I see."

Her jaw dropped. "No, you don't—"

"Yes, I do," he said dully. How could he have been so stupid? "You just looked at me like they all do."

Edie's eyes were sparkling. "No, it isn't like that—"

"Isn't it?" Frederick shot back, turning away and pulling a hand through his hair.

How had he managed to convince himself that Edie had cared about him—truly cared about him? All their conversations, their talks, she had never said... There had been no mention of affection.

And Edie had just considered him with the same fear everyone else in the *ton* did. The concern that if they got too close to him, they'd become tainted with the same stain he had borne the whole of his life.

"I hesitated," said Edie, stepping around and trying to take his hand. "Is it so wrong to hesitate?"

"I don't you want you to hesitate. I want you to want me!" Frederick said, agony in every syllable as his heart tore in two. "I never hesitated with you!"

There was a sharp look in her face as she said, "I am not so sure of that. It took a certain amount of convincing for you to agree to a false engagement, let alone a true one."

"That's not true. I intended—"

"Was it not?" Edie shot back. "Was that not exactly what happened?"

Frederick growled in his throat, irritation threatening to pour out of him. "I just offered you my heart, and you said nothing!"

"I didn't. I just wasn't sure if you... I cannot just immediately—"

"Why not?" he persisted. Desperate though he was to be close to her again, Frederick knew if he got too close, all ability to think would seep away from his mind. "It's my parentage, isn't it? Isn't it?"

Again, a hesitation, and this time, a tormented look of pain across Edie's face. "That is a low blow."

He swore quietly under his breath.

"How could you even think that? You don't underst—I thought *you* were the one who... And this isn't a small thing you are asking of me, Frederick!"

"It isn't?" He laughed darkly, hating the twinge that shot across her expression as he did. "I thought it was the rest of my life I was offering you. I must agree—it isn't a small thing!"

"You have lived like this your whole life, I know. You have no idea what it is to—"

"To be accepted? To be a part of Society?" Frederick said, his voice breaking.

Oh, he was such a fool. What had he been thinking—that someone like Edie would risk everything, risk her reputation, her place in Society, her vouchers to Almack's, the good opinion of the world... just for him?

Edie's voice was a tad higher as she retorted. "I just mean... Yes, I am the flourishing rose of the year's Season, but—"

Frederick stepped away, unable to bear it. "You hypocrite—you said you didn't want to be treated just as someone beautiful!"

"You aren't letting me explain—"

"You said you didn't want the title, we—we talked about it! Unearned title, I remember," he said, blinking back tears.

Oh, God, he hoped she did not notice. The drawing room he knew so well was swimming before his eyes, and he could not understand how this had all gone terribly wrong.

Of course she did not want to leave behind the comfortable and respectable life that she had lived. Of course he wasn't good enough for her. Had he not known, his whole life, that love and matrimony were not in the cards for him?

Edie was speaking hastily, her words intermingling so much it was hard to follow her train of thought. "I've had to live up to so much. Dragged this way and that, told what to do, whom to dance with. All this year—but even before then. My father, he has always wanted, always planned—he's wanted what's best for me!"

The words echoed around the drawing room like a malediction.

Frederick cleared his throat as he tilted his head. "So I'm not the best."

"I didn't say—"

"Dear God, I should have known—the Countess of Dalmerlington's comment should have opened my eyes. You could have a duke, the very best—and here I am, the bottom of the barrel. Because I'm illegitimate," he said flatly, self-loathing rising. "Just half a Chance. Not the real thing. I don't have the impressive title your father wants, though mine is greater than his own—"

"Frederick—"

"Or the riches or the position that others have," Frederick said, barreling onward because he could only see one end to this conversation and he wished to get there as quickly as possible. *Get it over with.* "I can't say I'm surprised. Hurt, but not surprised."

Edie was blinking back tears, and he didn't know why. He wasn't the one who had shied away from a proposal, a true proposal of marriage. He wasn't the one who was clinging to the expectations of the *ton* so tightly it would mean relinquishing a chance of happiness.

She was trying to smile. "You think so little of me—"

"It's *you* who thinks too little of me. This should be easy, Edie—the easiest thing in the world," Frederick said, stepping toward her and cupping her face in his hands. *Oh, the craving to kiss away those tears... to show her that they could be together, no matter what.*

But she would have to stand with him against the world, would she not?

And if she could not do that here, in the privacy and safety of their own company...

"You care too much about what the world thinks. You've read that scandal sheet, that *Whispers of the Ton*, and you think—"

"It's natural to consider what the world thinks!" she shot back boldly, color high and eyes bright. "Most of us are forced to live within the bounds of Society. There are certain expectations—"

"And some of us are born outside those bounds," Frederick countered bitterly. "And that's too large a step for you, isn't it? Stepping outside of Society, toward me."

"I will not be talked to like this," Edie whispered, staring into his eyes. "Because *you* are so used to being brave, to ignoring everything Society says about you, you look at me, fawned over in the papers, and you think I—"

Something hardened within him. "I'm not brave, Edie. Bravery suggests a choice. I haven't had a choice, this has been my life—it's been handed to me and I've had to learn to live with it. But you... you have a choice."

"I know," she said, her voice so quiet he could barely hear it. "And... And I would have made it. But you don't respect me. You laugh at my position in Society—"

Frederick released her face and turned away, groaning as the pain of her rejection filled him.

"I don't—I can't..." He barked a dry laugh, tugging his cravat, which was inexplicably tightening. "I suppose all ladies are like this! No one wishes to ruin their reputation. I would know if I'd taken up Lindow's offer to meet Miss Quintrell."

The instant the words were out of his mouth, Frederick knew he had made a mistake.

Edie grabbed his arm, turning him around to face her—and now there was not indecision or hurt in her face, but anger. "Oh, so you have been lining up the next woman to kiss in a library and trick into an engagement?"

Frederick blinked. "Wh-What? No, no, it isn't like—"

"So what was it?" she said sharply.

How had this happened? How had this conversation descended into such chaos, such a disaster?

A crushing sensation was pressing against his chest, making it almost impossible to speak. Impossible to think.

"It was just something Lindow said," Frederick muttered, trying to avoid the accusatory glance in her gaze. "And it's not as though—I mean, this engagement isn't real! It's all been pretend, hasn't it? None of it has meant anything!"

"Hasn't it?"

He knew it was too late to take back his words when he saw Edie's face. All life was drained from it—the perfect, impassive lips, the dull, tired eyes. It was strange; William had once accused Frederick of shutting out the world with his expression when he did not want to be hurt.

He'd never understood what his half-brother had meant... until now.

"Good day, my lord," said Edie quietly. "Please consider this pretend engagement, which meant nothing to you—"

"Edie—"

"—which meant nothing to you, to be at an end."

Chapter Seventeen

December 10, 1812

THOUGH HER STOMACH rumbled, Edie pushed the carefully fried trout about on her plate. The eye of the fish, lifeless and now unseeing, looked up at her.

She sighed heavily.

Luncheon was supposed to be one of the calmest parts of the day. Visiting hours were approaching, and there was usually an evening engagement to be enjoyed. Luncheon, however, was the pleasant genteel meal she shared with her father, and her father alone.

Mrs. Teagan had been most insistent, when she had accompanied them to London. *"A girl needs her father, Miss Stewart. Far be it from me to come between you!"*

Now she came to think, Edie had absolutely no idea where Mrs. Teagan took her lunch. Surely not with the servants downstairs. But then where?

"You are very quiet."

Edie jumped and looked up guiltily—though what she felt guilty for, she was not sure. At least, not in this conversation.

"Most of us are forced to live within the bounds of Society. There are certain expectations—"

Oh, she had plenty to feel guilty about when it came to *that* discussion—but her father did not know about that, did he?

A further strain of guilt tightened around her, squeezing her tightly. She ought to tell him—she knew she must… but for each passing minute she did not tell her father that she and Frederick had broken with each other, she could almost believe it had never happened.

"Am I? Quiet, I mean?" Edie tried to speak with the same cheer she always had, but it was clear her father was not convinced. She rallied. "I am just eating my food, that is all."

"Indeed," said Lord Stewart wryly. "The food you have barely touched."

Forcing herself to stick a morsel of fried trout onto her fork, Edie brought it to her lips. It was delicious—she knew it was. Cook never failed, and the trout had been freshly caught only a few days ago, apparently.

It tasted of nothing.

The dining room was elegantly laid out, as it always was when they were taking luncheon. The fresh flowers in the vase by the window were starting to wilt. The cake that stood on a stand to her left looked a tad stale—or was that just her imagination?

The image of another cake, a different cake, flashed before her eyes. A cake she had never gotten the chance to taste.

The scandal sheets had made no mention of it. That had been a surprise, for Edie was sure the viscount's servants would have heard the loud voices and spread the news by now. Yet *Whispers of the Ton* did not even contain their names.

It would all come out eventually…

"You should tell me about it," said her father softly. "You know you can always talk to me. You always have."

Edie's lungs tightened.

Yes, she always had. There had been no mother for her to turn to, only a gruff father who had never expected a daughter and had found himself left without a wife to mediate between them. It had been a strange time for them, but now… now Edie could not imagine her life without him.

For the first time in over a decade, however, there was a topic about which she could not speak to him.

"I don't want to talk about it," she said quietly.

Edie dropped her attention to the waiting fish on her plate. It prevented her from seeing any hint of disappointment or concern on her father's face—expressions that would make it all the harder for her to stay silent.

She could not tell him. Revealing that the whole engagement had been a farce was more, she was sure, than her father would bear.

Bad enough that she and Frederick—that she and *Lord Pernrith* had been caught kissing, and rather more, in a library. Bad enough that of all the gentlemen in the *ton* she could have been compromised with, it was a man whose reputation was low in the eyes of Society. Bad enough that they had been forced to marry.

But if her father discovered it had all been a sham... that she had lied to him, moreover, to him and Mrs. Teagan and everyone in Society...

No. Edie was not going to lower herself in his eyes to that extent.

She would wait until dinner, then tell him the engagement was at an end, Edie decided, fiddling with her fork and pushing a roast potato back and forward across her plate.

And that would be it.

"I'm not brave, Edie. Bravery suggests a choice. I haven't had a choice, this has been my life—it's been handed to me and I've had to learn to live with it. But you... you have a choice."

Her grip tightened painfully on the fork, just for a moment, as the memory of the argument rippled across her mind.

Words had been spoken that could never be unsaid. She had seen the pain in Frederick's eyes, felt it viscerally scatter across her body.

He had decided her character to be less than it was, less than she had thought she'd proven it to be. And he would never forgive her. Never.

"My dear Edie," said her father softly. "Do you mean to tell me—

or not tell me, as the case may be—that your pretend engagement with Viscount Pernrith is at an end?"

Edie dropped her fork with a clatter as she stared, astonished, at her father.

Lord Stewart's face was a picture of soft concern, and it only made her heart ache all the more. How had she managed to disappoint and hurt the two men in her life who mattered the most?

"I—you don't—we never told... How on earth did you know that?"

Edie supposed she should have attempted to keep her face straight, prevent him from knowing the truth—but as her father appeared to know, what was the point in hiding from him?

Her father placed his own knife and fork onto his almost empty plate and leaned back in his seat. When his gaze met hers, it was a kind one. "My darling girl, haven't you noticed?"

"Noticed... Noticed what?" Edie said, her voice hoarse.

Dear Lord, if her father was about to tell her he suspected that she and Frederick... if he had worked out they had... if Mrs. Teagan had any inkling that they...

Heat blossomed across Edie's chest.

But not shame. No, she could not feel ashamed of having shared the most intimate of things with Frederick Chance. He was the only man in the world with whom she wished to share such things, and it was a joy to look back and know that, even though it had ended terribly, she had still managed to have that experience with him.

Even if he despised her now.

"Oh, Edie," said her father kindly, shaking his head. "I presumed you had noticed. These walls, they aren't that thick. You can hear most of a conversation from the next room."

Edie's mouth fell open.

"It is remarkable how clear those voices are. The walls must be made of paper."

She had known that—but she had never considered that someone might have overheard her and Frederick...

Lord Stewart's eyes twinkled. "I heard every word of your little plan before you and Lord Pernrith came into my study. 'My father will force you to marry me, so we must pretend we are engaged,' I think it was?"

Edie had never been so astonished in her life. It was like discovering that one's father had secretly been working for the Prince Regent in France, or one's grandmother had been an actress on the stage.

Attempting to fit into her mind that her father had known, from the very beginning, that the engagement between herself and Frederick had only been for show...

"You—You knew!" Edie spluttered, food quite forgotten. "From the moment we went into your study?"

"I have to say, I was impressed," said her father lightly. "I knew you would consider your fate, keep your options open. Having a false engagement, one that could be broken at a later date with no feelings harmed... It was a clever idea."

Yes, it had been a clever idea. She had done it for Frederick as much as for herself. She could not force a man into marriage. No feelings harmed... that had been the plan.

When had it started to go so awry? When she had hesitated most awkwardly yesterday, too stunned to accept he really did want to marry her? When they had danced at the Duke of Sharnwick's ball? When they had lain together, joined together, fast and hot, slow and luxurious, at Wickacre Hall?

Or had it started before even that? Had Edie started to lose her head well before visiting Frederick's home in the country? Did it go as far back as when she had read their names entwined in the gossip sheets—when *Whispers of the Ton* had considered their engagement to be a scandal?

"But..." It was difficult to wrap her head around the fact that her father had been so well-informed the last several weeks. "But you went along with it! I mean, you organized the announcement in *The Times*. You hosted his family!"

Edie could not understand it. What had possessed him?

"And you knew about his reputation, you knew that... well. He was not well regarded." She swallowed. It felt treacherous even thinking such a thing, let alone saying it. "You were eager to ensure I never spoke to him after Lady Romeril's ball."

Lord Stewart shrugged. "So I was. Yet I could not deny that being engaged to a viscount, a clear step above me in title and rank... I could not see how it would hurt. Additional eyes would be on you, even more than those that had been attracted after being declared the flourishing rose of the Season. Who knew what earl, or marquess, or duke would covet you?"

And Edie's hopes sank.

Her father had not bothered to put a stop to the sham engagement not because he'd been concerned about her, or because he'd thought Frederick a good match... but because he'd hoped it would spark the interest of another.

Another with greater wealth, and more of a chance for her to become "Your Grace."

"I see," she said listlessly.

"I don't think you do," countered her father gently. "You see, amongst all those reasons was another."

Edie leaned forward. "Yes?"

"I was curious," said Baron Stewart gravely.

She slumped back in her seat. *Curious*. Had not Frederick mentioned how people in the *ton* gawped when they discovered his history? That he had been forced to put up with the most unpleasant of interviews by those who were trying to identify if he could truly be called a gentleman?

No wonder Frederick hated Society so much. No wonder he had been so pained when she had hesitated, the shock and surprise of his sudden proposal mingling with the parts of her which she despised.

The parts of her that wanted to be adored, and admired, and the center of attention in Society. She could not deny those feelings were, in small part, true, even if she'd been offended by the viscount's insistence that she was led by those desires.

"You wanted to see what half a Chance was like," Edie stated dully.

Lord Stewart raised an eyebrow. "Dear Lord, no. I suppose that would have been interesting, but I had quite another motive."

She frowned. "You did?"

Her father nodded, and there was a sad sort of look in his eyes that Edie rarely saw. In fact, it was typically the expression he wore when he was discussing... her mother.

"I wanted to see if he could make you happy."

Edie started, heat curling around her lungs.

Happy.

Her father had never said anything like that. It was always "Make sure you dance with every gentleman in the room" or "I'll just find out what his fortune is per year." Often "Go on, play one more piece on the pianoforte, just to make sure they remember you" and "Matrimony is a serious business."

Never before had Lord Stewart mentioned anything about her happiness.

"And he did for a time, did he not?" Her father looked wistful. "Make you happy, I mean."

Edie had never felt more wretched in her life. Was this what she would have to endure now, the months and years ahead? Regret and anguish, always wondering what could have been and why she had managed to talk herself out of an engagement with the man she loved?

"Please consider this pretend engagement, which meant nothing to you—"

"Edie—"

"—which meant nothing to you, to be at an end."

"It's just..." she said aloud, hardly knowing what she was going to say. "The more I tried to—and the plan was to break it off eventually, I knew it wasn't going to last for... And I thought..."

Edie swallowed.

If only she had not spoken so hastily. Frederick's clear anguish at what he'd perceived as a rejection—which she hadn't actually done—had forced her to speak without thinking, and the unthinkable had been spoken, and she could not take it back.

No matter how much she may wish to.

"And it's not as though—I mean, this engagement isn't real! It's all been pretend, hasn't it? None of it has meant anything!"

"Hasn't it?"

The unsettled pain in her stomach lurched most uncomfortably and Edie pushed her plate away.

They had stood there, her hands in his. He had looked into her eyes and there had been such love there.

True, he had not said the actual word. But then neither had she, and she had felt it for many weeks now.

And what had she done? Not thanked him for his kind words, not flushed and giggled at the intensity of it all. No, Edie had envisioned the headlines of *Whispers of the Ton*. The focus that would be on her for the rest of her life if she accepted Frederick's hand. The way she would never be able to walk into Don Saltero's Chelsea Coffee House, or Almack's, or anywhere without people staring.

People who would always presume the worst. People who would gossip about her behind her back and simper when she approached.

Never again would she know whether someone was a true friend, or just curious about discovering more about the scandalous Viscount Pernrith. Never again could she slip into a room and be ignored.

He was right. She *had* thought those things. They'd been fleeting thoughts, washing through her head, but then he'd gone and accused her of thinking those things—and worse. Accused her of thinking him beneath her.

She had been wrong to worry about such things, but she could not deny them—nor the pain her hesitation had clearly afforded.

"You hypocrite—you said you didn't want to be treated just as someone beautiful!"

The pain on Frederick's face was still so clear, she could see it in her mind's eye. And in that moment, she had known it was over. Whatever had been between them, it had been gone.

There was no possibility Frederick would ever forgive her, would ever be able to see her as someone who could respect him.

"You have to try—"

"The engagement between us is at an end," Edie said stiffly, speaking over her father. She would not permit him to continue in this conversation under a misapprehension.

His stare examined her steadily. "But if you love him—"

"Love is not always enough," she said, her chest tightening. "You know that as well as I do. Better than I do. Love cannot always keep those we care about with us."

It was perhaps a cruel thing to say, and Edie saw the pain flicker across her father's face. But it was true. Her parents had adored each other, from the little she could remember. And they had been separated.

"Your mother was taken from me." Lord Stewart spoke quietly, grief dripping from every word. "That is not the same."

"It ends up the same way."

"True love, a love I myself have known, is always worth risking for, fighting for, trying to have," said her father quietly.

Edie raised an eyebrow, unable to help herself. If he was going to speak about true love, then it was only fair she pushed back with both barrels. "So you are going to profess your intentions to Mrs. Teagan any day now, are you, Father?"

It was Lord Stewart's turn to look aghast. "I haven't—not until I—but how did you…"

She could not help but laugh as her father's jaw worked furiously, but no sound came out. "It was hardly difficult, once I started noticing the signs."

"'Signs'?"

Edie lifted a hand and started counting off her fingers. "You take her hand onto your arm at every opportunity, I keep catching you looking at her, you've spent far more on her Christmas present than mine—do not fear, I am not offended—and when she mentioned that book you immediately went out and purchased it for her—"

"I'm a man who encourages reading," her father said faintly.

She narrowed her eyes. "What book am I reading right now?"

Lord Stewart threw his hands to the heavens. "How am I supposed to know?"

"And what book is Mrs. Teagan—"

"*The Castles of Athlin and Dunbayne*, by Ann Radcliffe," her father said. Then his eyes widened. "How the devil do I know that?"

"Because you love her," said Edie simply. "It's... It's obvious, when you know the signs of what to look for."

And she had managed to get herself so entangled in the falsification of an engagement that she hadn't noticed the strength of her feelings. Frederick had become a part of her life quickly—far more quickly than she could have imagined. And now he was gone from it.

Gone, merely because she had hesitated. Because for a fleeting moment, she had cared more what *Whispers of the Ton* had thought about her than the man she loved.

"You should say something to her," Edie said softly.

Lord Stewart gave a laugh. "I don't want to be seen as... She's under my protection, you understand. And she's a good fifteen years younger than I am!"

"And you think the opinion of others should stop you from reaching out for love?"

Only then did she realize she had walked into her own trap. She would have noticed on her own, naturally, but her father's snort placed more emphasis on it.

"We're not too dissimilar, are we?"

Edie sighed. "No, I suppose not. You do love her."

"Almost as much as you," her father said solemnly. "In truth, it's been hard to keep my hands off—"

"Father!"

Her exclamation was joined by a sudden screech and a thump that appeared to occur close to them.

Very close to them. Both Edie and her father turned to the wall that adjoined the dining room with that of the parlor—the parlor, now she came to think about it, Mrs. Teagan had claimed as her own.

"Oh, dear," came Mrs. Teagan's voice weakly through the wall. "I... ah. I appear to have dropped my book."

Edie stifled a giggle.

"Ah, there it is. I'll just... Ahem. Go upstairs."

There was the sound of a door opening, then hurried footfalls up the staircase.

"What did I tell you?" Lord Stewart's face was pink, but he held his daughter's gaze steadily. "Walls as thin as paper."

She could not help but grin. "I suppose you have no choice but to propose now."

"I shall just have to hope I have not been convincing myself of her returned regard," her father said quietly. "That's what has held me back for so long, you see. I suppose that is what held young Pernrith back from speaking to you. I suppose you broke it off before either of you could admit your feelings."

Edie's smile faded. "Not... Not quite."

For a moment, she thought her father was going to inquire into precisely what had happened, but he appeared to think better of it.

"Well, there we are," he said cheerfully. "I haven't had the bravery yet to speak to the person I love, but that does not mean that you shouldn't. Are you brave enough, Edie?"

Swallowing hard, Edie whispered, "I don't know."

"You have to ask for what you want," Lord Stewart said seriously. "If there is even half a chance—"

His words were interrupted by a snort from Edie that was half laughter, half pain.

"Damn," said her father with a shake of his head. "But you know what I mean. If there's the slightest chance of happiness, won't you ask for it? Fight for it?"

Edie took a long, deep breath.

Her father was right. In every other situation, his advice would have been perfect.

But he didn't know—no one could know how deeply she had hurt Frederick. By hesitating at his proposal, by making it clear without a word just what she would be sacrificing to become his wife, she had treated him just as the whole of the *ton* had.

With barely concealed scorn.

And she'd had the gall to be hurt he'd think so little of her.

She thought little of herself now.

Yes, she could ask for forgiveness. She could ask for his hand, for his love. But Edie could not help but feel that the half chance her father spoke of was unlikely to turn out in her favor.

"I will try," she said shakily. "But will he want to hear it?"

Chapter Eighteen

"—AND BEFORE I truly knew what was happening, which to be honest started far before that, I was pointing out that the whole thing had been a farce anyway," said Frederick wretchedly, standing by the fireplace at Cothrom House with his hand against the mantel. "And before I had a chance to explain, or even think, she was gone. Edie, she... she just walked out."

He was not sure what he had expected after he had explained the whole debacle. Not applause, certainly, but something. A pat on the back, maybe, or a clearing of the throat, or a sigh before a speech about how he had done the best he could, and it was unfathomable how the whole thing had come to a sticky end.

Instead, Frederick was met with silence. Silence, save for the cracking of the fire.

He turned around, his spine stiff, as it always was when with his brothers. "Any thoughts?"

The two words were almost spat out into the air.

It had taken a great deal of courage to write to all three of his brothers and request that they meet him here. Frederick had never... They could come to him for aid and support, and over the years, they had. Even George.

But he, go to them?

No. He had no wish to be indebted to a trio of men whom he could never repay. It wasn't in his nature.

Yet to whom else was there to turn? He had no other family, no friends in the *ton*, thanks to their distaste of his position. There was no one else to ask.

Of course, based on the response he had received to date, he may as well have not asked a single person.

William, Duke of Cothrom, was shaking his head as he sat in the window seat, one leg crossed over his knee. John, Marquess of Aylesbury, was blowing out his cheeks slowly as he sat in an armchair. Most unusually, George, Earl of Lindow, was pacing. That kept his eyes away from Frederick.

Precisely what I would have expected, Frederick tried but failed not to think. The bitterness rose as frustration mingled with pain.

He had never asked for much. Could have demanded money, jewels, property. He could have demanded his due as a full brother, recognized as he had been by their father.

He had never requested the title of Viscount Pernrith. He would never have claimed it had William not urged him to.

Here he was, asking for help with the one thing that truly mattered... and all they could do was stay silent?

"Do you not have anything to say?" Frederick said aloud, his voice testy as his hands clenched into fists by his side. "You three—well, two of you—have come to me with your problems, and I've always sought to guide you. Can you not offer me the same compassion?"

John cleared his throat. "Well... I mean, it's a lot to take in."

"I had no idea the initial engagement was a hoax," William said quietly. "I am sure we would not have interfered, had had dinner with the young lady and her father, if we had known."

Despite himself, despite every fiber of his being knowing it was a bad decision, Frederick glanced at George.

Who scowled as he continued his pacing. "I knew."

"You knew—" William started.

"Yes, I knew," George muttered darkly. "But what did I care what the man did? It's not up to me to decide what a man does with his time."

The retort was cold, precisely what Frederick would have expected from the man.

There had never been any love lost between himself and George, and in a way, he didn't think there ever would be. There was such a thing as too much water under the bridge.

Still. He had hoped the man would at least *attempt* to be civil.

Doing everything he could to retain the calm and unruffled disguise that had been his automatic response with his brothers, Frederick inclined his head. "I apologize for not informing you all on the true nature of—"

"I don't see how that matters," interjected John with a curious expression. "How the engagement started is not relevant. The point is, you wished it to become true."

Frederick's jaw tightened and he turned to the fire, unable to meet the eyes of his brothers. "Yes."

Yes, he had wanted it to become true. He had been desperate to know the woman he had fallen in love with felt anything for him in return.

Well, that wasn't quite true. Frederick could hardly lie to himself. More than marriage, he'd wanted Edie to adore him, to love him, to crave him—to desire him as deeply as he desired her.

And now...

"You hypocrite—you said you didn't want to be treated just as someone beautiful!"

"There must be a way to rectify this." Frederick was astonished to find the seemingly calm and almost cheerful voice was his own. "This cannot just end. It can't."

"I thought it was the rest of my life I was offering you. I must agree—it isn't a small thing!"

"Well, I must say, I am not sure what we can do," came William's voice behind him.

The eldest Chance brother always saw disaster and scandal in their midst, and most of the time, he was right. It did little to help Frederick's confidence that William believed nothing could be done.

"It does sound... Well, forgive the phrasing, but like a mess of your own making," John said apologetically.

Turning, Frederick saw the second Chance flushing—actually flushing.

"I am not saying she acted perfectly," John added hastily. "More that... Well. Did you not expect such a response? At all? Considering... Considering how Society treats you?"

Considering how Society treated him... Yes, Frederick supposed he should have considered that it would be a rare woman, indeed, who would happily join him in that particular flavor of ostracization.

But he had thought Edie Stewart to be that rare woman. Believed she'd understood, that she had taken the time to get to know the man behind the scandal. She was one of the few people with whom he had been open. He'd thought he'd known that she too, in a small way, loathed the way Society adored some and ignored others.

"I just offered you my heart, and you said nothing!"

"I didn't. I just wasn't sure if you... I cannot just immediately—"

"Why not?"

Frederick pulled a hand over his face as he remembered the words from their argument the day before. *Oh, hell.*

"I must apologize."

His hand fell away as his eyes widened. Surely, he could not have heard those words from—

George, Earl of Lindow, tensed his shoulders. He had ceased his pacing just before Frederick, and his eyes were serious for the first time in Frederick's memory.

"'Apologize'?" Frederick repeated stiffly.

This was unprecedented. Lindow hardly spoke to him at all, if he could help it. When he did, it was usually a cutting remark or unpleasant quip.

And now he was going to apologize? What the devil for?

George nodded. "I should not have sent you that letter."

Frederick blinked. "Letter?" What on earth was the man talking about?

"About Miss Quintrell. It was an honest mistake, and by that I mean, I did not intend harm," said George stiffly, not quite meeting his eye. "Which I know is a difficult thing to believe when it comes to you... you and me."

Frederick's jaw tightened. He was certainly correct about that. Most of his childhood had been spent in fear of the youngest full-blooded Chance. Fear of retribution. Fear of reprisal. Fear of rage.

And now here he was, admitting he was wrong... and most irritatingly, Frederick did not agree.

"The letter caused no direct harm," he said tautly. "It was I who brought up Miss Quintrell to Edie, I who—"

"But if I had not sent the letter in the first place, her name would not have been available for you to speak," insisted George in an unbending voice.

Frederick could hardly believe it. Would the man not relent? "But if I hadn't—"

"Will you just accept the damned apology, man," George said with a glare far more reminiscent of the man he knew. "You're not likely to get another."

Out of the corner of his eye, Frederick could see both William and John staring at the pair of them. There was a look on the elder's face, almost as if—

He tried not to groan. *Oh, God, it's hope.* They were hoping this terse scene would lead to a renewal—not even a renewal, a beginning of a friendship between the two of them. Between himself and Lindow.

Dear Lord.

Frederick sighed, then forced himself to meet George's eye. "Look. I don't hold any ill will toward you, Lindow. In truth, I never have.

Not directly."

The youngest Chance met his eye and swallowed, the crease in his brow deepening.

Then George resumed his pacing. "Good."

Somehow, a great deal of tension had managed to lock itself into Frederick's shoulder blades. As he forced out a long, slow sigh, some of it melted away without the bulk of the pressure at his temples diminishing.

"*You have lived like this your whole life, I know. You have no idea what it is to—*"

"To be accepted? To be a part of Society?"

Edie.

Try as he might, it was impossible to force her from his mind. He could not stop thinking about her from one minute to the next. Everything reminded him of her. The glitter of sunlight on water—she was the flourishing rose. The warmth of the sun—the hit to his stomach whenever he saw her. Any of those damned scandal sheets—how much Edie loved them.

Perhaps loved them too much.

If he cared about her less, Frederick was certain it wouldn't hurt. But how did you turn off your heart? How could you remove the person you thought about every single moment from your thoughts? Was it even possible to get your heart back?

"The question is," Frederick said aloud, half to himself and half to the room at large, "what do I do now?"

There was a slight *thump* somewhere else in the house. All four men turned in that direction, then glanced at William.

He shrugged. "When Pernrith said he wanted to talk, I asked Alice to entertain Florence and Dodo with a game of cards."

Just for a moment, there was a flicker of mirth on George's face. "In that case, that sound was probably one of the wives getting irritated at Dodo's expertise."

"The wives know better than to get involved with Dodo and cards, surely?" John's eyes blinked rapidly. "You think they're actually playing?"

The conversation washed over Frederick. It hardly concerned him, and more, it did not interest him. But it did tug his emotions in a way he could not have expected.

The wives.

For a few hours—almost a whole day—he had believed Edie would join that group. That there would be four of them, and he would somehow be a part of the family in a way he never had been before.

It certainly wasn't the reason he'd wished to marry Edie. If marrying her meant being snubbed forever from Society and spending the rest of their days at Wickacre Hall, he would have done it, and gladly.

But Frederick could not deny to himself, at least, that something else had thawed his heart.

A way into the Chance family. An opportunity to be a part of it as an equal, to see his wife… his wife be a part of it.

Frederick swallowed. Now that opportunity was gone. Perhaps forever.

"—told her not to win every time, but that's Dodo's way," George was saying, his chin high. There was a strange sort of look on his face. One of pride. "And when she wins—"

"I think we should be focusing on Pernrith and his lady troubles," William cut across him with a meaningful look.

Frederick groaned. *'Lady troubles'? Dear Lord, that sounded awful.* "I wondered what you all thought I should do. What each of you thought, I mean."

For some reason, his three half-brothers were staring in complete astonishment.

"You… You're asking us?" George prompted curtly. "Each of us? You care?"

The aggressive tone could not be hidden, and Frederick felt the hackles on the back of his neck rise in response.

It had always been this way. William made him feel inadequate, like he was always fighting to be considered a Chance. John made him feel as though he were on his second chance with the family, and that any slip would precipitate his removal from their good graces. And George... Well. George made him feel like an outsider, someone who would never truly belong.

When it came to facing all three of them together, Frederick slipped into his defensive strategy of saying little and remaining as stiff and polite as possible.

And now here he was, baring his soul and asking for their help.

Perhaps I should not have asked them, Frederick could not help but think, hopes sinking. *Perhaps I've taken a liberty, going directly to them.*

He was only half a Chance. Yet here he was, bothering a duke, a marquess, and an earl—merely because he had not convinced a woman to marry him. As he had known he never would.

"Do not worry about it. I should never have asked... It was foolish." The tightness around his torso was painful, making each word a challenge. But still, he spoke. "I apologize for bothering you."

If he had hosted his three half-brothers, Frederick would have been able to stride across the drawing room in four steps and would have already reached the door to usher them out. But as it was William who had insisted on hosting, his drawing room was quite a bit larger than his own.

That was why he had only managed to get halfway across the room when the most unexpected thing happened.

George put out an arm.

Frederick walked into it. He halted, then looked in unconcealed astonishment at the gesture his half-brother—*that* half-brother had made.

"We... Oh, hell." George sighed. "We may not have behaved the best in the past—"

"Speak for yourself," cut in John with a grin.

Both Frederick and George turned to glare.

The Marquess of Aylesbury put his hands up in mock surrender. "Just a jest. Merely a jest..."

Frederick turned back to George, hardly able to believe what he was hearing. Was his brother... was the Earl of Lindow, the brother who had so actively hated him for so many years, actually attempting *to be nice*?

George cleared his throat. "We have definitely not behaved in the best way in the past. I more than the others, you know that. But... damn it. It doesn't mean we're not brothers. Of a sort. And it doesn't mean we won't try to act in the best way now. So sit down."

"'Sit... Sit down'?" Frederick repeated.

He was surely dreaming. There was no possibility the gruff, angry man he had known for decades was actually trying something different—something new?

"Sit down," George repeated gruffly. "We can fix this."

Frederick's eyes widened. "We can?"

"I hope so," said William, rising from the window seat and walking over to them. He clapped a hand on each brother's shoulder while John remained seated. "And I hope to God this will be the last time I save one of you boys from a mess of your own—"

"'Boys'?" said John and George together.

"'Last time'?" repeated Frederick, who had never received—as far as he was aware—much help from William.

"'Mess'?" said new three voices.

Frederick hesitated. "'Mess'?"

The door to the hall opened and the three wives poured in. From their positions, Frederick rather suspected they had been leaning against the door for some time. Listening. Listening to their conversation.

He recalled the thump the Chance brothers had heard minutes ago as the wives burst into hysterical laughter at the looks on their husbands' faces. Perhaps it had not been a passionate round of cards…

"Dear God," Frederick muttered, face burning.

How long had they been standing there? Had they heard everything—had they been doing so merely to laugh?

But as his pulse raced with the embarrassment and shame of it all, he saw to his surprise that it was his brothers who looked mortified. It appeared, by the tenor of their groans and the way William was shaking his head ruefully, that this was not a new occurrence.

Which I would know, Frederick thought with an awful lurch of his stomach, *if I were truly a part of this family.*

"What have I said," said William heavily, sighing all the while, "about listening at doors?"

His wife, Alice, grinned as she slipped an arm around his waist and kissed him lightly on the nose. "You said a great deal, though I have to say, I thought it was for Maudy's benefit more than anyone else's."

Despite himself, Frederick grinned. His niece, Maude, was a complete handful, and like his two half-brothers, he doted on the little girl. She was a treasure, and if she grew up anything like her mother, she was going to be a rascal.

"D-Don't complain t-too much," said Florence, embracing her husband, John, swiftly before releasing him. "You should be th-thanking us on bended knee!"

And Frederick's spirits rose. There was a look of confident delight on the three wives' faces, each one of them—a confidence that could surely only mean one thing…

"I hope you have decided to come with solutions," he said formally. "Good day, ladies."

"And that's the first kind word offered, and of course it's from Lord Pernrith," said Alice with a nudge of her elbow against her husband's side.

"Ouch!"

"He always was the best gentleman of the four of you," said Dodo severely to her husband.

Frederick cast a worried look at George to see how he would take this remark coming from the woman he had so recently married. It was hardly the most politic thing anyone could say.

Apparently, however, George was happy to take criticism from his wife. "Undoubtedly."

"Solutions," Frederick repeated, his pulse starting to race. The sudden influx of people into the drawing room had ceased to be a concern—how could it? If these ladies could help him win Edie's heart...

"Of c-course we have s-solutions," Florence said, drawing herself up.

Dodo was grinning and she exchanged a look with her two sisters-in-law before jerking her head to the husbands and saying calmly, "What, you thought you were going to get actual help from these dolts?"

Chapter Nineteen

December 13, 1812

"**A**ND YOU ARE certain it has not arrived?"

Edie had not intended her voice to be harsh, but then, she had been waiting what felt like forever. Certainly all day.

She glanced at the grandfather clock in the corner of the morning room. Oh. Well, a few hours, at least. It was ten o'clock, which was admittedly at least five hours earlier than she thought it was.

How was it possible that she had waited so very long and it was only ten o'clock in the morning?

"I will tell you the moment that it arrives," said her father soothingly. "And I am sure it will not be long. It is getting closer to Christmas, after all. You know how everything slows down. The newspaper—"

"I thought it would be here by now," said Mrs. Teagan absentmindedly. She was embroidering what appeared to be a large cushion cover, sitting by the window to get the little daylight that the wintery December morning afforded. "I mean, it's past ten o'clock."

Edie caught the warning glance her father shot the woman who would, in a week, become Lady Stewart. Unfortunately, her former chaperone was so absorbed with her embroidery, she did not notice.

"It is late, isn't it?" Edie said wretchedly. "The one day I want to read it—"

"I've been saying for years that you should be reading the newspaper. It's an excellent source of information about the world," pointed out Lord Stewart mildly.

He was seated halfway between the two ladies of his life, a book open on his knee. It was a book of maps, as far as Edie could make out. There had been threats—mention, that was, of himself and Mrs. Teagan taking a tour overseas once they were married. It had been something Mrs. Teagan had always wished to do, apparently.

Edie had tried to smile when he had told her, though it had been a challenge. Was she to lose father and chaperone simultaneously? Where was she to go? Off in the company of some distant relative? Would her father hire her a companion?

"I read about the world," she said aloud.

Her father snorted. "Those scandal sheets do not count as—"

"They certainly told me more about what was happening in Society than any of those newspapers of yours," Edie said hotly.

She knew the irritation bubbling inside her was not truly directed at her father. Lord Stewart had done nothing to upset her, save, perhaps, for proposing matrimony to Mrs. Teagan yesterday—who had, according to her father, accepted in floods of tears. But then again, Edie herself had encouraged it. Well, perhaps, she had not encouraged the *speed* at which her father had moved.

Lord Stewart had taken great pains to ask Edie whether this was a good sign or a bad sign. *"The floods of tears, I mean."*

And Edie had comforted him with the little knowledge she had about such things, mostly based on the novels she borrowed from the circulating library, and the paragraphs and paragraphs she had eagerly consumed from the scandal sheets.

"Yes, Father. Yes, I think that's a very good sign."

It wasn't Mrs. Teagan's fault, either, that she was getting her happily ever after and Edie was not.

In truth, Edie could think of much worse ends to the year. Christmas was almost upon them, and there was going to be laughter in the house from a happily married couple—something the Stewart house had not known for many years.

The new Season would soon be upon them, and some other flourishing rose would be named... But then, Edie hadn't always liked the attention the title had brought her. This was good news, surely.

So why did her heart ache so painfully? Why was it impossible to sleep through the night without tears? Why was everything so difficult when she knew Frederick was out there in the world, believing she cared more about her reputation than him?

"You are certain it was not taken straight to the kitchens?" Edie could not help but ask.

Her father sighed. "You have asked me that already."

"I know, but—"

"All the servants have been given strict instructions to bring the day's newspaper to you, not to me, and most certainly not down to the kitchen to be ironed," said Lord Stewart, turning a page in his book. "Honestly, I cannot remember why we started doing that. It makes no sense. It must be such a waste of time..."

Edie allowed her father to continue as she sighed and curled her feet under her in the armchair.

She had been certain her plan would work. It was foolproof—at least, it had felt so at the time. There was little she wouldn't do to reach Frederick, but merely turning up at his house was absolutely out of the question.

After all, why would he even bother to see her? After she had hurt him so terribly...

The door opened and Edie's head jerked up. "Yes?"

"The newspaper, miss," said the maid nervously.

Edie had launched herself from the armchair and wrenched the carefully folded newspaper from the woman's hand before anyone else could make a sound.

Only then did her father exclaim, "Edie!"

"Now that is hardly ladylike behavior," tutted Mrs. Teagan.

But Edie didn't care. Her pulse was thumping so wildly, it was almost impossible to hear what they were saying. She had rushed back to her armchair, fingers already thumbing open the newspaper, desperately searching for the announcements page. It had to be in here somewhere, didn't it? They wouldn't have forgotten—

"Ah," she breathed slowly, slipping her feet back under her again as her gaze raked over the page.

This was one of the reasons she despised newspapers. How was one supposed to find anything in a thing this big? And the print was so small, it was a wonder anyone could read it. At least *Whispers of the Ton* ensured it was easy to digest every morning. Not a behemoth like this…

Ink smeared on her fingers as Edie brushed her fingertips across the columns, desperately trying to find it. But no matter how her attention flickered across each line, she could not find what she sought.

… announce the sad demise of…

… welcome the newest arrival to…

… has lately returned to town and is eager to return to…

Words flickered before Edie's eyes, but none of them were the ones she had carefully penned.

What had gone wrong?

"You took my instructions to the office on Fleet Street, did you not, Father?" Edie asked, looking up.

Her father glanced up from his book of maps. "I beg your pardon?"

"The note and the instructions I gave you," she repeated, as patiently as she could manage. Which in truth, was not that patiently. Could he not understand just how crucial this was? "You took them to *The Times*'s office, did you not?"

Edie had wished to take them herself. What did she care about the expectations of Society? Caring too much about what the world thought, even for a fleeting moment, had only brought her into this mess—surely, the swiftest way to get out of it was to cease caring at all?

Her father was not sure about that, and Mrs. Teagan was quite certain of the opposite. No woman under *her* care was going to do anything so rash as walk into a tradesperson's office! Even if that tradesperson was almost respectable.

"Office?" Lord Stewart said vaguely. "Oh. Oh, yes, I gave them the note and tried to explain as best I could."

Edie's hopes sank as her stomach lurched. "'As best you could'?"

"Well, it was a tad unusual, my dear," said her father fairly, as though she were being most unreasonable about the whole thing. "Truly, I had never heard of such a—"

"It was an idea I had, that was all. It was not supposed to be the sort of thing that you would have heard of," Edie attempted to explain as a knock at their front door sounded through the house. "I never expected it to be a common thing. That was the whole—"

Both she and her father turned to the door to the hallway. A strange commotion was slipping under the door—a noise Edie had never heard before.

Shouting? In the hall?

"What on earth is going on?" asked her father blearily, his mind firmly in Rome, the map of which was open on his lap.

"I have no idea," said Edie slowly, her gaze and attention dropping once more to the announcements page in *The Times*, which remained on her own lap. "Mrs. Teagan?"

"It sounds like trouble, whatever it is," said Mrs. Teagan primly, her attention remaining on her embroidery. "And where there's trouble—"

The door to the hall burst open and there, panting and with Jenkins the butler clutching his shoulder, attempting to remove him from the room, was—

"Frederick," gasped Edie.

"Pernrith?" said Lord Stewart.

"My lord!" exclaimed Mrs. Teagan.

Her father blinked rapidly, then waved a hand. "That will be all, Jenkins."

"My lord, he—"

"*That will be all.*"

Jenkins let go of Frederick, then bowed stiffly before stepping away. The four of them stood there in silence, all staring at each other. It appeared none of them quite knew what was to happen next.

Edie could see the confusion. Mrs. Teagan was waiting for Lord Stewart to say something, but her father was evidently thrown by the fact that Frederick was not wearing coat or cravat, his shirt open at the neck in a manner quite improper. And she...

How could she say anything? What she had hoped for had occurred. Frederick was here, and he could only be here, surely, if he wished to speak to her.

But then why did his expression look so cold, so distant? Why did he not speak?

"What is the meaning of this?" Frederick said quietly, pulling something out of his waistcoat pocket.

Edie's pulse was thundering painfully, but it skipped a beat when she saw what he was holding.

A scrap of newspaper. A scrap of a newspaper that looked, from this short distance, very similar to the one in her lap.

Silence fell in the morning room.

Then her father cleared his throat. "Ah, I have just remembered, I haven't—"

"I believe I am needed elsewhere," said Mrs. Teagan, rising hastily from her seat and depositing her embroidery upon it. "Somewhere else, at any rate. David—"

"I quite agree," Lord Stewart said swiftly, offering her his arm. "Anywhere but here."

Frederick watched, apparently bemused, as Lord Stewart and Mrs. Teagan pushed past him out of the morning room into the hall, the latter slipping the door shut between them.

And that left them. Just Edie and Frederick.

Her pulse was throbbing painfully in her ears, and it was all she appeared able to hear. Precisely what she had thought this conversation would be, she had not been sure—but she had never expected Frederick to arrive half-dressed and looking half-possessed.

Had she done the right thing?

Yes. Edie had been unable to think of any other method to convince him that this, this whatever it was between us, was more important to her than her reputation.

Short of turning up at his house and banging on the door, pleading to be let in.

In fact, if her father had asked her mere minutes ago to justify her plan, Edie was fairly certain she could have done a good job at it.

All those arguments fled her mind as Frederick stood there, chest heaving as though he had run here all the way from Pernrith House.

With it went her certainty. What had she done?

Well, she couldn't maintain the silence much longer. However this conversation was going to go, it needed to happen. She couldn't live much longer in this limbo of hoping and not knowing.

"My lord," Edie said formally. She rose, placing the newspaper on the armchair behind her with shaking hands. "H-How pleasant to—"

"Did you do this?" Frederick asked, thrusting a finger at the scrap of newspaper he was holding as he took a hesitant step toward her.

Edie swallowed but stepped forward in turn, her curiosity propelling her forward. "Oh, did you find it? I had the devil of a time attempting to find—"

She cut off her words as Frederick marched past her seemingly without a second look. She heard the rustle of paper.

Turning, she watched as Frederick picked up the newspaper she had so recently discarded, placed it on the console table just to the left of the fireplace, and spread out the announcements page.

"This," Frederick said quietly, his voice soft once more, all fire gone. "Was this you?"

Hardly knowing how she was managing to walk, let alone breathe at the same time, Edie moved to stand beside him.

The intoxication of his presence almost overwhelmed her. Oh, it had been too long since she had been with Frederick. His scent, a medley of sandalwood and vanilla, was paired with the heat from his torso, the very evident strength in his arms as the tension in him roared.

Edie swallowed. Tempting as it was to look at what he was pointing at in the newspaper, a much greater temptation was curling itself around her heart, begging to be heard.

A temptation to take that hand and place it on her waist and kiss him—

"Miss Stewart," Frederick said stiffly. "Did you write this?"

Edie swiftly forced her outstretched hand back to her side. *Miss Stewart.* Well, she had known what would happen when she had stormed out of Pernrith House all those days ago. She just had not known how much it would hurt.

Her gaze drifted to the announcements page, falling onto the small paragraph she had been seeking to no avail.

> *The engagement is announced between Frederick Chance, the Right Honorable Viscount Pernrith, younger son of the late Duke of Cothrom, Stanphrey Lacey, and the Honorable Miss Edith Stewart, only daughter of David Stewart, the Right Honorable Baron Stewart, and the late Lady Vanessa Stewart, Woodhurst. This second engagement is this time founded on love and affection, and the wedding will occur very soon.*

A small smile curled around her lips. Well, they had put it in precisely as she had requested. That was something. One never knew with newspaper people.

Edie looked up slowly, half fearful, not knowing what expression she would find on Frederick's face.

And her lungs tightened as she saw—

Hope. And pain. And confusion, and a longing that mirrored her own.

It had been a bold move. Edie would have been astonished at any other lady in the *ton* doing such a forward thing, but she'd had to do something. She knew how much Frederick relied on, trusted the newspaper.

"She'll be as right as rain in the morning, as long as you have a copy of The Times *for her to read at breakfast."*

"Well, thankfully, Mrs. Teagan and I share a taste in reading."

What better place to announce her love and affection?

"Was this you?" Frederick asked softly, his hazel eyes fixed on hers. "I thought for a moment... Lindow. But I don't think he would do something so cruel."

Edie flinched as though the blow had been a physical one. Cruel? He believed it cruel?

Well, there was nothing to do but confess. She had tried, and she had done what she had thought was right. She could not be blamed for getting it all so entirely wrong.

Swallowing hard, she whispered, "Yes."

"Yes?" Frederick said, catching the word.

Oh, he was only a few inches away. If she just leaned forward—

Edie stopped herself just in time. "Yes, it was me."

She expected remonstrances. She expected a critique. She expected Frederick to say just how cruel and unfair it was of her to do such a thing without his agreement.

What she did not expect was for Frederick to gently lift a hand as though to cup her cheek, only for that hand to fall back to his side.

Edie leaned closer toward him. All she wanted was a touch. To know he did not hate her. That though they evidently could not be together, because he so clearly did not wish it any longer, that he did not loathe her.

Then Frederick said something she could never have predicted. "You... You did not read yesterday's scandal sheets, did you?"

Edie blinked, startled by the sudden change in topic. "You mean *Whispers of the Ton*?"

"Yes, that one. Or another. Or any of them," Frederick said, his voice soft.

Heat blossomed in her cheeks. She had not read a single scandal sheet since she had argued with Frederick.

"You care too much about what the world thinks. You've read that scandal sheet, that Whispers of the Ton, and you think—"

His words had rung in her ears far longer than, perhaps, he had expected. Each time she had attempted to read one, a strange sense of sadness had overwhelmed her. She hadn't even picked one up this morning.

"I haven't read any of them," Edie admitted, swaying as she stood. First away from him, and then... then toward him.

She wasn't sure how much longer she could stand here and not be touching him. After sharing so much with Frederick, the divide between them was distressing. An agonizing, uncrossable distance.

"How could you have known that?" she wondered aloud.

Frederick grinned, and it was as though a second fire had been lit in the morning room. Heat poured through Edie, a sense of comforting closeness she had desperately craved the instant she had lost it.

The moment she had walked out of Pernrith House.

"Here," he said gently, moving his hand.

Once again, Edie thought he was going to touch her, and once again, she was disappointed. Frederick's hand pulled something from another pocket—a scandal sheet, from the look of it.

He was still smiling when he handed it to her. "Look."

Edie took it but continued to stare, unsure precisely what he was doing. How on earth had he known she had not read a scandal sheet since they had parted?

"I... I don't underst—"

"The very bottom of the second page," Frederick said gently, and there was a genialness in his eyes that softened every word he spoke. "Read it."

Edie's stomach lurched. *Oh, no.* What had happened—what had been written about her?

Frederick Chance, Viscount Pernrith, suffered on a daily basis from the gossip that people muttered about him, she knew. Had she now brought even more disrepute onto his head?

"Read it."

Turning over the paper, unsure how she was still standing when such emotions poured through her, Edie let her focus meander to the bottom of the page. Past snide mentions of fashion disasters, past a hint that someone's husband was in fact not as faithful as the *ton* believed, past a delicate reminder that so-and-so's child had been born only six months after their wedding...

Her heart jolted.

> *It has come to our attention that a certain gentleman wishes to apologize to a certain young lady—and we say that advisedly, because the gentleman in question has done the unbelievable and actually written to us. Viscount P., whose recent engagement announcement surprised the ton, now wishes it to be known that he was an absolute rogue to the delightful Miss S., and he hopes that she will one day forgive him. His love, it appears, will continue whether he is forgiven or not.*

Edie had forgotten to breathe. Inhaling a sudden gasp of air into her lungs, which were painfully crying out for relief, her eyes flickered over the paragraph once again.

His... His love?

Looking up, Edie saw that there was a quirk on Frederick's lips.

"It appears we had much the same idea," he said quietly. "I do love you, Edie."

Somehow, his hands were about her waist. Edie could not recall him moving, but then, it did not matter. He was where he should be. Close to her.

"I am so sorry for what I said—more, what I did not say," she said in a rush. "Oh, Frederick, I can hardly believe I acted in that—"

"I expected a great deal from you, and worse. I judged you the moment I thought you could not abandon everything you had ever been taught," Frederick said fiercely, as though the blame were all his.

Which it wasn't. Edie knew she shared much of the fault. "But I love you, Frederick, and I should have—"

"It's how we were raised. Even I think like that sometimes," Frederick said with a sigh as he pulled her close. "It's not your fault. It's—what did you say?"

Edie blinked, suddenly shy. "What?"

"You..." He leaned forward, nuzzling her nose with his own. "You love me?"

"Of course I love you. You're the most precious man I've ever met." Edie gasped as she lifted her lips for a kiss.

It was like coming home. The searing heat of Frederick's lips was matched only by the thrumming need to deepen the kiss that poured through Edie's lungs. Pleasure tingled through her tongue and sparked at her breasts as she pushed them against his own broad chest.

This was it. This was everything. This was her Frederick.

How long the kiss lasted, she was not sure. All Edie knew was that when they finally broke apart due to lack of breath, her hair was mussed, his lips were stained, and she wanted to do nothing more than kiss this man, like that, every day, for the rest of her life.

"You really don't resent me?" It was the fear that had remained with her for so long.

"Edie, you mustn't—"

"Because you'd be within your right to. I behaved abominably," she said in a rush. "I should never have hesitated. I should never have made you think—I *did* think, a little, about what Society would say. I know you said it's how we were raised, what Society expects, but—oh, Frederick, I want to be better than that!"

"And we will be," he said ardently, kissing her swiftly on the mouth. "Edie, I adore you. I could never have imagined… We will have the rest of our lives to be better. Better than the rest of them. Better to each other."

Better to each other…

Edie sighed happily as she lifted her lips for another kiss. "I like the sound of that."

Chapter Twenty

December 23, 1812

"You know," Frederick jested as the carriage jostled them, "it would have been a great deal easier to just stay engaged."

Edie laughed and a glow spread through him. It always did whenever he was able to make Edie laugh. It was a gift. Having her in his life was a gift. And now...

"Yes, I can see how difficult wedding planning has been—for you," she teased, tucking a curl behind her ear. "Getting the special license, sending out invitations for the wedding a mere week in advance. You poor thing!"

Frederick grinned. "Glad to see I am finally getting the recognition I deserve!"

Their carriage filled with their giggles and he wondered whether he would ever again be this happy.

It was starting to become an occupational hazard of being around Edie—being ridiculously happy. He had been happy that morning, when he had first seen her at the end of the aisle. He had been even happier when Lord Stewart had stepped with her along the nave, placing Edie's hand on his with a stern but fair look. Frederick's happiness had increased as the vows had been spoken, as he'd heard them echo around the small church. When they had stepped out of the church, their families processing out of it, and Frederick had stolen a kiss—

Well. Happiness was not really the right word for the sudden spark of contentment that had soared through him at that moment.

And now here he was, only minutes later, traveling back to the Stewart house with his wife beside him.

His wife.

"My wife," Frederick said aloud, knowing he would never tire of that particular phrase.

Edie raised an eyebrow. "Yes, husband?"

His stomach lurched, a pleasant sensation. A sense that finally, his dreams of the future had come true. That the hopes he'd had for a life with Edie, a life he had thought lost to him forever, was actually his.

Not just in the grasp of his hand, but a world he could now walk into.

"Did you enjoy our quiet wedding?"

Edie snorted. "Quiet wedding?"

"Well, we only invited nine people," Frederick pointed out fairly. "Your father and stepmother—"

"I still can't believe they got their own special license and married before us," she interjected with a shake of her head. "My father was hardly quick off the mark."

"—and my three half-brothers—"

"*Brothers*," Edie corrected with a knowing look. "You know that's how they think of you."

Frederick did not bother to argue with her. She may have been a Chance now—in his opinion, the finest one of the bunch—but that did not mean she completely understood the decades-long complexity of the Chance brothers.

"My brothers, then, and their wives," accepted Frederick with a small shrug. "And Maudy. That is only nine people. I never expected—"

"Did you not?" Edie laughed, her veil shimmering in the watery winter sunlight. "I knew half the *ton* would turn up."

How, he was not sure. It had certainly been a shock to watch the little church they had chosen fill up, and up, and up, until it had been standing room only at the back. And even that had been almost full.

"Why on earth they would want to—"

"You are jesting with me, aren't you?" His new wife narrowed her eyes. "You cannot honestly be surprised so much of Society wanted to watch the scandalous marriage of two very non-scandalous people?"

Well, she has a point there. "The flourishing rose and the thorns?"

Edie nudged him in the ribs. "You do talk nonsense."

"Something like that," Frederick said lightly.

His chest did not feel light. Oh, the wedding had happened, and she was his, and there was nothing that could separate them now—nothing. Yet there was still that fear something terrible was going to happen. A sense all this goodness was not his, that he had not earned it. That at any moment it could all be taken away.

Frederick swallowed. *And the thought of Edie being taken away...*

"Besides, I think in truth that most of them were disappointed," she was saying calmly. "After all the things we had printed"—Frederick laughed—" I believe they thought there was going to be a duel at the altar, at the very least."

"So you're telling me you think we should have given them more of a show?" he teased.

Edie nudged him again as she giggled, the carriage rattling along the London streets. "I don't know what we could have done!"

"Oh, I don't know," said Frederick, a flicker of need dancing just below his stomach. "Something like this, perhaps..."

He had taken the precaution of ordering the very largest carriage to transport them from the church to the Stewarts' house. Not because Edie's gown was particularly voluminous. In fact, it was a rather elegant thing that swept down to the floor with very few layers, as far as he could make out.

But after their journey back to London from Wickacre Hall in which he and Edie had pushed the space within the small hired carriage to the limit, Frederick had been determined. This time, the carriage would be large.

At least large enough for this...

"Frederick!" Edie exclaimed in apparent surprise as he leaned over her and pressed a kiss on her neck. Then, "Frederick..."

He had taken a second precaution too, which Frederick was delighted he had foreseen. A little coin pressed into the driver's hand had ensured that instead of taking them directly to the Stewarts' home, where the wedding breakfast was to be hosted, he would drive them...

Well. Anywhere.

The instruction was to keep moving until Frederick told him to head, finally, to the Stewart house. And not a moment sooner.

Which meant that unlike Edie, gasping and squirming with delight under his lips and fingers, Frederick knew they would not be disturbed. Not until they wanted to be.

"We can't—we mustn't—" Edie gasped.

How she was managing to do that, he did not know. He was doing his utmost to make it impossible for her to speak.

"Be quiet and kiss me," Frederick said in a rasping voice quite unlike his own.

"But we—"

"I paid the driver," he said hurriedly in a low voice, lowering his mouth so it reached the cresting peaks of her breasts. *Oh, God, but she was perfect.* "We'll be driving around until we're done. Until you *are* undone."

Edie's gasp may have been one of desire, or surprise, he did not know. He did not need to know. Frederick's fingers had finally managed to discover the hem of her gown and were now creeping up her leg, past her knee—

"Frederick—"

"Do you want me to stop?" he asked raggedly, halting.

Pulling back, Frederick looked at the woman he adored in fear that he had perhaps gone too far. Unlike so many of the gentlemen of the *ton*—though thankfully none of his brothers, and as far as he knew, no one in the Dulverton Club—he did not consider a woman to be property after marriage.

Edie had her own desires and her own needs. Sometimes, that need could be for him to halt.

"I... No," she admitted, face flushed and lips parted. "But someone will hear—"

"You'll have to be quiet, then," Frederick said with a teasing grin as he returned his lips to hers and his fingers continued stroking up her thighs.

It was heavenly, to taste the sweet, aching need on her lips, to delve his tongue into her wet mouth just as his fingers slipped into her welcoming folds.

Edie squirmed against the carriage seat, her breathing quickening. "Frederick—"

It did not take long. He knew precisely what she wanted, how she needed him to ease, to slowly build a rhythm around her nub as his fingers darted deeper, deeper, stroking the wet ache in her until Edie's whole body shuddered and she moaned in his mouth.

When she finally fell back against the seat, Frederick's need for her was exquisite.

Well, that was just something he would have to learn to live with. It wasn't as though—

"Edie?" he murmured, confused.

Because it did not make any sense. Why on earth had Edie slipped onto the floor of the carriage, kneeling there as though she were searching for a hairpin she had dropped?

"What are you—"

"I think it's about time that you received a little attention in this marriage, my Lord Pernrith," Edie said slowly, leaning forward and twisting him so that he faced her, diagonally, across the carriage.

For one heartbeat longer, Frederick did not understand. "But what are you—"

Then her fingers started unbuttoning the front of his breeches.

His eyes widened. "You can't—"

"Oh, can't I?" Edie said wickedly, mischief and desire in her eyes. "You think I have never wanted to do this?"

Frederick groaned. This was too much—yet if she didn't follow through on what she was suggesting, he was half-certain he was going to come in his breeches, anyway. "But if I groan or shout—"

"You'll just have to be quiet, then," said the minx, repeating his own words back to him.

He had a very cutting and witty retort to shoot back at her—and would have done, if Frederick hadn't suddenly been forced to tilt his head back and bite his lip as Edie took his manhood and—

Oh, Christ, this is heaven. Her wet lips parted and gently kissed the leaking slit at the end of his manhood, and Edie slowly inched him into her mouth, taking him deeper and deeper until Frederick could no longer hold himself back. He thrust forward, sheathing himself in her desperate mouth, and he groaned.

"Edie, oh, Edie…"

With his head back and his fingers splayed in her hair, Frederick could do nothing but lie there, helpless in the wake of her sucking mouth, a rhythm building slowly as she acclimatized herself to his length.

It did not take long. Frederick had been yearning for her the moment they had agreed on their real engagement—agreed they would not touch each other again until they were husband and wife.

When he exploded into her mouth, Edie suckled and twisted her tongue around him, expanding the pleasure through his whole body. Without saying a word, she released him and returned to the seat beside him.

The two of them lay back, panting, otherwise silent. Frederick was certain the world would stop spinning at some point, but he wasn't sure when.

Eventually, after blinking for several minutes, he turned to his wife. "We should—"

"I know," Edie said ruefully, attempting to tug her gown into a more decorous position. "They'll be wondering where we are."

"Ah, the vagaries of London busyness," Frederick said with a grin. "We can't be blamed if there was a carriage overturned, or a cart halted across a road, or... or something."

He tapped the roof of the carriage most reluctantly, and the vehicle took a left at the next turning.

"True," said Edie quietly, slipping his arm around her waist and pressing a kiss onto his neck. "But until we get there..."

Frederick entirely lost track of where they were, but no one could blame him. A beautiful woman who was now his wife kissing him furiously? No man could be expected to be aware of one's surroundings in such a situation.

It was slightly awkward, however, when a person cleared their throat. Loudly. And it wasn't Edie.

Frederick and Edie jerked apart. The carriage had ceased to move—moreover, the door was open, and a Stewart footman was standing there, pink in the face and eyes averted.

"I didn't—we weren't," Frederick began. Then realization dawned and he chuckled. "We are married, Edie."

His new wife was just as pink as the footman. "Yes, I know that."

"That means we can do whatever we want," he said cheerfully. "Excuse me, my good man."

Edie began to laugh as the footman, confused, took a step back. "Frederick, you can't—"

"I can, and I have," he said, snapping the door shut and returning a modicum of privacy to them.

"But you can't intend for us to sit in the carriage on the drive, and... well, and *kiss* while our guests wait for us?"

It sounded an excellent idea to Frederick. In fact, he had never heard better. "And why not?"

Edie stared, open-mouthed, her lips bruised by the fervor of his so recent attentions. Then she wet her lips, causing a dart of lust to shoot through Frederick. "Well, if that is what you wish, who am I to deny my husband?"

Frederick groaned as she returned to his arms. "Dear God, I love you..."

Minutes passed. How many, he was not sure. But when Edie's head was tucked into his neck and he was stroking her mussed hair—the veil had been lost long ago—Frederick knew he had to say something of what was in his heart.

"I... I cannot believe it. I am married. To you."

Edie's chuckle was gentle, but pressed as she was into his side, he could feel it as well as hear it. "You were waiting for me for a long time, were you?"

Frederick's stomach lurched. "You cannot know how long."

All those years he'd thought he would never find anyone who would wish to reduce herself to his circumstances. All that time he'd spent in company, knowing not a single woman there would even consider him as a partner.

God, his life had been empty. He had always known himself to be alone, but Frederick had not known how truly lonely he'd been until Edie had walked into his life.

When she had walked into that little alcove at Lady Romeril's ball, with no idea who he was...

"My life is so full with you in it," Frederick breathed, his voice choked.

Edie lifted her head and stared seriously. "You do know I love you, don't you?"

"I do know. Of course, I would like to hear it every day. You could have married anyone—"

"I married you," she said firmly.

"But you didn't have to." Frederick could hardly explain just what it meant to him that she had chosen him. Her! Miss Edith Stewart, the flourishing rose of the year's Season!

Edie's golden-brown gaze was steady as she examined him. "Yes, I suppose there might have been... Well. Other options. But my father wanted me to marry a good man, and I have."

He well knew the hopes Lord Stewart had had for his daughter. Hopes that had now been dashed—though Edie's revelation that her father had known of their foolish scheme from the very beginning had certainly been an eye-opener.

"But I think I have done one better," Edie continued softly, splaying her hand against his chest. Surely, she could feel his pulse, rushing forward at a great pace. "I didn't just marry a good man. I married the best man I have ever met."

Frederick's mind rebelled against the notion. "My heritage—my background—"

"That is just the beginning of your story." There was fire in Edie's eyes now.

It was strange; since their re-engagement, for want of a better term, she had been almost vehement in her attempt to convince him his scandalous beginnings were not so very scandalous after all.

She had not quite convinced him—but Frederick had to admit it was a pleasant sensation to know how he had been born did not matter to the person who mattered the most.

"Well, if that is just the beginning," said Frederick with a raised eyebrow, "does that make this my happy ending? Ouch!"

Edie had tapped him on the chest. "You do not think you have got enough already while we've been in this carriage?"

"I'll never have enough of you."

Her expression softened. "Oh, Frederick."

"Besides, I did not mean it like that," he added with a chuckle. "You have a far more scandalous mind than I do."

"That is what comes, I suppose, of reading the *Whispers of the Ton* every day," Edie quipped with a grin. "Anyway, I don't think this is an ending, not really. It's more… the beginning of a new story."

Delight spread across Frederick. This woman. This kind, and caring, and soft, and delicate, yet strong and determined woman.

There was no one like her. Never before had he encountered someone with the ability to learn and adapt as Edie Stewart. They may not have been made for each other—they were from entirely different walks of life, his title of Viscount Pernrith notwithstanding.

But they had loved each other, and that had made them right for each other. Over time, there would undoubtedly be difficulties. There was no real life without challenges. But having Edie by his side would make them infinitely more bearable. Besides, he was starting to think Edie would be far better suited to facing the world than he was.

"If you give me half a chance," Frederick said seriously, placing a hand over her own on his heart, "I'll… I would do anything to make you happy, Edie."

She leaned forward and kissed him. "I don't want half a Chance—I want you, all of you."

"Oh, you know what I—"

"And you know what I meant," Edie cut across him with a wry expression. "Time to stop thinking of yourself as half of anything and start allowing the people who care about you to love you. I'm… Well. I'm honored to be your wife."

Frederick's affections seemed to expand. "You are?"

Edie nodded, and ignoring the waiting footmen, the waiting guests, and their family, who were undoubtedly concerned about where they were, she moved back into his arms. His hands came around her, pulling her tightly into his embrace. He breathed her in, felt the movement of her, and knew this happiness was one he simply could not believe.

"I am honored to be your wife," Edie murmured.

He swallowed back tears. "And I am honored to be your husband."

"Well, that's settled, then," she said lightly with a kiss pressed onto his chest. "We'll be the Chances together. Two whole Chances, wholly in love."

And Frederick knew the happiness he felt, that expanded with every moment with Edie, that he could not contain and did not understand—that happiness would only grow with every passing day.

"No longer half a Chance, but two Chances," he murmured. "I like it."

Epilogue

December 25, 1812

"Happy Christmas!" The voices rang out all around the drawing room at Stanphrey Lacey, and Edie smiled shyly at the ruckus it caused.

Her family had always been small. Herself, and her father. Then Mrs. Teagan. And now...

"My goodness, this brandy is excellent stuff," her father said happily, emptying his glass. "But you young people have far more stamina than most—I'm afraid I'm going to have to retire."

Edie had been surprised her father had managed to keep up with what he called "you young people" for so long. After all, he was getting on in years, and the last few months... Well. They could hardly be described as restful.

"I will accompany you to bed," said the new Lady Stewart, flushing at the mention of a bedchamber. "I... Ahem. Yes. Tired."

Smiling broadly, Edie squeezed her stepmother's hands. "Thank you for a wonderful day. Your company has been invaluable."

Her former chaperone flushed, demurred, and very happily took her new husband's arm—a husband that, to Edie's eyes, looked ten years younger.

The luxury of Stanphrey Lacey had undoubtedly had its effect. Edie had never seen a manor house more ideally suited to hosting, and the Cothroms had been insistent that everyone join them for the festive season.

The drawing room had been decorated to the hilt, covered in ribbons of red and gold, holly and ivy garlands festooned all over the place, and more candles than was surely safe. And yet Edie rather had the impression that the place was dazzling at any time of year. The marble statues situated in the small alcoves were stunning, as were the huge portraits that lined the walls, elegant vistas and refined landscapes that told of a family who had been on the Grand Tour for many generations.

And within the splendid room: a family.

"Oh, such a shame," said Alice, the Duchess of Cothrom, with a sparkling laugh. "But does this mean you'll be sufficiently rested for the Boxing Day hunt?"

"I hope so, my dear lady, I do hope so," said Lord Stewart, beaming. "Good night, all! Good night, my flourishing rose."

Edie permitted her father to brush her head with a kiss, squeezing his hand as he and the new Lady Stewart departed the drawing room.

He truly loved his daughter—and he wanted the best for her even if they had, at times, disagreed precisely on what the best was. Her mother had been his flourishing rose, and he had been determined, for a while, to hold on to her daughter in much the same way.

But he had given her his blessing, freed her from the constraints of being the perfect flourishing rose Society had wished for. And that had meant she had—

"You do look rather dazzling," said Frederick quietly, seated by her on the sofa. "A flourishing rose, indeed."

Edie snorted quietly as she pulled his arm around her, snuggling into him with a level of intimacy she would have been mortified at mere months ago.

No longer. The Chance family, rowdy and busy and confusing as it was, had welcomed her with open arms. Though she was still growing accustomed to so much noise about the place, it was impossible to deny that she was not a part of this boisterous family.

"I'm not saying you're wrong. I'm just saying that I am right," said John, the Marquess of Aylesbury, in a teasing voice.

The oldest Chance brother, William, Duke of Cothrom, was standing beside him with a testy look on his face. They had been helping themselves to drinks, as far as Edie could see, but had got waylaid with an argument about—

"I am not about to give you a second wedding present," William said warningly. "You married an heiress!"

"Excuse m-me," pointed out a beautiful woman with fiery-red hair and a twinkle in her eye. "I can hear you, you know!"

Laughter echoed around the room as the two men flushed. Florence, the heiress wife of the Marquess of Aylesbury, grinned as she sat in an armchair near the fire.

"Don't worry about them," said George Chance, the Earl of Lindow, in a mock-whisper that surely carried. He was seated on another armchair, his wife beside him scribbling down something in a notebook. "I'm the easy brother to get along with. You don't have to worry about them."

"I'm sure," said Frederick quietly beside her.

Edie tried to ensure her smile did not falter. She could hear the pain in her husband's voice, even if no one else could, and it hurt to think that so much time had been lost between men who should have been the heart of each other's lives for so long.

And yet the Earl of Lindow and Frederick had been... Well, not at loggerheads. That was perhaps too simple.

The frostiness had melted, however. Edie watched as Frederick met George's glare, and though both of them looked discomforted, there was no denial of the latter's words.

They were trying. Trying was all one could ask.

"You boys are taking too long with those drinks," Alice called over. "Hurry up!"

"Yes, my love," said William quietly, hurrying over with a glass of lemonade for his wife.

Edie gave a sigh of happiness as Frederick's fingers curled around her waist, pulling her closer.

It was bizarre, indeed, to see a man as stiff and formal as the Duke of Cothrom call anyone something as intimate as "my love"—but then, it was impossible to deny the deep affection that was so obvious between William and Alice. Between each of the Chance brothers and their brides.

She sighed happily. This was a family in which affection and friendship were important. It was more than she could have ever hoped for.

"Lemonade never tasted so good," Alice said, taking a large gulp. "You know, ever since I discovered I was with child, I've lost all taste for liquor. It was the same with Maudy."

Maude, Alice's and William's daughter, had gone to bed long ago. Edie had not completely worked out how that had happened—from what she had read, the Cothroms had married but six months ago, and Maude was at least three years old, though she had been delicate enough not to remark upon it. *Another scandal,* she mused with a wry smile, *the Chance family had weathered.*

"Oh, I'm just the s-same," said Florence lightly. Then her cheeks pinked with a scarlet that looked almost painful and she covered her face with her hands.

"Florence!" hissed John, hurrying over to her. "We said we weren't—"

"I know, I d-didn't mean to!" Florence stammered behind her hands.

Edie's lips parted. "You mean—"

"You can't mean!" said Alice, leaning forward with evident delight on her face. "You're not!"

All the Chances had seated themselves now around the fire: Edie and Frederick on one sofa, Dodo and George on another, William standing behind his wife's chair, and John kneeling at Florence's feet.

"We had said we'd wait," said John with a laugh. "And yet it appears that we can't!"

"Oh, but why hold on to such good news as that!" Edie said, unable to help herself. When the entire room turned to look at her, she swallowed. It was going to take some getting used to, this family. "I mean, a child!"

"Quite right too," said Frederick.

Edie's heart lurched.

They hadn't spoken on that topic much. There were so many other things to discuss, so many things to do—so many carnal desires that they ended up getting distracted by, hungry lips reaching to give pleasure, now that they could. Now that they were married.

Children had not precisely been the top of the list, when it came to discussions.

Perhaps now, it would...

"Well, in the spirit of not holding on to good news like that," said Dodo slowly.

Edie stared as George took his wife's hand.

"We hadn't even decided when to tell people," he said, an unusually shy look on his face.

Alice threw up her hands in her excitement. "Not you as well!"

Dodo's blushing nod caused even more calls of congratulations to flow through the room.

"Goodness me, all three of us," said Alice in wonder. "No offense, my dear."

"No offense taken," said Edie, laughing as she leaned into Frederick's comforting strength. "Why, we've only been married ten minutes!"

"Not that that stopped us," he murmured into her ear.

She flushed, but thankfully, it did not appear that anyone had heard him.

Not that it would have been the end of the world. Edie was no great mathematician—certainly not in comparison to her sister-in-law, Dodo—but by her reckoning, it shouldn't be possible for the Lindows to know whether they were with child yet.

Which meant...

Well. She had certainly married into the right family.

"—ch-children all over the p-place," Florence was saying with a grin.

"It'll certainly make things more interesting," said William dryly.

"Just think, cousins for Maudy, as well as a brother or sister," his wife said so softly that Edie only just heard him.

The only response her husband gave, as far as Edie could see, was a squeeze of Alice's shoulder.

Everyone in this family was so different, so unique in their expressions of affection. And yet they had true affection for each other, that much was plain. Even Frederick and George. Of a sort.

"Congratulations on the impending expansion of your family," her husband was saying to the earl formally.

George's jaw appeared a little tighter, just for a moment. "Thank you."

Edie saw the tension in her husband's face and spoke into the silence. "Well, I shall have to hurry up and join you all—I wouldn't wish to get left behind!"

Laughter and other conversation flowed at her remark—so much so that when Frederick leaned his mouth close to her ear and murmured, Edie was certain no one else could hear him.

"You're right, my love," he whispered, his breath on her neck. "And I think we're going to have an awful lot of fun trying."

Thankfully, Edie was able to blame the nearby fire for the heat in her cheeks when Dodo asked if she was feeling well. Wild horses would not have dragged from her what Frederick had just said.

She smiled, trying to show him in the silence of her expression just what she thought of that suggestion—and Frederick's answering look told her that he knew very well.

Oh, this man. To be sure, they had not perhaps married in the most traditional of ways. Their clever scheme had ended up tricking both of them into something they could never have predicted.

Standing against Society and all their expectations had never been something Edie had thought would be a part of her future.

But she would not change how things had happened for the world. He was her world. Frederick Chance, Viscount Pernrith, and all his pain and joy and complexity? He was the one she wanted, and would want, for the rest of her life.

The conversation had continued while they had shared their moment.

"—think they'll get on?" William was asking.

"Who?" asked Edie, eager to rejoin the conversation.

"The cousins, of course," said John with a laugh. He had sat on the floor beside his wife's chair, leaning against her legs as her fingers played with his hair. "Poor old Maudy isn't going to know what hit her. A sibling and two cousins, all in the same year?"

"I suppose they'll get on splendidly," said Dodo. "The odds are—"

"What, like we all do?" George said dryly.

There was a moment of silence as he met Edie's gaze. His eyes flickered over to her husband beside her.

Edie held her breath. It was a delicate moment.

Frederick chuckled. "I suppose so."

"We are all very different people," said William solemnly.

"But we are brothers," John pointed out with a snort. "We always stand by each other. And we always have."

Edie watched as the four men—three of them so alike in appearance, and then her husband, Frederick—exchanged looks. Nods.

Some of the tension that had suddenly built melted away, and if the expressions on the other three wives were anything to go by, she was not the only one.

"We shall just have to hope the next generation goes on to be as lovely as we are to each other," John said cheerfully.

George snorted. "Or more so."

"As long as they don't make all the same mistakes you lot have," said William darkly.

"William!"

"Well, they have," he protested against his wife's remark. "All the nonsense they've put me through—"

"You don't think we've had to suffer you?" remarked John with a teasing grin.

Frederick slipped his hand over Edie's as the good-natured teasing continued around them. He squeezed her hand, and she squeezed it back.

This was what she had wanted. Not just a husband—her future had always contained a husband. That was simply what ladies of the *ton* expected.

No, she'd wanted this. A family. Laughter, and nonsense, and teasing—and yes, the awkward moments. Disagreements slowly worked through, and misunderstandings that in time only brought people closer together.

And a man, like Frederick, who adored her. Who was worthy of being adored in turn.

"—that's what I think, anyway," said George firmly. "What say you, Pernrith? You've been awfully quiet."

Edie sensed the tension cascade through her husband. He did a remarkable job hiding it. How long had Frederick been hiding his true thoughts, his deep feelings? How long had he felt like an interloper in a family in which he so obviously belonged?

And the tension somehow disappeared, his hand soft and loving once more.

Frederick grinned. "Well, I'm only half a Chance," he said easily. "But the way I see it? I think the next generation of Chances will have plenty of new mistakes to make of their own…"

A Short Letter From the Author

Hello! Thank you so much for reading *Half a Chance*, the fourth novel in my The Chances series. I truly hoped you enjoyed it and fell in love with Frederick and Edie just as much as I did.

I've always wanted to write a series of brothers, but I could never 'meet' the characters who were quite right. After waiting years to meet them myself, I have had a lot of fun writing the four Chance brothers—and I think Cothrom's, Aylesbury's, and Lindow's stories are just as much fun. Make sure you go back and read them!

I simply can't leave the Chance family alone, so make sure you keep reading the series to find out what Maudy and the rest of the next Chance generation gets up to. I can promise you that it'll be scandalous…

Being an author can be a lonely business, but knowing that there are readers from all over the world who are going to adore my stories makes it all worthwhile. Thank you for the support, and I hope you love reading more of my books!

Happy reading,
Emily

About Emily E K Murdoch

If you love falling in love, then you've come to the right place.

I am a historian and writer and have a varied career to date: from examining medieval manuscripts to designing museum exhibitions, to working as a researcher for the BBC to working for the National Trust.

My books range from England 1050 to Texas 1848, and I can't wait for you to fall in love with my heroes and heroines!

Follow me on twitter and instagram @emilyekmurdoch, find me on facebook at facebook.com/theemilyekmurdoch, and read my blog at www.emilyekmurdoch.com.

Made in United States
North Haven, CT
14 January 2025